# False Ceilings

# False Ceilings

**Amit Sharma**

LiFi Publications Pvt. Ltd.
New Delhi

*Published by:*
LiFi Publications Pvt. Ltd.
211, 2nd Floor, Gagandeep
12, Rajendra Place, New Delhi–110 008, India
*Phone :* (011) 2574 1000
*E-mail :* info@lifipublications.com
*Web :* www.lifipublications.com

ISBN 13: 978-93-82536-89-5 ISBN 10: 93-82536-89-2



First published in 2016

**Cataloging in Publication Data—DK**
[Courtesy: D.K. Agencies (P) Ltd. <docinfo@dkagencies.com>]

**Sharma, Amit,** 1979– **author.**
False ceilings / Amit Sharma.
pages cm
Novel.
ISBN 9789382536895

1. Indic fiction (English) I. Title.

PR9499.4.S53F35 2015 DDC 823.92 23



Printed in India by D.K. Fine Art Press (P) Ltd., Delhi–52

*For my demons*

# Acknowledgement

It wasn't easy to write this story because so much of it is derived from true incidents. It wasn't easy to absorb feedback on these real life events either. But the people who read the book were kind, insightful and supportive and were elemental in shaping the book to its final version. I would like to thank Poonam Sharma and Soniya Sundaram for their detailed feedback. I would also like to thank Rickie Khosla, Ruchira Shukla and Rachna Srivastava Parmar for their valuable suggestions and comments. In the end, I would like to thank my wife Anuja and my family for all the patience and love.

# *The If-Else Statement*

*04 February, 2001*

When Aaryan came across the If-Else statement for the first time while trying to comprehend how to create the Schrödinger's wave using a computer program, he smirked. It was scintillating in the way it mimicked life. The smirk broke into a guffaw not because of the innocence of the statement but because of its intrinsic irony, because something as obscene as life could be explained by something so effortless. Wasn't the If-Else statement also an artistic ode to life? Aaryan completely comprehended why he was laughing. He was angry. Maybe he would not have displayed the fit if he knew that 43 years later, when he would finally succumb to death, he would write the If-Else verse on a coarse white sheet of paper and split his sides for the last time.

Aaryan sat in a dingy computer laboratory in the Department of Physics. The department was a part of the age-old Delhi University buildings, decrepit and crumbling. It had seen better times, when students genuinely interested in Physics would pursue a Masters Degree from there, but now it was filled with students who could not make it to any Engineering or Medical college. The professors were aware of this reality and had made peace with it. Most of the students ended up doing a Bachelors of Education course after they were through with their Masters and would land up in various schools and engineering colleges as lecturers. Aaryan found that ridiculous. It was a vicious circle of doing Masters and Bachelors till you land a job. A selected few would end up doing a PhD, then a post doctorate and then some more research. He found that doubly ridiculous. He was magnanimously directionless.

The computer laboratory of the department begged for a makeover but no one was bothered. It was made up of dying walls shedding skin like a snake, cobwebs bellowing in the corners of the ceiling as four rickety fans tried to churn air, and an array of long wooden tables on which the MS-DOS based superannuated computers sat like dead bodies. The computer allocated to him was a peculiar specimen. It moaned loudly like a porn star whenever Aaryan turned it on and the creaking afterwards, as it woke up to life, annoyed him even more.

His partner for the practical class, an ugly satyromaniac named Ritwik, had bunked the class for the nth time as he was off to some movie with his nth girlfriend, where he was successfully trying to push his tongue into her mouth in one of the remote dark corners of the theatre. Aaryan was used to working without him and he felt comfortable this way. Ritwik was more of a distraction because he was always whispering about his conquests in Aaryan's ears and what new position he tried with the last girl he slept with, which nauseated Aaryan to no end.

"I have no interest in your sex life," Aaryan told him once matter-of-factly. Ritwik ignored the fact and continued whispering, which made Aaryan bang the Escape key so hard that it got stuck inside the keyboard and refused to come out.

The program Aaryan had written was puking some error. He had to redo a part of the code. Instead, he started to scribble the equation on his notepad.

```
if (condition)
{ //this happens }
else
{ //that happens }
```

He frolicsomely erased 'condition' and wrote 'my partner would not have been a dick'. He then erased a few more lines rapidly and scribbled a few.

```
If (my partner would not have been a dick)
{ He would have helped me solve the error }
else
{ I'll do it myself. Fuck him.}
```

As Aaryan stared at what he had written, he chuckled again. The Professor, who appeared to have travelled to the present from the times when monkeys were in the middle of evolving into humans, and who behaved as a monarch ruling the laboratory and who had overlooked Aaryan's earlier display of merriment, swiftly came to his side. Aaryan turned a page, cleared his throat and tried to look serious.

"Do you find the equation funny?" the Professor asked, raising a singular eyebrow.

"No, just the parallels. Sir, have you noticed how superbly it echoes life – What could be and what is?"

"And what is that supposed to mean?" The Professor made a face, which tilted his evolution timeline more towards monkeys.

"There is an error that I am supposed to resolve."

The professor floated away with a nod.

Then there were the if-else-if conditions, which complicated things – more conditions, more choices and more forks.

```
if (Condition A)
{ //this happens }
else if (Condition B)
{ //this happens }
else
{ //this happens }
```

And there were the nests, one statement inside another and almost brushing life – decisions, lost opportunities, frustrations, happiness and complications.

```
if (Condition A)
{ //this happens }
else if (Condition B)
{if (Condition C)
{ //this happens }
else
{ //this happens } }
else
{ //this happens }
```

"Ah!!!" Aaryan chuckled loudly and the lecturer again gave a hint of gliding towards him. He was visibly annoyed now and his expressions were making Aaryan giddy. Aaryan promptly returned to his work.

✦

12 Oct, 2060

Lipi was not sure why she was upbeat that day. There was

nothing to be jubilant about. Her husband passed away two years ago and she had lost the will to carry on. She was the ghost of the house, wandering aimlessly as far her walking stick would allow. She sat in her enormous bedroom for a larger chunk of the day, staring at the lush gardens outside or going through her envious collection of photo albums of her past. There was a whole wall dedicated to them. She had very few photographs of her before her marriage. Most of these albums were of the wonderful time she had spent with her husband – the last one being that of a Euro tour which their son had gifted them on their 50th marriage anniversary. That was also the year her husband died. The albums were her reason to go through another day. Her son had offered many times to digitalize the albums but she had vehemently refused.

"You can hang the digital photos in the air all around you, touch them and expand them. It's a new technology, Ma, and it's great. Try it," he had offered her but in vain. She wanted them on paper, just as they were, so that she could touch them with her wrinkled fingers. Besides, there were flavours in those albums, essence of her husband. His smells.

Her son was one of the most affluent businessmen in Delhi and she lived in a house that was nothing less than a five star hotel, but then it is always easy to overlook immoderate improvidence, especially when someone is desperate to feel sad and has no catalyst. Today, she was in one of those moods when she wanted to understand the reason for her chirpiness and that, invariantly, turned her philosophical.

"Life is not about how things happen, but why they happen. You must always ask *why* or you would turn into a cabbage," Lipi told her twin grandchildren while sighing at the end of the sentence and looking in the distant past. They sat in her room, comfortably embedded in the bed while Lipi juggled her mind desperately for a fairy tale. The twins were not in a mood to endure it, neither the fairy tale nor the philosophy. There were other things on their mind.

"So, *why* are you telling us this?" one of her grandchildren asked, while the other yawned in tandem with her sigh, creating a sad symphony, and she knew instantly that he was missing his new Virtual World Play Station. There was a time when the twins wouldn't leave her side, running their fingers in the folds of her skin searching for hidden stories. She used to tell tale after tale, stroking their heads placed in her lap, but they were growing fast and so were their distractions. There were far more exciting gadgets available in the market to replace their decrepit grandmother.

Just the thought of the Play Station made her giddy. She had tried the new console once out of curiosity and if it wasn't scary enough to wear the high definition 3D laser glasses and to be transported in another world, the perfectly real demons were enough to give her a heart attack. And then, before she knew, she was running with the dragon on her tail while her grandchildren desperately tried to annihilate it. The only thing she favoured was that she was able to run in that world just like she used to run as a child, even though she was actually sitting on a chair. But then with a dragon trying to burn off your butt? She wasn't that desperate. Whatever happened to the good old snakes and ladders, she wondered. Since when did children start having thrills by slaying three headed fire spitting monsters? Her son too had grown up playing them, but they were milder versions and less realistic. She hated those as well.

"Go play with your Half Life," she sighed again as she shoved her grandsons out of the room.

Lipi looked around the suddenly empty room. She sighed again.

"Dim the lights please."

The lights dimmed on her command. The automatic systems always fascinated her. She had a suspicion that someone secretly listened to her instructions and dimmed the lights for her, pulled down the shades, switched on the television or started the taps. This world was beyond her flights of fancy. She was brought up in a different world where telephones were kept on a table and you had to press buttons to dial a number. Now, they were wrapped around your wrists and you have to just speak the name. She had heard of an upcoming technology where you have to only think of the name. Televisions were now thin vertical wires hanging in mid air. All you had to do was to say 'start' for the wire to split vertically into two, creating a screen between them. She was brought up in a different era, but then isn't every era a different one, she wondered? Isn't every generation brought up so accustomed to something that it wonders how the previous ones lived without it?

Her eyes suddenly rested on the almirah. She stared at it for an unbearably long interval. The woodwork on the almirah was old and dusty now. Nobody made wooden almirahs nowadays. There were brown patches here and there on it but no chips were hanging out. It was not a very elegant design but had an old world charm to it, and the wood was robust. It reminded her of the house in which she grew up. Her son Sunny had offered many times to repolish and repaint the wooden ghost but she wanted it to be just as it was when she got it sixteen years back, with no coats from the present; just a fine spray of the sadness it had witnessed and the mysteries it carried.

Lipi got up from the sofa with difficulty, composing a few lines of pain on her forehead, and moved towards the almirah. She did not pull the knob immediately but ran her fingers over it, bringing her nose close to it and breathing in the smell of wood, suddenly transporting herself back. Then, an eternity later, she pulled out the knob, creaking open the door to give out the old forest odour. She relished that smell and inhaled a lung-full of it, feeling a bit crisp.

*Thank God the almirah was never filled with those bottles of whisky.*

It was empty except for a single piece of a rusty sheet of paper on the top shelf. She did not pick it up, as she was afraid that it might just crumple to shreds. She adjusted her glasses and narrowed her eyes to read the paper in the dim light, completely forgetting that she could zoom in her glasses or ask the automatic light system to increase the intensity. A few lines were scribbled on the sheet with a blue ball pen. The terseness of those lines always made her wonder. Lipi could not curb the gooseflesh every time she saw those if-else statements. She had no idea what those empty statements meant. That paper was found next to a dying man, a man who had laughed hysterically on the night he died for reasons she could not understand. It was a mystery she knew she could never solve.

"What were you trying to say, Aaryan?" she asked the piece of paper.

"Tell me what you saw?" she asked the almirah.

The almirah stared back. No, Lipi had no idea why she was happy that day, but she wasn't anymore. Not after seeing that piece of paper.

✦

*19 April, 2062*

The car was waiting as Sunny descended from the helicopter. He rushed away from the helipad as the rotor slowed to a halt. He was not sure why he was here. It was a faded memory. In fact he was not even sure whether it was a recollection or his mind just cooked up a story. As he sat in the car, he looked at the driver and smiled.

"How are you, Sir?" the driver inquired.

"Confused. And you Alan?" Sunny asked.

"I am in high spirits, Sir. This is a beautiful place to live – mountains, fresh air and greenery. To your hotel, Sir?"

"No. Take me to the villa."

Alan started the car and snaked down the road off the helipad.

"You will be staying there, Sir? I would have switched on the cleaner pod there. It will be dusty. Should I do it now? It will be partially clean by the time we reach there."

"No, I have no intention to stay there. I just have to find something and then we will go to the hotel. I hope there is a room for me there," Sunny said and smiled.

"What are you saying Sir? You are the owner," Alan said, shaking his head.

As the car encountered one turn after another, Sunny looked around and a pang of nostalgia hit him. Dalhousie had some of his most memorable memories and now that his mother was no more, he could not stop tears from welling up in his eyes. There were numerous summer holidays which he had spent with his parents in this hill station as a child. The villa was his mother's, passed from one generation to another in her family. It was a very old building, more that a hundred years old. It had been revived and revamped numerous times in the last few decades. His mother was always very sure of keeping it standing.

He recalled the times spent in the Villa when he sat with his parents in the balcony of the bedroom which faced the mountains and watched the Sun as it went down and hid behind the giant peaks. More than the Sun, he liked to look at the face of his parents changing colours from tangerine to orange to amber as the Sun gave way to the Moon. Lipi once told him that the villa was constructed by her grandmother's father and this bedroom was his. One hundred and thirty years ago, he sat here with his wife in the balcony and watched the sun go down!

"I heard about Lipi madam's demise. Sorry for your loss Sir," Alan said, pulling Sunny out of his past.

"Thanks Alan. She went peacefully." Alan nodded.

His mother's death was the reason he was back here. It was the reason he was chasing all his memories. He had been connecting dots ever since the carpenter brought the secret hidden in the false ceiling of that wooden almirah to him. He had turned it over so many times in his head but there were no answers. He was not sure that he would ever know what exactly happened because everyone involved were dead long ago. His mother was the last thread, but he was convinced that she was not aware of the secret because she had no grounds to hide it. All she had in that almirah was that crumpled piece of paper with the if-else statement written on it.

The lump in his throat grew bigger as the car approached the villa. He asked Alan to wait in the car. Sunny's legs were feathers as he reached the main door and scanned his eye to open it. There was a week old layer of dust inside and the cleaner pod blinked the date when it was last used. It was such a modern house that no one would have believed that it was more than a century old. The memories of the house ran amok in his brain, and for many seconds he stood glued to the ground, unable to move. He shook himself out of his thoughts and moved to the store room at the back. He scanned his eye again and entered a password in the panel next to the door. The room was accessible only by his family and that is why there was an extra layer of security. It contained old things; some of them had been in the house even before his mother was born and some were as old as the house, dating back to pre-independence era.

He commanded the lights to switch on and rummaged through old carpets, exquisitely carved copper utensils, paintings, boxes full of century old showpieces, classic English novels, horse saddles, preserved crumbling drawings of guest houses until he finally saw what he was looking for. The painting was almost hidden behind a large trunk. It was covered with a coat of a plastic like material which consisted of a chemical to safeguard it. Lipi, in a fit to conserve the memories of the house, had applied the coat to everything which needed to be saved. Sunny picked up the painting and stared at it. He must have been fifteen years old when he had seen it for the first time. It was of a handsome man – light brown eyes, wavy hair, slightly uplifted cheeks and a well defined jaw line. There was a hint of a smile and the head was held high. Sunny's eyes went to the bottom right corner of the painting. That is what had brought him here, the memory of something written there. As he scanned the corner, his eyes rested on the name written there with a wavy hand – Kanshi Ram.

It could have been the painter's name but he knew that it wasn't. It would not make sense then.

"So, you are the one," Sunny said to the painting.

Another piece of the jigsaw had fallen into place. Sunny suddenly had goosebumps wondering how many decades he had gone back to his roots. He was not sure that he would ever find the whole truth but he was getting somewhere. For a second, he thought of taking the painting with him but then he kept it back where he had found it. He would never know Kanshi's world, never understand the decisions he made, the kind of life he led, what gave him happiness, how he died. He went into Kanshi's bedroom and opened the door to the balcony and stood there for a while. The Sun was far from setting. Alan looked up at him and smiled.

"Let's go to the hotel Alan," Sunny said.

# *Shakuntala*

Shakuntala's eyeballs finally stopped moving when she took her last breath. They had been moving like a pendulum from the last seven days, wide open as they had lost contact with the brain and had forgotten how to close, blink or see. They watered every five minutes and someone from her family had to wipe off the water dripping from the corner of her wandering eyes. They turned red because they had been in constant contact with air. She looked like a helpless, petrified deer that had just been shot and was counting his last breath as he watched the hunter walk towards him. Her hands and legs were lifeless, hanging like the sparse hair on her head and flailing when someone changed her position. The only sign of her being alive was the breathing sound and her meandering eyes. The doctors had refused to keep her in ICU because it was pointless. There was nothing they could do, other than wait for the breathing to stop. By the seventh day, the family was praying to God to do so. No one knew if she could heed voices around her or perceive people. Her eyes wandered as if searching for something and her family liked to believe that she could distinguish them and take notice of them. They sometimes called her name and asked her if she wanted anything. Shakuntala never replied. Her tongue hung out of the corner of her mouth. She was dreaming with open eyes.

By the seventh day, her breathing became shallow and by nightfall it almost trickled into the next day. She was given food and oxygen through pipes but then these supplies rarely work when the body has given up the will to live. Everyday, a nurse would come to wipe her body and change her clothes. The doctors would do their daily rounds to check if she was still hanging on to life. People came to visit her – distant relatives who were still alive or their children, and would sometimes shed a tear seeing her plight. The old ones would get anxious and pray to God to give them a peaceful end; not as dramatic as hers.

Shakuntala's family was relieved when the eyes finally stopped scanning the room and looked at the ceiling fan, emulating a tired expression. Now that they have ceased to wander, her brother Madan tried to close the eyes but they would pop up half way back as soon as he removed his hand. They had been open for too long. The doctors were surprised that she survived for seven days. It was a mini miracle that her heart pumped even though most of her body parts had lost contact with the brain.

She was elephantine. It took a lot of manpower to shift her to the ambulance, which took the body back home. It took even more manpower to carry her to her first floor apartment from where she was to finally depart to the cremation grounds a few hours later.

✦

Shakuntala was mundanely hunky-dory on that fateful day, ruminating over a spicy namkin mix and watching her favorite afternoon show on the television as she spread comfortably on her double bed in her nightgown. The doctor had strictly forbidden her to eat anything remotely spicy, but she loved to refute him.

"I can't live like a bloody beggar,"she rebuked him as he gave a look of utter despair watching her sugar level touch the sky.

So in spite of the fact that she had heart problems, that she was suffering from diabetes and that she had a diameter greater than Jupiter, she kept on living her life as if she was immortal. She added extra chilies in her dal, chicken and vegetables and would eat every sweet she could lay her hand upon, even if that meant stealing it from the refrigerator. Except for hypnotizing her, her family had tried everything else to dissuade her. She cooked separately so there was no check on the masala and chillies.

As she flattened herself on her bed, she looked like an element of it. Her body looked like a water mattress wobbling over the wooden bed, her stomach spilling on both sides. The nightgown was one of the many flimsy nightgowns she had. It just hung from her obese body like an oversized car cover. It was sleeveless, torn a bit from the armpits and showing parts of her breasts. She was politely and rudely asked many times by her son to stitch it up and put a stop to the vulgar display of hanging skin but she was past caring. She wore her gown the whole day and never cared to change to another set of clothes in the morning. She had stopped wearing undergarments a long time back. It was too much of an effort and something that was dispensable now.

As she watched the show about a scheming daughter-in-law trying to steal away the property of her father-in-law, Shakuntala had a revelation. It was catatonic for the initial few seconds, much similar to how a somnambulist might feel if he wakes up suddenly in the middle of a busy road and realizes that he is naked. Shakuntala gasped and then gulped.

"What the hell am I doing?" she mumbled.

Somehow, the fact that she was going to depart this life soon manifested itself and it changed everything. Maybe it was her sixth sense. She had a sudden urge to get up from the bed. She pushed her legs out by holding the edge of the bed firmly with her right hand and then channeling all her energy, pushed her whole body up with a jolt. As she sat at the corner of the bed now, she spread her legs and bent down slightly. She had to get out the old iron trunk which was always kept locked and shoved under her bed. She reached out for it as God the Father reached out to Adam as he breathed life in him. The trunk came out with a screeching sound, trying to oppose the sudden turbulence in its peacefully prosaic existence. It was a black, old sad thing, which had spent much of its life lying calmly under her bed.

"The key! Where is the key?" she looked around as she cupped her head with one of her hands.

She found the key in her almirah in one of her many boxes buried under the debris of old buttons, pins, pieces of clothes, some torn photographs and pre-independence era coins. She walked back towards her bed and sat on it with a thud, with legs wide open and the trunk linking her legs. She bent down and opened the old rusty lock, which turned out to be a more arduous job than getting up and opening the almirah. And there it was, wrapped in a faint yellow piece of cloth of the size of a small tabletop. Her secret. It lay on top of some old sweaters and some of her husband's old shirts littered with mothballs. She picked it up.

'I have to do this,' she told herself. Maybe it was delayed now. Maybe her son would snort at her. Maybe he will slap her, curse her and then abandon her. She hesitated for a moment. She had always thought of this bundle as a curse.

'No, its not,' she told herself and was about to get up when everything went blank as the nerve ruptured in her brain. It was so sudden that Shakuntala lost control of her hands instantaneously.

Her legs went weak, crumbling under her weight. Her eyes adjusted to a hazy focus. The cloth and its enclosures fell back into the trunk and Shakuntala fell back on the bed.

So there she was, lying on her bed, staring at the ceiling with her legs dangling and a trunk sitting between them on the floor. She could whisper but could not shout for help. She was able to budge her hands a bit but not the rest of her body. There were sparks of light in front of her eyes. So this is it, she contemplated. This is how you die. Her past life was dancing in front of her eyes in a luminous haze announcing the fall of the curtain, the end of an era. She was overwhelmed with an avalanche of old memories and gasped. She could feel those moments, those horse rides with her father, the wooden radio that her father gave her as a gift, the owl on her bed announcing the inevitable, the man with a flute sitting beneath a tree, the potato fields, the day of her marriage, her husband's body against hers, the nauseating smell of death, snowflakes, a blinding life shattering jealousy and a meaningless existence thereafter, which culminated in the ridiculous situation she was in right now. Yes, she could see it all. She stared at the images with serenity. It was frightening to sense her old memories to be so vivid. They were like the name of an old forgotten friend, which tastes alien when spoken after ages. She could sense shadows around her, urging her to come with them, telling her that its time. The ceiling of the room had turned into a semblance of the past, a clamour of images whirling around by the slowly rotating fan. Shakuntala was not ready to let go. She was forcing herself to stay a bit longer. She had a task to perform.

Her granddaughter passed through her room twice and was considerably surprised to see her grandma resting in such a comical pose, especially because she would never display the contents of her trunk so unabashedly to any member of the family.

It was the smell of urine, which finally brought help. She had lost control of her bladder. Three hours later, as a final act of desperation, her eyes started oscillating. When her faeces stained her overused nightgown and the bed, her family decided that it was time to take her to the hospital.

She had started dreaming with open eyes.

✦

Shakuntala was born on a balmy July morning in 1930 in a lush hill station called Dalhousie situated in the lap of Himalayas in the Gurdaspur district of Punjab in northern India. For any other family, arrival of a female would have been a miserable day, but her father Kanshi Ram was delirious with joy.

"The first child in your family and it's a girl! God knows what bad karma have we performed in our previous birth," Shakuntala's grandmother said while she twisted her lips to the extreme left corner of her face. She hated the girl the instant she was born. When the midwife announced that it was a girl, Shakuntala's grandmother gave her the most ridiculous expression she had received in her entire career of forty years. Shakuntala's father, on the other hand, gave the midwife a one-rupee coin. She burst into tears at his kindness and cleaned the child more rigorously with a wet cloth than she had intended and wrapped her up in an expensive silk cloth before presenting the girl to her father. His legs were weak with delirium and he had to sit down.

Shakuntala's mother was too weak to say anything. She just sighed and went back to sleep after the umbilical cord was snipped. She saw Shakuntala after she woke up almost a day later. Kanshi was sitting next to her bed with Shakuntala in his hands.

She took the baby from him and stared at her.

"She has your nose," she said after studying her for some time. Kusum kissed her daughter on the forehead and gave her back to her husband. She wanted some more rest. Her hands were shaking. She was scared all of a sudden.

It took Kusum almost two months to come out of the cycle of sleeping, eating and sighing. The servants were hovering all over her as instructed by her husband. She wasn't much interested in Shakuntala. She knew what was expected of her and thus would feed her daughter at regular intervals. She knew that she had failed to produce a son, no matter what her husband said. For days, she could not muster enough courage to go in front of her mother-in-law. Kusum's parents had been staying at Kanshi's house for the delivery for a week. Earlier, her mother insisted on having the delivery at their house in Chamba as per the rituals, but Kanshi did not agree to it. He was not going to let Kusum out of his sight for a single minute. After the girl was born and Kusum's mother-in-law made her caprice sufficiently visible, her parents left in a hurry before they could be further humiliated.

Shakuntala's grandmother Radha Devi did not reside with her son permanently. She did not live permanently with any of her sons. She had five of them and she alternated amongst them with a dedicated regularity. She was a frail widow and was ready to go to the ashram in the outskirts of the hill station where all the old toothless widows stayed, but her sons were quite adamant and never allowed her to take that drastic step. Radha Devi too, in truth, was in no mood to spend the rest of her life in that hellhole of an ashram, but it was a sword she liked to keep. She just had to turn it slowly after oiling it with tears, and there was nothing that her sons wouldn't obey.

So Radha Devi, the 60-year-old toothless widow and a grandmother of 27 children, revolved with the regularity with which the Earth revolves around the sun. Her nomadic existence took her to each of her son for two months and then she moved on to the next one. Kanshi was the only exception to this rule as Radha Devi had decided to stay for four months in a year with her favorite son. He was the youngest and the most successful and she was especially proud of him. He was her trophy. It was but obvious that she stayed the longest with him.

"He frequently has tea with the Bade Gore Sahib, the Englishmen, you know!" Radha frequently bragged in front of other toothless old ladies, who like her, had not yet contemplated going to the ashram.

For considerably apparent reasons, whenever Radha Devi left the house of one of her sons to move to the next one, there was a unanimous wave of relief in the house she had abandoned and a predictable wave of terror washed over the house she was about to enter. Her sons were quite oblivious to either of the waves or chose to be so, even though their agonized wives and daughters made it quite conspicuous. It's in her blood to bicker, so get used to it, they would tell the women in their families.

Radha Devi's whole clan lived in Dalhousie. The brothers inherited the farms from their father, Jeevan Ram, after a bear ate him up one day as he went to collect wood in the forest. Three of the brothers – Kulbhushan, Sitara and Shambhu kept their terrace farms where they grew potatoes. The fourth son Raghubir sold off his share of the land and opened up a cloth shop. He sold expensive homemade shawls and carpets to the rich British ladies who just couldn't get enough of the beautiful designs. Kanshi Ram too sold off his share of the land and ended up being a builder.

Dalhousie was turning into a bustling hill station during the 1920s and the 30s. It all started in 1853 when Lord Dalhousie acquired five hills from the Princely state of Chamba and in return, reduced the taxes which the king of Chamba paid to the British Raj every year as compensation. The hills of Kathlog, Portreyn, Tehra, Bakrota and Balun were then named Dalhousie after the Lord on the recommendation of Sir Donald McLeod, thus establishing the sanatorium and giving birth to the hill station at the foot of the Dhauladhar range. It wasn't as popular as Simla but soon became a close second. Simla was the established summer capital much before Dalhousie came into existence. It had an added advantage of the Kalka-Shimla railway line as far as accessibility went; something that Dalhousie never had. The wealthy British officers and their families preferred Simla to Dalhousie as a summer retreat during the unbearable summers of Delhi, but then Dalhousie was not very far behind. It had an unsurpassed beauty, a charm to it, and a silent and collected serenity that was soothing as the winds gushed through lush oaks, deodars and pines. Since it did not had the maddening rush of Simla, a lot of British families and the elite from Lahore, the capital of Punjab, started preferring Dalhousie which catapulted Kanshi to instant success and turned Radha Devi into that bragging bitch, as she was notoriously called.

Kanshi's father's elder brother was a local builder who constructed summer houses and took him under his umbrella as soon as Jeevan Ram's chewed body was found in the jungle. By the time Kanshi was eighteen, he was almost a partner and had sold off his share of his father's land to invest in the successful business.

In a year, Kanshi had built three beautiful summer houses for the Gora Sahib and had become quite proficient in English by then. He had almost taught himself with an undying support from one Lord William who lived permanently in a summer house built by Kanshi's uncle because he had fallen in love with Dalhousie the moment he set foot there. He took it as a personal challenge to teach Kanshi some English words, and once Kanshi started to absorb the language, Lord William was taken aback by the ease with which he grabbed the nuances.

As Lord William had no intention of leaving Dalhousie, he started giving regular lessons to Kanshi and within a year, he was lending his books to him. By the time Kanshi turned 19, his uncle had already left for Haridwar, the holy Hindu city, as he wanted to be near God in his last few days, leaving all his wealth and business to Kanshi as he did not have any children of his own. That year, Lord William presented Kanshi with an old copy of David Copperfield. The same year, Kanshi expanded his small one bedroom house and added two more bedrooms along with a large hall on the ground floor. He added two rooms on the first floor and carved a wooden staircase from the hall to the lobby connecting the upper rooms. The lobby opened into a small balcony, overlooking the surrounding mountains. There was another balcony in the bedroom upstairs. His house stood at the mouth of a valley overlooking the terrace farm he had sold earlier and which was now the property of another farmer who lived at the other end. The farm ended abruptly at a cliff from where one could see the dense forest of pines and oaks below. Behind his house, there were stairs carved out of the mountain till the main road that connected to the main market area. There were narrow walkways to carry mules and horses to the road.

Getting Kanshi a wife was a monumental task for Radha Devi. She had set some very high standards and Kanshi was getting restless as his mother was taking too much time. He was well past the marriageable age and his mother had already rejected ten girls. Most of his friends were married by now and some even had children. His brothers sometimes descended on their mother like a huge tidal wave urging her not to be so picky, but she was taking her own sweet time.

"Even the Maharaja of Jaipur will not reject so many girls," Kanshi said to his mother one evening during dinner. Radha Devi was furious. She had had enough of her five sons teaching her how to find a bride. She knitted her brows and gritted her teeth.

"What am I supposed to do?" she said as her voice tipped a bit towards a high-pitched shriek, "shouldn't I check the girl out properly? Ramdev's daughter didn't even know how to cook Madra! Can you believe that? And Chauhan's daughter was a mess. She tumbled in front of me, spilling the hot milk on my feet. Do you want me to marry you off to such girls? Have faith in me. I am trying my best."

"All I am saying is don't take so long that no one is left to marry your son," Kanshi said.

Radha Devi understood the gravity of what her son was trying to articulate and so Kanshi was promptly married to the next best match she could find. Kusum was the daughter of a wealthy contractor from Chamba, a hill station on the banks of Ravi. Kusum was sixteen, but very mellowed and cultivated for her age. She handled Radha Devi well during her interview, giving all the answers deftly. The interview lasted for almost an hour with the topics ranging from cooking, sewing and other important household chores. The wedding was a spectacle and was talked about for days later. No one had seen a wedding ceremony of such magnitude before in Dalhousie in their living memory.

Kanshi had not seen Kusum before their marriage. He was sure that his mother wouldn't let him down after so much nitpicking, and he didn't want to risk it by giving her another chance. Who knows how long she would take if this girl got rejected, he thought. He saw Kusum for the first time when they were exchanging garlands during the marriage ceremony. Her face was partially hidden behind a veil when they stood facing each other but he could clearly see her nose and lips. When Kusum raised her hands to put the garland around his neck, their eyes met for a second. That one second was enough for Kanshi to be besotted by her. It was a match made in heavens, said Radha Devi when she blessed them later.

A few days later, when Lord William invited the couple to dinner, he told them that he had never seen such a fine couple in his life. Kanshi translated it for Kusum and she blushed. Kanshi received a copy of *Wuthering Heights* this time and Kusum received a beautiful shawl.

Kanshi had been training Kusum to eat rice with fork and drink soup and dal with a spoon. When they sat to eat, she was a bit awkward initially, which made Lord William smile, but she was fine a few bites later. Lord William was very fond of Indian food, and had ordered his cook to go to Kanshi's house and come back with a list of food items that Kusum liked. That day, Kanshi acted as a translator as Kusum talked with Lord William, telling him that the food was very delicious and the shawl was very pretty and he was very kind.

Kusum brought the much-required stability in Kanshi's life and the much-anticipated jealousy in Radha Devi's. She never gave Radha Devi any reason for complaints and that infuriated her even more. Radha Devi left no stone unturned to unearth a single mistake committed by Kusum, but she could never go beyond the extra salt in the food, which surprisingly Kanshi found to be always perfect. When Kusum came to their house, she brought two servants with her. Her father was a rich man and sent the servants as gift, which Kanshi gracefully accepted. This arrangement killed any chances of nitpicking for Radha Devi.

Kanshi was now at peace with his life. It wasn't very difficult for Kusum and Kanshi to fall in love. Both of them were uncomplicated humans with a good heart. Radha Devi's occasional bickering did not bother Kanshi and soon Kusum also got used to it.

"Mothers are supposed to scold," she told Kanshi.

Radha Devi, who had lost her son to this new woman, was deeply disappointed at her son's behaviour. He wasn't spending much time with her nowadays and was always in his room upstairs with his new wife and there was no one to complain to. For a while, it seemed that Radha Devi was subdued, but four months after the marriage the news of Kusum's pregnancy was broken to her by the midwife and she got another opening.

"I hope it's a boy," she kept saying for the next nine months.

"I don't care," Kanshi kept telling his mother.

Kusum was suddenly terrified. It was one thing to be scolded for an extra pinch of chillies in the food and another thing to be reprimanded for the rest of her life for giving birth to a girl. She prayed to God for a boy and then prayed again to forgive her for what she was asking. Kanshi kept telling her that she was worrying unnecessarily.

"You do not understand," Kusum said.

Shakuntala was that first mistake, the light at the end of the tunnel for Radha Devi. Her saviour.

"Look at your brothers. Each of your brothers had a son as their firstborn. This girl has cut off a branch of my family tree. Shakuntala! Huh!" Radha Devi repeated these lines innumerable number of times on the dinner table. The lines unfortunately had an instant effect on Kusum. She always left the room crying which gave Radha Devi the same pleasure which a man would get on seeing an oasis after travelling months through a desert.

For the next four years, the four months that Radha Devi spent with the family every year, ended up pushing Kusum into a deep melancholia. Kanshi sympathized with his wife and helped pulling her out of the depression for the rest of the year, and so Kusum ended up like a polar bear, going into hibernation in the presence of her mother-in-law for those terrible months and was her normal cheery self for the rest of the year. She never asked her husband to request his mother to stay away from the family and neither did the thought ever occur to Kanshi.

At the end of the fourth year, Kusum was eight months pregnant and was under the constant supervision of the midwife and the two servants in the house. In spite of the fact that she lived like a queen attended round the clock by servants and her husband, Kusum was deteriorating. No one could understand why. The midwife told Kanshi that it was more of a mental ailment rather than something physical. In reality, Kusum was terrified.

'What if it's another girl?' The question was constantly hammering in her brain. The question was pushing her into the abyss of depression and before she knew it, she had turned into a sad, weak and annoying woman. She constantly threw tantrums, shouted at the servants, told the midwife that she was bad at her job (which made the midwife cry), slapped Shakuntala for minuscule mistakes and almost stopped talking to her husband. She was not ready for a lifetime of oscillation between depression and happiness depending on which month of the year it was. She wanted a boy, and very desperately. She wanted the branch of the family tree to grow and loop around the tongue of her mother-in-law, impairing her ability to traumatize her. The last four years had choked her. She wanted to put an end to the chronic emotional swaying she was subjected to year after year.

Kanshi was the epitome of patience with Kusum. He took all the tantrums, her shouting and her depressions in his stride. Sometimes, he was able to pull her out and tried his best to convince her that nothing else mattered but the love they shared. He was the only thread by which Kusum was hanging above the pit of insanity. If she shouted at him, he would kiss her, which would make her smile. He would reassure her numerous times that it did not matter to him if it was a girl again. I would be dancing with joy, he said.

Sometimes, when the weather was a bit warm, they would sit in the balcony of their bedroom and stare at the mountains surrounding them. Kanshi would then throw a shawl around both of them and Kusum would place her head on his shoulder and his hand on her stomach, making him feel the child inside. It calmed her and she would forget everything else. Kanshi would sit with her and watch the sun go down behind the mountains as it splashed its last fading orange smear over the trees and the sky before bowing to the night.

"No one but us will know this moment, that we sat here like this and saw the sun fade away and then one day, this moment will be lost with both of us. There will be no one left to tell our story," Kusum said one evening as they watched the sunset.

"But it is our moment, our sunset."

"Yes, yes you are right," Kusum said taking a deep breath and closing her eyes.

Kanshi smiled in silence.

Shakuntala had turned into a cherub. She was undoubtedly the most beautiful child in the whole clan. Radha Devi never had the nerve to mistreat Shakuntala in front of Kanshi. She was polite with her but never showered her with any affection. Kusum too felt a bitterness, which she herself couldn't comprehend. Shakuntala was her daughter, but the mood swings had drained away Kusum's capacity to love her. Deep inside, she held Shakuntala responsible for her own condition. There was always a knot in her heart and Shakuntala was never more than a blot of guilt within the layers of her mind. She showered enough love on Shakuntala to stop her daughter from hating her but anything more than that was beyond her calibre. Kusum blamed Shakuntala for being a girl and Radha Devi blamed Kusum for producing her. Thankfully, the bitterness did not cascade to Kanshi and he made sure that all the wishes and demands of his daughter were granted even before she uttered them. If she asked for a piece of mithai, her father asked the local sweet shop owner to send a servant to their home with all the varieties available. If she liked a toy, her father made sure that she got tens of them. He would play with her in the snow in winters and make Yeti for her. He would surprise her with pets. She had two rabbits, a parrot and a dog by the time she was four. The parrot was bought when he was a chick. He was white as flour and Shakuntala could not believe that it was a parrot. Kanshi would write words on a piece of paper and give it to her to teach to the parrot. She loved the way his fingertips bent outwards as he held the pen. Kanshi placed the chick in an earthen pot and would ask Shakuntala to whisper the words to the parrot by cupping her mouth on the pot. She named the parrot Ram, after Lord Ram, because that was the first word she taught him. The parrot soon turned green, relieving Shakuntala of all her doubts and he did pick up a few Hindi words and repeated them with all diligence.

Of all the merriments bestowed upon her, the evening horse rides were the best time of the day for Shakuntala. Years later, when the nerve ruptured in her brain, she distinctly remembered those charming horse rides with her father, with the fading sun behind a distant mountain and the elongated shadows of the pine trees. Kanshi had bought a horse for himself a few months after Shakuntala was born. He got her a brown pony when she was four. She named him Oliver, as her father suggested.

Sometimes Kanshi would walk her to the G.P.O, one of the three bustling market places, called malls, built by the British in the early 1880s in Dalhousie. G.P.O was the most vibrant and the busiest. It was full of shops and people who socialized in the evenings. Kanshi always had one business or the other at the Post office, so he would leave Shakuntala at the sweet shop and disappear for a few minutes. Sometimes, he would walk her to a road from where they could see three, sometimes four of the five mighty rivers of Punjab, fading away in the horizon.

"That is the Sutlej, that one is Beas, the one at the corner is Ravi and can you see the faint shimmer at the corner? That is Chenab," Kanshi told Shakuntala as they sat together on the grass near a mountain slope.

"How do you know for sure?" Shakuntala asked.

"Everyone knows. They have always been there."

He would take her to Khajjiar, the stunning Spring Valley. Father and daughter would sit next to the lake till dusk.

Every time the father-daughter duo would leave the house, they would entreat with Kusum to give them company but she hardly obliged. She rarely left the house.

Each of Radha Devi's sons had a bunch of children, but not Kanshi, and this turned into another bone of contention. The eldest son Kulbhushan had eight children, followed by seven from Sitara, six from Shambhu and five from Raghubir. Kanshi's score was just one till now and that too a girl. It was unnatural for Radha Devi. It was unacceptable by any standards of the society. But Kanshi was never convinced.

"I just want two children. Do you know what will happen after fifty years if we keep having babies like this?" he said to his mother one day when she told him that his score was displeasingly low.

"Why do you care? Do you know how difficult it is to explain it to people? Everyone thinks that Kusum has some medical problem, that she can't bear a child that frequently."

"I don't care what people say. Why do we always have to explain things to people? I just want two children."

"What if both are girls?"

"Then so be it. I wouldn't mind another Shakuntala," Kanshi smiled.

"Hey Ram! What will become of this boy! Are you crazy, Kanshi? Do you even understand what you just said?"

It was a boy and Kusum died during childbirth. She was twenty. The midwife had warned the family numerous times that Kusum was too fragile to bear a child. She had grown too weak in the past few months despite constant caring. But there was no choice other than to go ahead with the delivery. It could not have been undone. The only way out was to make Kusum eat as much as possible so that she gained some strength, but the terror of the impending doom killed her appetite. She never saw the face of her son. She slipped into unconsciousness as soon as he was born and never came out of it. Radha Devi was sorry for her for the first time in her life. She was sad mainly because she could not celebrate the extension of her family tree. After all, you can't celebrate life when there has been a death in the family. When the midwife informed Kanshi about the tragedy, he quietly went in the room where his wife's dead body lay, and took her in his arms, rocking her gently as if putting her to sleep. Shakuntala sat at her mother's feet and wept soundlessly. The midwife had taken away the newborn from the room and given him to Radha Devi who looked at him with sad eyes. The poor boy would never know his mother, she thought.

Kusum's death turned the house upside down. Swiftly, all the brothers descended with their families. Then there were the neighbours who dropped at any inappropriate time to pay their condolences. People who knew Kanshi from work poured in, which included the head of a very influential British family for whom Kanshi was building a summer house. Lord William appeared too and grieved for the children. He had met Kusum on a few occasions in the last four years but not as frequently as he had wished. Lord William had also met Shakuntala a few times and felt that she was a bright girl. He had suggested Kanshi to send Shakuntala to the famous Sacred Heart convent in Dalhousie. Kanshi liked the idea but never actually had the time to think about it. Lord William again fanned the idea but Kanshi was not in a position to think through the suggestion. He had just given away his wife to the fires.

The house had turned into a mad house with people always on the move, food being served all the time, children running here and there, Madan (his newborn son) crying all the time as if mourning his mother's death and in the middle of it all, the last rites of his wife were being performed. Sometimes, Kanshi wanted to scream and ask everyone to leave. He wanted a moment to himself for the tragedy to sink in, to understand and mourn his loss. He felt hollow, with a bottomless pit in his chest. He wanted to sleep for days. But soon, once the last rites were performed, everyone started dispersing and Kanshi went to Haridwar to disperse the ashes of his wife in the holy Ganges.

When he returned, the house was as quiet as a cemetery. Radha Devi decided to stay with her son for some more time. She had become inseparable from Madan, as if Madan had just sprouted out of her arms and could not be detached. Shakuntala was completely neglected by her and spent most of the days in her room staring out of the window and crying.

Kanshi was not himself for the first few days. He had stopped going to work and wandered through the house like a ghost, remembering some incident or picking up things that reminded him of Kusum. He would sit alone in the balcony in the evenings and would lose track of time and would have to be reminded by the servants to take his food. Radha Devi tried to cheer up her son with Madan but to no avail. Kanshi did not touch him. Shakuntala was confused and terrified. She could not bear to see her father like that. She missed him. She missed the evening horse rides. She would go and sit with Oliver in the shed that her father had constructed behind the house, feed him grass and talk to him. The pony listened to her with all the attention he could muster.

Lord William paid another visit and urged Kanshi to return back to work. A few summer houses Kanshi was working on were unfinished and he was on the verge of losing a few good contracts.

"And send your daughter to the convent. She is a bright and sharp girl. It will do her good. Get her out of this place," Lord William said. "Now pick yourself up. You are only twenty-three. You are young and there is a whole life ahead of you."

And so, reluctantly Kanshi returned to work and Shakuntala was sent to the Sacred Heart. It was a very difficult separation for both father and daughter. Kanshi told Shakuntala that he wanted her to stay at the hostel so that she can shed her fears and inhibitions, but in reality he wanted her to be away from his mother. He wanted her to meet people, make friends. Shakuntala was devastated. She thought that her father was sending her away. He was shunning her, holding her responsible for the loss of her mother. She cried, stomped her feet but Kanshi was adamant and so finally she had to leave.

"Have you gone mad? Who sends girls out of the house to study and that too with *firangi* girls? Oh! How will I explain this to everyone! Oh! How will I bear the shame! Oh! The laughter! The gossips! She will turn into one of them and then you will realize what a blunder you have made!" Radha Devi cried when she heard of the incredulous decision.

Kanshi kept quiet and did just as he wanted. Radha Devi turned to Madan for consolation and talked to him at length about his father losing his mind. Madan yawned, laughed and sucked his thumb.

The convent boggled Shakuntala. There was not a single Indian girl there. All of them were British. She was terrified initially but thankfully, the British girls were kind enough to include her in their circle. The fact that Shakuntala could speak fluent English helped. A new window was opened for her and after staying in the hostel for sometime, she was thankful that her father did not bend by her initial resistance. She loved the piano classes, the Western Music and Geography. She had no idea that there were so many countries, so many different worlds she was unaware of. She had no idea that there were so many stories to be read. Her English improved considerably and in a year she finished reading an abridged version of Oliver Twist borrowed from the convent library. She had always wanted to read it after her father named her horse Oliver and told her about this book. Shakuntala was an above average student. She was never part of the cream but then she was never expected to be.

Kanshi visited her regularly and brought her sweets and clothes. Sometimes he brought Madan with him who could walk now and end up at places where no one could find him. Shakuntala liked him because he was her brother but there was no other connection. She hardly knew him, and this disturbed her at times. Kanshi had shed off his initial apprehensions about Madan. As better sense prevailed, he realized that his wife's death was not Madan's doing.

Sometimes Kanshi took special permission from the warden and took Shakuntala for a ride on her pony. He took her to Panjpula one day and they sat next to the waterfall staring at the lush green valley beneath and then he took her to Dainkund, the singing hill.

"Did you know that Rabindra Nath Tagore came to Dalhousie

once?" he asked her as they sat beneath the singing hills.

"Did he? When?" Shakuntala was intrigued.

"Oh! Long time back. In the 1870s I think. He was just a boy. He remembered this place for the rest of his life."

"And who else?"

"Well, Subhash Chandra Bose is here," Kanshi said cautiously. "He is going to reside in Dalhousie for some time. He is staying at a house on Panjpula road."

"Can we meet him?"

"No. And we should not. He has just been released from jail and he is taking a rest. Also..." Kanshi hesitated.

"What?"

"Look Shakuntala, you are old enough to understand that I am not a freedom fighter. I also work for people against whom our entire nation is fighting. I give them houses where they enjoy their life. I am giving them the exact opposite of what the nation wants to give them."

"And what is that?"

"A kick."

Shakuntala laughed and rolled over the grass to keep her head in Kanshi's lap. Kanshi was quiet for sometime as Shakuntala looked at the shadows of the pines shifting with the sun.

"Do you feel guilty?" she asked finally.

"Guilty? No! I like my job. I like building houses. It does not matter to me who lives in them. The money has provided for my family. I am able to educate you. What else does a man want?"

"Do you feel guilty at times of not being a part of the independence movement?" Shakuntala asked. Kanshi sighed.

"I don't feel the hostility. These people have been nice to me but yes, sometimes I do feel as if I am betraying my nation. It's a fight that I have to fight daily with myself. I can't let you down. I can't pack everything and jump into the struggle and leave you and Madan to God. When you grow up, you might consider me a coward but some choices are hard to make and I don't have the courage."

A few years later, when the questions she asked her father that day started making sense to her, she did not think of her father as a coward. She liked to believe that if he would have been around for longer, he may have jumped into the freedom struggle. He was on the brink, balancing the sanity. Besides, Dalhousie was practically untouched by what the nation was going through at that moment. The heat was on in the bigger cities, where the leaders dwelled.

During one of Shakuntala's regular visits to her home on weekends, Kanshi closed her eyes as they entered the house and took her to the hall. It was a surprise, he said. After he removed his hands and Shakuntala's eyes adjusted to the light, she saw a brown wooden box of the size of a small trunk lying on the corner table. It had a dial on the right with a needle that could be rotated over a semicircular area covered by glass. There were a few knobs just below the dial. The left side of the box was covered with alternating wooden and metallic strips above a mesh of metal.

"A radio!" Shakuntala squealed with delight.

Kanshi rotated the dial to the correct frequency and there it was, the All India Radio, buzzing the house with human voices. Thereafter, it almost became a ritual for Shakuntala to come home during weekends and spend some time with her father listening to songs and news. Sometimes, Madan would sit with them and abruptly start dancing as a song played and make them laugh.

Later as she grew old, Shakuntala never let anyone sell the radio and always kept it with her. The day she died, the radio was in the house, sitting in a corner of the drawing room, unused and covered by a pretty crosia. It had turned into a piece of art, something that could have been in a museum, but she clung to it as the last reminiscent of her past. It reminded her of how much her life had changed.

Kanshi turned his business back to how it was. He was neck deep into work and a time came when there were around a hundred of his workers building summer houses at various locations. Money was flowing in and so was the envy of various other small-time builders. Kanshi had inherited the company of his uncle who was a well-established builder himself, but he had increased the profits and the reputation almost ten times in the wake of rising demand.

In the course of next six years, Shakuntala acquired the graciousness of a lady. She had read many books. She could make proper tea using kettle and cups. She played the piano reasonably well. She knew mathematics and geometry. She was what every girl of her age during that era in her country could only dream to be. Kanshi couldn't hide the tears of contentment every time he saw her.

He was by now the most sought after builders of the area and a proud father. Even though he had turned a bit aristocratic, there was never any ostentatious display of wealth. His house remained modest in appearance, although he added three more rooms later. The larger the house became, the lonelier he felt. He missed Kusum. During a few rare evening horse rides for which he went alone, he wondered how life would have turned out if Kusum had been alive. He wanted to fit her in the present, to be a part of the life he was leading, to see what a congenial lady her daughter had grown into. Sometimes he would close his eyes and imagine Kusum sitting besides him. He would try to imagine how happy she would be to see all this, what words she would utter when she would meet Shakuntala, how she would fly through the rooms of her house, sometimes turning and giving him a mischievous look as he followed. The ache was as unbearable as the cold winters of Dalhousie.

"It was supposed to be our moment together. Why did you leave?" He would ask her as he sat alone in the balcony of his bedroom sometimes, watching the sunset.

Kanshi could never bond well with Madan. It was partially because he was overworked most of the times and partially because Radha Devi would never leave father and son alone. She had started spending almost the entire year at Kanshi's house on the pretext that someone had to take care of Madan in the absence of his mother. Kanshi did not object. Madan was spoilt silly by his grandmother. Shakuntala had never thrown tantrums but Madan was a different breed. He would turn the house upside down and throw things at his grandmother and servants if his demands were not met. He sometimes ended up being slapped by his father, something that had never happened with Shakuntala. Radha Devi would throw her arms around Madan and kiss his slapped cheek later.

"*Hai! Hai!* How can a father slap his son like this?" she would shout at Kanshi.

One day when Madan got a beating and Kanshi stormed back into his room, Radha Devi followed him and saw him standing at the window, staring at the mountains. She swallowed the venom she was about to spit. She looked at him for a while from the door.

She felt pity for him. Not even thirty and gone through a lifetime of pain. For a second, she wished Kusum were alive.

"You should get married again," she said calmly.

Kanshi was silent. His mother came close and stood next to him.

"What if the woman I marry gives birth to another girl?" he said serenely.

His mother recoiled, hit by the bluntness of the statement. It dawned upon her that her son held her responsible for Kusum's death.

"I did not kill her, Kanshi," she said, plucking her son's shirt. She turned him around and looked in his empty eyes. Kanshi stared at her and in that moment she realized that her son was never going to forgive her, no matter what she said. Slowly, she let go of his shirt. Her legs were shaking. She feebly walked towards the bed and sat at its foot. Kanshi walked out of the room, closing the door behind him. Radha Devi sat there for a long time watching the shadows elongate on the floor as the Sun made its calculated sweep in the sky.

"I am going to Delhi," Kanshi told Shakuntala after a few days.

"Delhi? For how long?"

"Only for a few days; I have to see a piece of land there. If I like it, I'll buy it and build a house for us on it."

"Are we moving to Delhi?" Shakuntala asked, terrified at the thought of leaving the convent.

"No! Why should we? It's just an investment. Besides, I want things to be secure for my children."

Kanshi was gone for almost ten days. When he returned, he was ecstatic.

"I liked it. It's at a beautiful location, trees all around, quiet and serene. I will be going again to sign all the papers and close the deal," Kanshi told Shakuntala.

"Why, Papa? I have never seen you show any interest in Delhi. What is it?" Shakuntala asked, but got nothing more than a pat on the head.

Kanshi had not taken the decision in haste. The Second World War had started almost a year back and Kanshi was afraid of the changes it might bring with it. India was forced to enter the war by the British Empire without consultation with any of the Indian representatives. As a result, the entire Congress leadership resigned from the local councils. The Empire was now fighting a world war in addition to the internal resistance from India to leave the country. It was just a matter of time before they would buckle under the pressure and kneel down. There was too much on their hands to handle. But this was not something that Kanshi feared. The Lahore resolution was passed in 1940 and that was what was troubling him. There was a fear in the air. He could sense it. He was not aware which parts of India would go in the separate country that was being demanded, but he was very sure that Delhi wouldn't go. He could sense the upcoming uprooting and countrymen turning against each other once the external threat fade away. He wanted to invest in a place that he knew was safe so that when the time came, he could take his children away from trouble.

Shakuntala never saw him again. Instead, she saw the owl.

It was a harsh winter that year and it snowed quite heavily. So when the summers came and shards of sunlight started to melt away the frozen waters, it was time for everyone in the convent to air their beddings. Shakuntala shared her dorm with five other girls, and so one sunny Sunday morning all six girls picked up their beddings and took them to the huge ground in front of the hostel building. They covered the ground with old bed sheets and placed their mattresses on top of them. A few hours in the sun and the cotton inside the mattresses would be warm and fluffy. They would then beat the mattresses with wooden sticks to remove the dust and make the cotton softer. And then the girls would fall on their mattresses again and again, feeling the softness and crying Ah! in unison.

It was during such an exercise when Shakuntala went back inside to get a book she was reading. When she came out, she saw all the girls huddled in one corner of the garden. They were scared and pointing at her mattress. It took her some time to realize what she saw sitting there. Years later, when she recounted the incident numerous times in front of her grandchildren, she described it as round, ugly and with huge eyes, bigger than the big white buttons she had in her coat. The owl was sitting on her mattress as if he was born on it and had never left it. He was white and as Shakuntala approached, he turned his head without turning his body, just like a ghost. He stared at Shakuntala, blinking his eyes. She stared back. Owls were bad omens. Shakuntala realized that something terrible had happened, something in her existence had snapped. The river had changed its course. She felt vulnerable. Tears started filling her eyes and the book fell off her hands. Her knees weakened and she was unable to stand. And then, the owl expanded his wings. It was as if he wanted to embrace her, console her. He shifted his feet and suddenly there was a flapping sound as he took off. Shakuntala stared at him till he was out of sight with tears flowing down her cheeks.

In the evening, her warden called her and told her to pack a few of her things, as she had to go home for a few days.

"Your uncle is waiting in the visitor's room for you. Pack your bag and go," the warden said as her hands caressed Shakuntala's head. Her eyes were red. Shakuntala ran to the visitor's room. She saw her eldest uncle Kulbhushan sitting there. The moment he looked at her, Shakuntala knew.

Some people called it an accident while others thought it was a murder. No one knew what exactly happened, but there were whispers and gossips for years. A falling boulder crushed Kanshi and his horse during one of his evening rides. Falling boulders and landslides was not something uncommon in Dalhousie, but then Kanshi was a successful man with many enemies and jealous competitors. The chances of it being a murder were not ruled out and an investigation was carried on later but with no results. The boulder had thrown Kanshi and his horse deep into the valley and it took almost two days to locate them. When his body was recovered, he was unrecognizable. He was brought home covered in multiple layers of white cloth and a rope tied all around him. The smell was unbearable and he was cremated immediately. All this happened before Kulbhushan went to the convent to bring Shakuntala home. He could not bear the thought of allowing her to look at her father in that condition. He forbade anyone to inform Shakuntala.

By the time Shakuntala came, the last rites had been performed. She was fuming but she did not complain. Later, the feeling that her father was dead never sunk in as she had not seen his dead body. She liked to believe that her father was still in Delhi and would someday appear suddenly to give her a surprise. They hung her father's painting next to her mother's with a garland around it. Her aunts tried to make her cry by telling her what an unfortunate child she was but they couldn't bring a tear in her eyes. How could she when her father was still alive?

"You will burst like a volcano one day, Shakuntala. Spill out your tears, child, let them out," they would tell her. She just stared back.

Radha Devi went into a deep uncontrollable shock. After the thirteen day rituals were over, she quietly packed her clothes one night in a bundle and went to the ashram in the outskirts of the hill station. Before leaving the house, she went into Shakuntala's room and kissed her on the brow as she lay asleep. She stood there looking at her for some time. She did not tell anyone about her whereabouts till one of her sons inquired in the ashram. The sons descended there to implore her to come back but she was adamant. She told them that she had lost interest in her life. She wanted to be at the feet of the God and ask forgiveness for what she had done.

Radha died in the ashram eight years later in her sleep in 1948.

Shakuntala went back to the convent two months after Kanshi's death. The girls in the dorm were more than sympathetic. They would try to make her laugh and then would go and cry in the corridor as she would not respond. To Shakuntala, the thought that her father will never come to visit her again was unbearable. She was blinded by it. He is not dead, she kept telling herself. She kept mumbling this in her sleep and made the girls in her dorm cry in pity. She sometimes had a feeling that he was watching her, concealed behind a wall, smiling. Sometimes she felt that he would appear on a Sunday to meet her and she waited sitting on the stairs outside the visitor's room. This went on for six months.

"I want to go home," Shakuntala blurted out one day when

Kulbhushan came on one of his regular visits.

"What? Why? I always thought you wanted this." He was surprised.

"Not anymore. It's too painful and I am going mad. Please take me somewhere else," Shakuntala pleaded.

Kulbhushan had five sons and three daughters. The eldest was a son who was eighteen years old and the youngest was a daughter aged six. Their house was not as big as Kanshi's. All the children slept in one big room on the upper floor while Kulbhushan and his wife slept on the ground floor. The house stood somewhere in the middle of a mountain, halfway between the valley and the peak. The terrace farm on which Kulbhushan and his elder sons worked surrounded it from the front. Shakuntala felt awkward during her initial days there. She had met her cousins occasionally but had never envisioned that she had to live with them one day.

Kulbhushan was a burly man with a thick moustache with pointed ends. He had soft eyes and the lines around them oozed wisdom. He was almost ten years older to Kanshi. His wife Pushpa was a small, timid woman who would smile even if you shout at her. She welcomed Shakuntala like her own daughter. A few days into the house and Shakuntala started to absorb the atmosphere. The house was always buzzing with noises but she was used to it because of her hostel dorm. The house in which she was born was as tranquil as the ocean when she compared it to Kulbhushan's. It was empty now, locked away with dust-covered memories inside it.

All the five boys in the house studied at the local school and the girls helped their mother. Shakuntala started giving tuitions to the boys and helped them with their homework. She also started teaching English to the girls. She gained a newfound respect amongst them because of her knowledge. They were in awe of her. During the day, she helped Kulbhushan on the farm with whatever she could and helped his wife as well in the kitchen. To feed eleven people three times everyday was a monumental task in itself.

Kulbhushan never complained about the added responsibility. Kanshi's fourth brother Raghubir brought up Madan. He had the least number of kids (only five) and he was now the richest amongst the brothers. Ideally, Shakuntala should have been taken up by the third brother because he was the next in line with the least number of kids, but then Kulbhushan took up the responsibility because he wanted to. Of all his brothers, he had always loved Kanshi the most and was always overprotective towards his little brother and his family. Besides, he was proud of what Kanshi had turned Shakuntala into. He wanted Shakuntala to be his daughter.

The four brothers had decided to carry forward Kanshi's business in which they failed miserably because they did not have the required time and the business acumen. They had their own work to look after, which no one was ready to give up. There were disagreements with workers about wages. The brothers grappled with his business for a year before shutting it down. They somehow managed to complete the summer houses for which the construction had already started before Kanshi's death but did not take any new ones. There were losses and they had to return a lot of money. They heaved a sigh of relief after they returned to their plain and simple jobs.

Shakuntala was twelve now. She was not content with her life but she had settled in. After all, this was her choice. She was the one who wanted to leave the convent. Did she regret the decision? She asked herself this question many times. But the answer did not matter now. It all seemed so distant, like a fading dream. Sometimes, Shakuntala sat on the open terrace of Kulbhushan's house in the mornings, before anyone else woke up, and looked at the green valley down below. The valley was covered with mist in the morning. No one knew where it came from. Some said it arose from a lake in the jungle down below where fairies bathed at dawn. She sat there and looked at the mist wandering aimlessly, covering things, hiding them as it moved up. But then sometimes, sunlight broke from the clouds and in a few minutes, the mist vanished. This always made her smile.

More than anyone else, her cousins kept her busy. The days flew by as she told them fairy tales and played games with them, running on the narrow lanes in the farm. Sometimes she would almost forget her previous life but then there was always a slight pain in a corner of her heart. It wasn't as unbearable now as it was earlier, but it was there, with its slight buzzing sensation reminding her of its presence. A thousand times she had dreamed of her parents embracing and beaming at her but the reality was far less soothing. Kulbhushan and Pushpa did their best to ease her pain but they knew that it would take its own time to wear off.

Shakuntala asked Kulbhushan to sell off Oliver. Her parrot Ram had died a year after she left for the convent. Besides her clothes, the only thing that Shakuntala took from her old house was the radio. It sat in Kulbhushan's bedroom and every evening, the kids would huddle in and listen to the news bulletin in Hindustani. A few months after she moved in with the family, the Quit India Movement started in 1942. The Indian National Congress had demanded complete independence from the British

Raj. Gandhi and many Congress leaders were jailed the very next day and there were nationwide strikes and bloodshed. Kulbhushan asked the family to stay at home for some days and not to visit the market frequently. The Hill stations were still untouched by the upheavals the rest of the nation was going through but things were reaching a crescendo now. The struggle was intensifying.

Shakuntala started learning the basics of growing potatoes. It was not as easy as it appeared.

"You have to cut the potatoes properly otherwise you will end up with multiple sprouts in one."

"Dig it further. Further. It's not enough yet!"

"Face the sprout upwards. Do you want the plant to grow inwards?"

"Pull it out gently! Feel the potato first, then dig a bit farther and pull it out gently. Easy! That's it!"

Kulbhushan was worse than the nuns in the convent. This was his kingdom and he was the master of the art.

"I may not be as intelligent as your father was but I know how to grow potatoes," he once told Shakuntala. Shakuntala smiled as she placed a sprout in the ground.

The worst part was guarding the potatoes from the bears. The valley below was full of them and sometimes in the dead of the night, a few of them would visit the farm for a feast. There was no other way but to terrify them with fire, so someone had to be at guard. An approaching bear would always make some grunting or snorting sounds that would give him away. So, the male member on duty that night would quietly slip out of the house and light a fire to shoo him away. This was terrifying to Shakuntala at first but the family was just used to it as if it was a stroll in the pines.

Sensing Shakuntala's fear, Kulbhushan bought a dog to watch the fields at night. Shakuntala took up the responsibility of feeding him and taking him for a walk. She named him Tiger.

The potatoes were ready, so they were dug out and filled in jute sacks, which were sewn at the top with thick thread and taken to the market in a horse cart. This was an activity in which the whole family participated. All the sacks wouldn't fill in the cart in one go, so Kulbhushan would have to do multiple rounds. A few of them were sold to the local vendors but a majority of them went to other towns or were bought by the servants of the residing British families. It was during one of those multiple rounds when Shakuntala met him for the first time in 1946. She had taken Tiger along with her and was roaming around while Kulbhushan finished his business. She passed the post office when she sensed someone watching her. She turned around and there he was, squatting on the ground and chewing a thin broken stem. He was not very good-looking, just an average 18 year old. His eyes were intense and he had a perfect square jaw and neatly brushed hair. Shakuntala stared back because his jaw was so much like her father's, then raised her chin and marched ahead.

"Disgusting! Come Tiger!!!" she said as she gave the boy an icy cold glance and pulled her dog.

Next day, when she went to the terrace of her house to dry her hair after a bath, the boy was there, sitting under a tree and waiting for her. There was a pathway carved out of the mountain just behind Kulbhushan's house, which went up to the road and joined other arteries in the mountain. It was a short cut that the family used when they were not using the horse cart. The boy was sitting under a tree next to the stone pathway and could see the house below. When Shakuntala came out, her back was towards him and he stared at her for a long time as she rubbed her hair with the towel. As she turned to go inside and looked up the mountain, she saw him squatting under the tree. It took her a moment to place him and realized that the boy had followed them yesterday.

"What the hell is he trying to do?" she muttered under her breath as she stomped inside.

The boy started coming everyday. He had a flute with him and he played a beautiful tune to announce his arrival. Shakuntala never came out of the house but she listened to it as she sat inside and did her chores. It was weird how the boy was following her all the time. This went on for almost fifteen days. As his visits showed no signs of abatement and the tunes became more and more surreal, Shakuntala had momentary urges to have a look at him. She finally gave in one day and opened a window in the pretext of getting some fresh air and had a long look at him. His eyes were closed as his fingers moved in a rhythm playing with the air coming out of the keys, but then as if getting a cue, he opened his eyes. He saw Shakuntala standing at the window. As their eyes met, she smiled at him which made him blush instantly. The music stopped abruptly and the flute fell off the boy's hand. It was the first time she had acknowledged his presence with an approving gesture.

During one of her routine rounds to G.P.O with Kulbhushan to buy some groceries for the house, Shakuntala heard rumours of a famous Hindi movie director, Abbas, who was in Dalhousie to search for a location for his latest movie. Shakuntala had seen Achhut Kanya in theatre three times with Kanshi and she was fascinated. She just wanted to meet and talk to a person who knew the beautiful people on screen, a person who had seen them, touched them, worked with them.

"Can we meet him?" she implored Kulbhushan when they were returning from G.P.O.

Kulbhushan opened his mouth to say something but then closed it again. He was in a dilemma.

"What is it?" Shakuntala asked him.

"All right! Well, Abbas saw you in the market the other day..." Kulbhushan started.

"Did he? Why didn't you tell me?" Shakuntala almost fell off the cart.

"He came to meet me. I had no idea who he was but he was very polite and introduced himself as a filmmaker. He wants to cast you in one of his movies. He thinks you are very beautiful and can be a very successful actress. He offered quite an amount of money."

Shakuntala was quiet. She had no intentions to become a movie heroine. The prospect scared her. She just hoped that Kulbhushan hadn't said yes.

"I refused. We belong to a respectable family. People say all kinds of rubbish for actresses and it would be painful for me if you are subjected to that," he said after studying her face.

The sigh of relief that Shakuntala exhaled was almost audible. Kulbhushan smiled.

The incident had facetious effects on Shakuntala. She did not open the window or smile at the boy for the whole of next week. When she encountered him in the market place one day, she pointed her nose towards the sky and moved on. The boy was aghast. He could not understand what deadly mistake he had committed. Maybe he was not playing the right tunes. But he was there every single day in the morning, playing the flute below the tree and waiting for a glimpse of Shakuntala. Soon Shakuntala's whimsical behaviour started melting away as the flute threw one enticing tune after another in the air and it was just a matter of time before she opened the window again to give a smile. There was a faint sound as the flute fell again on the stone stairway. The smile turned into laughter this time. The boy grinned too.

Kulbhushan and his sons had eyed the stranger many times around their house and questioned him once. He told them that he liked sitting there and had no intention of harming anyone. He was a visitor in Dalhousie and would be leaving in a few days. They gave up the idea of forcing him away from their house, as he did not disturb anyone and he played the flute beautifully. It was very pleasant to listen to music as they worked in the fields. No one invited him inside the house. After all, there were unmarried girls in there.

They started meeting in deserted places, in houses built and forgotten, on farms invisible from main roads and narrow pathways, under dense trees, behind huge boulders. The boy had stuck a small handwritten note near the window and as Shakuntala opened it one day to have a look at him, he pointed his eyes at the paper protruding out of a slight crack near the window. That is how it started. He was smitten and Shakuntala was intoxicated. Both were young and their meetings often started with lustful kisses. He would push his hand beneath her kameez and run it over her bare skin and she would pull his hair and kiss him on the lips. It was a new world, terrifying and fragile and yet so beautiful. Shakuntala was surprised by the animalism. It was as if there was someone else hiding inside her waiting for this man to come along. Although she would never let him go to the extreme, it was getting harder for her to stop herself. Sometimes, they would sit quietly under the pine trees as the winds made soothing sounds and he would tell her about his family and his brothers. He was in Dalhousie with his elder brother Bhaskar. They came for ten days to attend a marriage of a close relative, but had stayed almost for a month because he had insisted. They were from Khanna, a village in Punjab – six brothers and three sisters. All of them were older and married except for him and a younger brother. She told him about her mother, her father, and the tragedies. She cried for the first time after her father's death, accepting the fact that he would not return. All the tears that she had accumulated over the years left her body and she felt light-headed. He held her close to him and kissed her and told her that he would take care of her for the rest of his life.

She never called him by his name, but always called him *Suno*. It was disrespectful to call your lover by his name. They met like this for a week before Suno told her that he wanted to marry her. Shakuntala said yes to the proposal. It was a decision made on instincts, on the warmth of love, on the promise of a future of passions. Yes, he was a bit of a stranger but that part of him was chipping off rapidly.

"And don't call me Suno. It makes me feel as if we are already married. Call me Manu. That is what everyone calls me at home," Suno said one day.

"I won't take your name in front of everyone else, but in private I shall call you Manu."

"Did I ever tell you about a girl in my village, who is madly in love with me. She worships me and thinks that I will only marry her."

"Oh! What will she do now? You have broken her heart," Shakuntala said as she kissed him on the cheek.

"My mother is very fond of her. She has already accepted her as her daughter-in-law. Wait till she hears this!" Manu laughed.

"Are you marrying me to make people jealous?"

"No. I am marrying you so that I can see you naked."

"Chi!"

Manu's elder brother Bhaskar came to Kulbhushan's house the next day. Kulbhushan finally understood the reason for the boy's continuous presence around his house and why the flute churned out one mellifluous tune after another. The family was surprised but there was no reason to say no. Manu's family was well to do and the boy liked Shakuntala. Besides, they did not ask for any dowry. Soon the local pundit finalized a date after matching the horoscopes to his satisfaction. Both the families started preparing for the ceremony amidst songs and shopping. Shakuntala was in a frenzy. The feeling had started to sink in that another change was going to hit her life, but hopefully for better this time. She was going to an alien place amongst unknown people. The only man she knew there was Manu and she clung to the thought. He will sail me through, she thought. She had come to accept Kulbhushan's house as her own and that feeling was leaving her now. She wondered how many times she will have to let go of this feeling of stability.

Just before the arrival of the groom and his family, Shakuntala sat in her room looking at her image in the mirror. She was wearing a red pahari dress made by Kulbhushan's wife for her. At one point or the other, the wives of her uncles had done some embroidery on the dress or added a few minor details here and there to make it look pretty. They had used golden strips of ribbons to make flowers, which had been later sewn in the dress. Shakuntala was wearing jewellery bought with her father's money. All her clothes were packed in iron trunks strewn across the room. She was lost in thought, thinking about her father when Madan entered the room. She had not seen him since a few months. He was 12 and had grown into a diffident handsome boy but Shakuntala could hardly relate him to the noisy brat she had known him to be. He had turned all right. He was shy now, much quieter. They had met on a few family functions and get-togethers in the last few years and had respectfully acknowledged each other's presence; and now Madan was standing at the door, smiling. It was at this explicit moment when both of them looked into each other's eyes and endorsed the fact that they were supposed to be together. There was a future, which they were supposed to carve together, which was theirs and was snatched away from them by destiny. Shakuntala smiled at his image in the mirror. Madan came forward and embraced Shakuntala. They sat there like this for a few moments, embracing each other, staring at their reflection in the mirror and smiling.

"You look beautiful," Madan said after a moment.

"I wish..." Shakuntala began to say.

"I know."

"Am I disturbing?" Kulbhushan asked. He was standing at the door and smiling.

"Oh no! I was just leaving," Madan said as he straightened up and left the room.

Kulbhushan closed the door as Madan went out.

"You are looking very beautiful. Just like a doll," Kulbhushan said as he kissed Shakuntala on the forehead.

"Thank you, thank you for everything."

"Not yet! There is one more thing I need to do. Something I haven't told you yet. Your father never made a will but then he was leaving that for old age. We four brothers tried to save the business but couldn't and we are deeply sorry for that. We kept the money aside for your future but much of it went in paying back the advance of tens of summer houses that your father was supposed to make. We spent a part of it on your marriage and we are going to spend the rest of it on Madan. Be assured that none of us will use it for our own amusement."

"Uncle..."

"Now let me finish. I know it doesn't matter and you know that I love you like my own child but still, some things should better be spoken. After your father passed away, I found this in his almirah," Kulbhushan said as he waved something wrapped in a yellow cloth with a thread at Shakuntala.

"I want you to take this and keep it safe with you. I haven't told about this to anyone. Remember, use it only when you think it is required. This is something your father would have wanted you to have," Kulbhushan said as he pushed the cloth towards Shakuntala.

"What is inside it? I don't want it. Please keep it with you, uncle. I can't handle such things."

"You will know when to use it. Believe me, you will," Kulbhushan said as he got up and took the key of the iron trunk lying next to Shakuntala's feet and opened it. He kept the thing wrapped in the yellow cloth on the top and locked the trunk and gently kept the key back with the bunch.

"Keep it safe and use it wisely. God bless you my child," Kulbhushan said as he got up and went outside.

That day, Shakuntala did not see what was there in the yellow cloth. She saw it a few days later, and decades later, when the time came to use it, the nerve wrecked in her brain. That was the irony of her life, which reached a blinding luminosity before plummeting into darkness, which came in tidal waves of happiness and distress and there was always a harbinger – first the owl and now her husband. She took the radio with her. She was a married woman now and life was beginning to smile again, at least for the time being.

Manu and his five brothers lived together in a modest house, which was just big enough to accommodate everyone. There were a host of twenty children in the house. Shakuntala's father-in-law died long ago and her mother-in-law was a crumbling old woman with a terrified look on her face and who spent most of her time in a small room provided to her on the ground floor. Shakuntala felt claustrophobic at times, lost in a crowd, but then she was running in and out of such thoughts. She had lost herself in a crowd earlier and living amongst so many people kept her occupied because she had a habit of going into cogitations when left alone.

The girl did come to have a glimpse of Shakuntala. She wanted to have a look at the woman who had taken her place. Shakuntala sat in the hall, her face covered with the end of her sari, while all the women of the village gathered around her. Every minute or so, a woman would hold the corner of the sari and gently pull it up to have a peek at her face. The woman then rotated a few coins around her head, bless her and place them in a cloth lying at Shakuntala's feet. Everyone was raving about her. Such a beautiful bride Manu got for himself, they were saying. Shakuntala wouldn't have recognized the girl had she not held the sari for a few seconds more than usual. She stared at Shakuntala, sizing her up and then smiled. Shakuntala looked up and it instantaneously struck her that this was the girl. The girl smiled again. A smile clad with pity for herself, a sad smile for the love she had lost. She never came to the house again and this was the first and last time Shakuntala saw her.

It was a difficult year. Independence was imminent and so was the partition. The British Empire's rule in India was dissolving and the nation was on the verge of being divided into two separate nations. The Cabinet Mission, a British delegation, met the leaders of Congress and the Muslim League in Shimla. The meeting failed and there was no consensus between the two groups. The riots started spreading from Calcutta where 5000 people were massacred in three days. After that, everything fell like a pack of dominos and the butchering spread all over the country like a wildfire. Any hope that the British had of leaving quietly was quashed. Lord Mountbatten was hurriedly dispatched from England to strike a fair deal without any further bloodshed.

Religious groups had started building all over Punjab which moved from village to village, leaving dead bodies behind. Night watches were arranged to make sure that no one sneaked into a village and created mayhem, but such measures hardly worked in front of mobs of hundreds of bloodthirsty men with swords and iron rods in hands. Seeing the volatile nature of the situation, a hasty agreement was reached between Mountbatten, Nehru and Jinnah and on 3 June, 1947 the three of them broadcasted the decision on All India Radio. India was to be divided but the question of which piece of land goes to which country was still hanging in the air, Punjab and Bengal being the major roadblocks.

Shakuntala and Manu sat in front of the radio that day and

heard the trio and wondered what things have come to.

"What is going to happen now? Do you think we should pack?" A visibly shaken Shakuntala asked.

"I think, yes, we must. I will inform everyone in the house," Manu said.

"Why do we need independence, if this is the price at which it comes? How can people who fought together kill each other after they achieved what they were fighting for?" she said.

"Ask the politicians. We are farmers. We are too small for all this."

"Do you think we might have to leave this house? The village might end up in Pakistan."

"No, I don't think so but madness has no direction. God knows in which way we might have to run to escape it. Shakuntala, I have to tell you something. My father had a friend in Delhi who might help us. After all this mess is cleaned up, we are going to shift to Delhi and live there. "

"Now where did this come from? I thought you liked it here."

"I cannot be a farmer all my life. I hate it. And there are chances of a better life there. I have a plan."

Delhi. Shakuntala was startled how that city never left the horizon of her life, how it was always leaping into her existence from one corner or another. The last time she heard about it was the last time she saw her father. That city made her uneasy.

Cyril Radcliff arrived in India on 8 July, 1947 to draw borders across India and Pakistan. The process was hasty and had to be completed in five weeks. People were completely disoriented during that period. They had no idea whether the land on which they were standing would lead them to death or life. Speculations were rife and a slight indication would make people pack and leave in hoards. When news spread that Lahore, the capital of Punjab would go to Pakistan, the rich Hindu and Sikh families started moving towards Delhi and its adjoining areas much before Radcliff submitted his report. Some of them left their belongings behind, in the hope that the news was false. Some stayed, adamant that they would not leave their home and ended up watching the densely populated Hindu and Sikh settlements of the culturally vibrant Lahore burn to ashes.

When it finally came, the conclusions of the Radcliff report were messy. The Radcliff line passed through densely populated towns, villages and sometimes even through houses. Radcliff was glad when he left India on the day of her independence barely giving two hours to the two sides to understand and agree upon the borders. Mountbatten did not reveal the plans till the last moment because he did not want the British to be blamed for the inevitable bloodshed. Some people said that this decision was what lead to the mayhem that followed. If Mountbatten would have revealed the plans two weeks before the day of independence of India and Pakistan, millions of people would have crossed the borders alive.

As the borders finally took shape and physically cut the nation into two, the mess which looked harmless on paper took a long time to clear in reality. As Pandit Jawaharlal Nehru unfurled the tricolour on the grounds of Lal Qila in Delhi on 15 August 1947, amidst thousands of Indians cheering and shouting slogans of Hindustan Zindabad, little did everyone know that independence would bring an unprecedented wave of destruction. The border between India and Pakistan was now finally revealed by Mountbatten and fifteen million people were uprooted from the land that they knew as their homes and thrown into unknown territories. Millions were butchered while crossing over and hiding. Riots broke out in every nook and corner of the bleeding countries. All those who had once stood together and fought against the British Empire were now cutting each other down. Trains that were filled with refugees in one country started arriving in the other filled with slain corpses, filled with jute sacks full of breasts. There were ample reasons now to rape women of other religions, to behead women and children and to hang men. There were reasons now to ask the women in your family to jump into wells to save your dignity while you try to escape alive. There were reasons now to forcibly convert people to your religion. There were reasons to strip schoolgirls naked and rape them in front of a crowd.

Khanna remained in India but the village that was now Shakuntala's home was not untouched by the madness. There were searches conducted in all the Hindu houses, as there was a possibility of Hindus hiding their Muslim neighbours who were not able to cross the border on time and those who were too old or sick to travel. Most of the Muslim households in the village were burnt down and the occupants were butchered. There were dead bodies in the fields, corpses hanging from trees, heads rolling on the ground, wells filled with slain men and women. The stench of terror was unbearable and it hung like a massive weight on everyone's heart.

One night, as Shakuntala lay on her bed thinking about her house in Dalhousie, she gave a sigh of relief that the hill station remained in India. A majority of the Gurdaspur district of Punjab, in which Dalhousie was located, stayed in India. The Radcliffe line was kind enough to pass it by. Punjab was the most difficult state to divide between the two countries because of its uniform multi-religion density. After much toying by the British, the Radcliff line squeezed past somewhere between Lahore and Amritsar, which were hardly 55kms apart. Shakuntala could not think of the horror her relatives would have to endure if they had to cross the border, but they were spared.

By the time it all ended, millions were dead or uprooted. There were scars that would never fade; lives that would never be the same and anger that would never subside. The unrest continued well into the next year, right from Mahatma Gandhi's assassination to Operation Polo to the first Kashmir War. Manu was biding his time and waiting for things to settle down before he could make his move. He helped his brothers in the farm and described elaborate details to Shakuntala about his thoughts of settling in Delhi. The two years which Shakuntala had spent in Khanna had been quite uneventful. The stir which Shakuntala's beauty had created when she entered the village had fizzled out in the wake of the partition. Most of their neighbours were gone and were replaced by unknown livid people.

One day, out of the blue, Manu asked for his share of the family land. Everyone in the house was furious except for the eldest brother, Bhaskar. Manu was too educated to be a farmer, he said. Although Manu had barely passed school, it was considered a big achievement as the brothers pressed their ink stained thumb in lieu of signature. So, amidst protests and collective boycotts from the family, 1/6th of the total land was carved out and given to Manu. Manu sold the land as soon as the papers came in his hands. All the women in the house refused to cook for Manu. Shakuntala was blamed for changing Manu after marriage.

"He was like a cow before and now look at him! How can a woman change a man so much?" The women in the house gossiped.

Shakuntala pleaded and cried in front of the whole family saying that she had nothing to do with it but she would stand by

Manu, as he had done nothing wrong. The drama of blaming and protests were silenced one night when Bhaskar lost his temper, and that was the end of it.

"What is wrong with everyone? He wants to move out of the village. I wanted to do that once but didn't have the courage. Let him go peacefully. Give him your blessing. I don't want to hear another raised voice in this house."

And so, Manu and Shakuntala left for Delhi in 1949. The whole family bid them farewell at the local railway station, some happily and some reluctantly. The family covered almost 3/4th of the platform and it took Manu and Shakuntala a while to touch everyone's feet before boarding the train. Manu almost missed the train in the process. Shakuntala was travelling by train for the first time. She was petrified initially as the train chugged out of the station but soon she gave in to the rhythm. The constant rattling and the wind blowing in through the windows soothed her mind. She turned several times to look at Manu and smiled as he sat next to her looking at the farms rolling out of their sight.

On reaching Delhi, Narayan came to receive them. He was Manu's father's very old friend and the reason why Manu was in Delhi. He had leased a two-room house near Bengali Market for the couple. Narayan had bought a double bed and some groceries and kept them in the house beforehand. Except that the house was quite bare. After a day's rest, Manu got busy buying all the household goods with the help of Narayan while Shakuntala got busy in setting up the house.

The plan that Manu had in his mind was to buy Narayan's shop in Connaught Place with the money and open a Shoe shop there. Narayan had come to visit the village four years back and had showed an inclination to sell it when he met the brothers in

Khanna. None of the brothers showed any interest but Manu saw a window of freedom. He wrote a letter to Narayan to hold the shop for him. I will buy it but give me some time, he wrote to Narayan. I had known your father since childhood, I will hold the shop for you as long as you like, Narayan wrote back. As the dust of partition settled down, Manu told Narayan that he was ready and then asked for his share of land from his brothers. Within a week after reaching Delhi, the shop was his. Narayan also arranged for two craftsmen to make all kinds of fancy and formal shoes and helped Manu to set up the Business.

Delhi bothered Shakuntala. It scared her. She wondered why there were so many people around. And why was everything so flat. There were no hills, no snow, no pines – nothing, just a disrobed piece of unending land. She was like a fish out of water. For the first two months, Shakuntala and Manu hardly went out except to India Gate that was quite close by or sometimes to the Bengali Market. They would sit at India Gate in the evening and gawk at the waves of bicycles and a handful of cars coming out of the Secretariat as offices closed. One day, as the couple sat there and looked at the President's palace devouring the setting sun, Shakuntala took out Manu's flute from her bag and gave it to him. Manu was startled.

"There are so many people around," he said.

"Close your eyes then. I want to listen," Shakuntala said.

Manu took the flute, closed his eyes and started playing. Four policemen standing a distance away wearing their Khaki shirt and shorts with red turbans on their heads stared at him and then smiled. People started to gather around him. The vendors selling various eatables took advantage and established themselves nearby. A row of barbers who were snipping off hair in their makeshift shop which was simply a cloth on the ground and a customer sitting on it, stopped and looked around for the source of the music. Ice cream eating children pulled their ice cream eating parents towards the tune. Manu kept playing for a long time oblivious to the flurry he had created. When he eventually opened his eyes, they met with the gaze of a crowd staring at him. He looked at Shakuntala accusingly and she smiled and placed her head on his arm. The crowd beamed and clapped before dispersing into their lives.

Manu had set a target date for the opening of the shop and wanted to finish the initial stock before the opening. He took Shakuntala to Connaught Place for the inauguration and she helped in decorations. As the shop opened and the customers started trickling in, Manu had some respite on Sundays. Shakuntala had never seen him work so hard before. He mentioned to her that it was almost a month and a half since they arrived in Delhi and they hadn't explored the place properly. Both of them started spending their Sundays traveling across the length and breadth of the city and that is when Shakuntala realized that she had only seen the tip of the iceberg. Manu took her to Qutab Minar, Chandni Chowk, Jantar Mantar, Lal Qila, Humayun's Tomb and many other places. Going to Qutab Minar was an arduous task as Delhi ended at Lodhi Gardens and there was only a makeshift road that went till the monument, so Manu bought a bicycle and he would tie a towel at the crossbar so that Shakuntala could sit comfortably on it. The bicycle soon became an integral part of their expeditions in Delhi. South Delhi and East Delhi did not exist at that time; Pusa Road and Daryaganj were jungles where people feared to roam at night. Traffic lights were being installed for the first time on the roads.

Sometimes, the couple traveled by the Delhi Transport Service's newly introduced buses or by the decorated horse carts called tanga. The more Shakuntala roamed, the more she had a glimpse of the rest of the iceberg. Delhi was huge, nowhere nearly as huge as it turned out in the next few years, but definitely a far cry from Dalhousie.

The city was full of refugees. People who had fled from Pakistan and crossed the border in search of a new life were swarming the city. Makeshift tents and refugee camps sprouted at Old Fort, Red Fort, Kingsway, Lodhi colony and hundreds of other places where people had to start their life from scratch. Some people started living in houses left abandoned by the families who had either fled Delhi for Pakistan or had been butchered before they could escape. There was poverty all around. Refugees were doing miniscule jobs to make ends meet. Some had opened roadside shops on pavements much to the discomfort of already existing shops in the areas; some were selling clothes or toys from door to door while some just begged. Narayan would narrate stories of refugees to Shakuntala on his usual visits. He would tell about people who were rich zamindars in Pakistan but had fled with nothing more than the clothes they were wearing. He told the couple horrid tales of murder and loot in Delhi when rioters looted whole markets and burnt them afterwards. The government had a humungous task of feeding and settling refugees in and around the city.

Sometimes Narayan would enter into rhetoric about the 562 princely states of India and how they were a pain in the ass, Hyderabad being the most painful. It was a year long jostle following independence after which Operation Polo ended the reign of the Nizam in Hyderabad and the state was included in India in 1948. While leaving India, the British had given up on the

Princely states, asking the government of India to deal with them on their own. It was not under the control of the British to merge them in either India or Pakistan. Shakuntala and Manu were quite unaware of the stories about how the princely states were merged one by one into India by Sardar Patel through persuasion and sometimes by force and Narayan would tell them the stories with relish over a cup of tea in the evening.

As the couple settled down, Manu's elder brothers started pouring in from Khanna for short visits. Soon the visits stretched and two of the brothers, Akhil and Sambhav, settled in Manu's house permanently with their families. Shakuntala and Manu were too anxious to ask them to depart, as they did not want to cause an uproar. Bhaskar, the eldest, tried to intervene and force Akhil and Sambhav to dart back to Khanna, but both of them wanted to settle down in Delhi and expected Manu to aid them. Manu told them as respectfully as possible that he himself was trying to find a foothold and was in no position to assist them. We would wait, the brothers replied. They had sold off their shares in their farms in Khanna and now had the funds to start anew in the big city. Manu could have taken Narayan's help but he refrained from doing so. Shakuntala wondered why she always ended up with a crowd staying in a small house.

"But why don't you take Narayan kaka's help? Your brothers lie in the house like snails without raising a single finger and would only untie their mouth to gobble. They are not providing us any finances to support their stay, then why are we suffering them?" Shakuntala prodded him.

"I can't go to Narayan kaka every time. He is my father's friend, not my father."

In 1950, India got its first President and the Election Commission. Manu and Shakuntala went and stood outside the magnificently lit dome of Darbar Hall of the Rashtrapati Bhavan, the President's House. A crowd has gathered there to have a look at the first president of India, Dr. Rajendra Prasad. The moment was electric with people chanting 'Vande Mataram' and Manu screamed with the rest of the crowd. Soon Dr. Rajendra Prasad appeared and greeted the crowd and gave a short speech. The whole city was in a festive mood. On 26 January, 1950, Manu and Shakuntala went to see the first Republic Day parade of the free nation. People sat on the ground on both sides of Rajpath as the President arrived in a horse carriage and stood on a small podium next to the road to take military salute during the parade. Later, the parade passed through various roads of the city which was thronged by crowds to view the spectacle. When the procession passed in front of Manu's shop in Connaught Place, his workers stood with the rest of the crowd between the white pillars and gawked in amazement. They were delirious with joy when they later narrated the whole sequence to Manu.

A few days later, Manu went down with jaundice. He was in bed for two months before he started to grasp that his business was inadvertently suffering. He could not leave the shop to Shakuntala or to the workers and ended up asking Akhil and Sambhav for help. Manu was nurturing the notion that he was going to meet his maker soon and wanted his brothers to take care of Shakuntala and his shop. He drew legal papers and gave the power of Attorney to his brothers.

Two months later, Manu ended up being alive and devoid of the shop. He shouted and screamed but nothing could be done. The shop was now the legal property of his two brothers. Manu asked them to vacate his house, which they shamelessly refused. The house turned into a war zone and Manu threatened his brothers with dire consequences but he knew very well that he could not do a thing legally. Narayan came to Manu's rescue once again. He cursed the brothers dramatically by sprinkling water specially brought from the holy Ganges and the brothers reacted equally vividly by jumping away from him as if he was a leper. He took Manu and Shakuntala with him to his residence. Manu was hesitant to take his help yet again.

Shakuntala was too shocked to react. This was diametrically opposite to how she had seen brothers of her father behave with each other in her family. She shuddered to think what would have happened to Madan and her if her uncles would have been like Manu's brothers. Her mind could not grasp what happened to Manu and her. It was all like a bad dream, just like the death of her father. Suddenly, they had nothing. If Narayan would not have been there, they could have lived with the refugees and nobody would have acknowledged the dissimilarity.

Narayan vowed to place Manu in a good position in a government job and used his contacts to get him a clerk's job in the Defense Science Organization. The money was ample for two people and soon Manu applied for a government flat. With a little nudge from Narayan, they got the flat quite soon. A part of Manu's salary went as the flat's rent to the government, but what was left was more than sufficient for both of them. Bhaskar tried calling Manu back to Khanna after he came to know about what happened, but Delhi was now their home. There was no turning back. The flat was not very big but for the first time in her life since her childhood, Shakuntala felt free. She had a whole house to herself, no matter if it was not copious. It was fulfilling.

She cherished Manu but she wished he had not trusted his brothers without doubt but then she chided herself – if you cannot trust your family, then whom to trust? She was afraid to admit this but she was also not positive if Manu had it in him to make a life on his own. He could not save the shop and this job was Narayan's brainchild. Was he capable of taking care of her? There were times when she was alone in the house and she remembered the past. What if she had not dropped out of the convent? Everything was so distant now, as if it happened in another life. She had it in her. She was different. At times, she questioned her stupidity of thinking too much about the past.

As time passed, the house that was ample and exuberant at first started feeling secluded. Loneliness at times oscillated her thoughts wildly and she ended up being restless. She passed her time by writing numerous letters to Kulbhushan and her cousins. She was constantly in touch with Madan as promised. He had finished his school and was ready to go to college. She listened to her father's radio, she knitted sweaters for Manu, she made his favorite dishes, she read books and English magazines and she kept the house in perfect order and ended up being the ideal housewife. But soon, the two-bedroom house started pricking her. Freedom seemed banal. Manu's presence soothed her, he was her fulcrum but she was hungry for more. The walls of the house were turning into slow poison; she had to get out before it devoured her.

Sometimes she stood in front of the mirror and applied makeup, thinking how her life would have been if her uncle had let her be a film actress, and then in the summer of 1951 as she had utterly made up her mind to have a conversation with Manu and Narayan about her further studies, she realized that she was pregnant.

# *Aaryan*

Aaryan was experimenting with his crayons on the front page of Hindustan Times when the doorbell rang. His father had fallen asleep while watching television after coming from office and his mother was cooking dinner in the kitchen. She hurriedly came out and opened the door. Aaryan looked up and saw his mother's friend Pinky, who was also their neighbour, standing at the door.

"Pinky! My hands are full! This better be urgent!" Aaryan's mother blurted out.

"It is. Come quickly. I have to show you something," Pinky said with a mix of trepidation and anxiety on her face.

"Wait. Let me run and turn off the gas." Aaryan's mother disappeared into the kitchen for a few seconds and hurriedly came out.

"Come fast!" Pinky said as she pulled her out. His mother forgot to close the door as she glided up the stairs.

"What is it?" she said while climbing up.

Aaryan's family lived in a modest two bedroom apartment on the first floor of a building that housed seven other families. There were similar buildings all around and they all formed a U shaped structure together with a park at the center. Pinky lived with her husband and son next door. She had locked her flat door from outside which piqued Aaryan's curiosity further as he got up to observe where the ladies were going. He had no idea that what he was going to witness in the next five minutes was going to haunt him for the rest of his life. It was a sweltering June of 1984 and although Aaryan was just five and did not understand the implications of what he saw, he cursed his mother later for not closing the door from outside that day. If she had, his life would have turned out all right.

As he stood at the open door, undecided whether to go ahead and follow the two women or to return back to his mutilation spree of famous political figures on the newspaper with his crayons, Aaryan could distinctly hear the snores of his father. The fear of being rebuked made him hesitate but then he told himself that no one will know, he could run quickly upstairs and dash down before anyone would notice. And then he ran. The building was four stories high and Aaryan was quite enthusiastic to know the secret, but by the time he reached the top, he was panting.

In the two corners of the wide top terrace, there were large cement drums, four on each side. The drums stored water for all the families living in the building. They were stationed on wide cement beams placed two feet above the ground. Children frequently used this area to play hide and seek. It was a popular spot to hide behind a drum by placing your feet on the beams. Aaryan was quite good at it and so when he saw the two women jump on one of the beams to have a better view of what was happening on the road behind their building, he tiptoed and followed them.

His mother had her hand on her mouth and was about to cry. There was something burning on the road. Aaryan looked closely and recognized it as one of the black and yellow Ambassador taxis which plied on Delhi roads. The taxi was on fire and there were people dancing around it with hockey sticks, cricket bats and swords in their hands. They were clapping and cheering like a couple of youngsters dancing around a bonfire in a picnic. Aaryan was amused. He couldn't understand what those people were trying to do.

Everything happened very rapidly after that. Aaryan heard a distinct scream and a burning hand came out of the broken window of the taxi. Someone from the crowd hit it with a bat and the hand went inside. A man was desperately trying to come out of the burning taxi and the people dancing around it were pushing the man inside using rods and bats. The screams which came from the taxi were blood curdling and Aaryan's mother dropped a tear and turned around, unable to watch anymore. Aaryan's eyes locked with his mother's. She didn't say anything but just got down from the beam and picked Aaryan in her lap. Pinky was surprisingly quiet too. Everyone came down the stairs without saying a word.

Aaryan's world had been disoriented from a week now. The school was shut down indefinitely and he was not allowed to go out and play with his friends. He saw police and army convoys making rounds of the colony and shoving people inside their homes and shouting at them. There is a curfew so stay inside, they yelled. Every time his father turned on the television, there was always someone playing a sad musical instrument or reading news. There was no *Chitrahaar*, the weekly programme of the latest Bollywood songs. There was no Giant Robot, his favorite evening show. Sometimes there were images of a woman and of people shouting and crying her name. His mother told him that she was the Prime Minister of the country and that is all he could get out of her.

It was years later when Aaryan actually understood what he witnessed that night. The reality did not dawn on him in one instant but it was gradual. Bits and pieces joined together over the years, television programmes detailing what happened, hushed voices from the people and newspaper reports completed the jigsaw for him. There was no Internet at that time for him to know instantly about what happened and neither were there hundreds of news channels providing a biased and spicy day-to-day account. It was a slow malignancy, something that turned him into a misanthrope eventually. He never pried into the topic in front of his mother. He did not get that close to her.

✦

When Aaryan died at the age of 65 in August 2044, he was alone in his one bedroom apartment provided by the University where he taught. He died in his sleep, lying across his bed on his stomach, with his fingers in his hair, trying to uproot them. The room was shabby, not cleaned since a few days; newspapers, clothes and utensils lay strewn across the room. The clothes that he wore for his lectures on the previous day were lying at the foot of his bed in a heap. A bottle of whisky rolled on the floor nearby and an empty glass was lying on the bed with large blotch of whisky coming out of it. The police found a number of such bottles in his bedroom. A paper was found next to his body with an if-else statement written on it. The neighbours told the police that they heard him laugh hysterically the previous night.

"After sometime, we were not even able to make out whether he was laughing or crying," a lady from the neighbourhood said.

The police also found a ransacked wooden almirah, but since there were no signs of a robbery, they concluded that the Professor must have done it in a fit of fury. They found it peculiar that the almirah was the sole bearer of the Professor's wrath. It was not a dramatic death but then Rohtak was not a very big city but a small town in Haryana and the University Campus was even smaller. News travelled swiftly and people talked about it for months. The inspector who was studying the case was not interested in investigating the death of a nondescript old man and promptly closed the case labelling it as a natural death.

Aaryan was past his retirement age when he died but he kept on asking for extension. He had been teaching in the university from the last 40 years and knew people who were considerate enough. He had known people from the time he was new in the University, people with whom he had grown old and who were now well placed in various administrative departments. It was a nice, little society where all the Lecturers and Professors teaching in the University lived. He was polite with everyone to the point of being in his or her good books but he never went out of the way to befriend anyone. Besides, weather, politics and cricket were topics that did not require him to disclose his innermost feeling to anyone and yet, discussing them easily made him an interesting part of any group.

All he wanted was to continue where he was. There was nothing that would have motivated him to shift back to Delhi and launch his life afresh. He had not been to the godforsaken city for years now. The last time he went there was when his mother died and that happened a lifetime ago.

Aaryan was considered the most venomous lecturer around. He could be really ruthless with the students and this always resulted in the best results in his subjects. He would shout at them and would throw them out of the class at the slightest provocation. The students were usually panic-stricken as Aaryan held their practical marks in his grip, which were usually the last resort of students to get a good percentage. The students knew that a slight instigation would land them in a hot soup, so they kept their swearwords to themselves. Aaryan was quite the opposite with his colleagues and neighbours, but then that was a façade he had to put. He loathed everyone.

✦

When Aaryan was born in 1979, his mother had become alarmingly sparse. She had difficulty feeding him and he cried all the time. No one was able to understand why he cried so much and he ended up giving his already exhausted mother endless, sleepless nights. It was only months later when he was able to gesture did the family realized that his legs pained. From then onwards, his mother helped him by pressing or massaging his legs at night till he fell asleep. At times when she was very tired, she took two of her dupattas and tied them around his legs. She would start from the thighs and move down, tying a little knot near the ankle. When she untied the knot in the morning, he loved the tingling sensation as blood rushed back in his numb legs and then even the slightest movement would send pinpricks of pain through them. He smiled as he coaxed his legs back into consciousness.

At times, when there was a power failure and there was no electricity throughout the night, the family slept on the top terrace of the building. Aaryan's father would take two folding beds on the terrace and join them together. He would then put up a mosquito net, tying the strings at the four corners to the television antennas or the lids of the water tanks. The family would then crawl inside. His mother would then ask him to count the stars as she pressed his legs or massaged them with oil.

Aaryan's father was a clerk in Defense Research and

Development Organization (DRDO) in Delhi and went to his office every morning on a bicycle. Mr. Iyar accompanied Aaryan's father to the office. He lived in the ground floor flat of the same building with his wife and three daughters. Every day, both men would ride to the office discussing the newspaper headlines. Mr. Iyar's youngest daughter Priya was of Aaryan's age and both of them had become fine friends. They ran around the square park in front of their house chasing each other and laughing. There were a few swings in the park and both of them would have a competition as to who could take the swing higher. Aaryan's favorite was the slide at the farthest corner of the park. It was made up of bricks and cement and had stairs like those in their flat to go at the top, only narrower. While sliding down, Aaryan would close his eyes and imagine that he was flying. Sometimes Priya would slide down just after Aaryan and kick him at the back. Priya would invite Aaryan to the tea party of her dolls while Aaryan would let her be a part of the jungle conference of all his plastic animals, which included a blue lion and a yellow giraffe.

Aaryan and Priya were put into something that would be called a playschool in modern times. The children were supposed to bring slates and chalks from home and were taught English and Hindi alphabets and the numbers. His father used to come back home for lunch and pick up Aaryan on the way. Aaryan would come home and demonstrate what he had learnt that day on the slate to his mother. She would make him practice it on a notebook and then in the evening he would run towards the park to play with Priya and other children in the colony. Sometimes they would bring water from their house, wet the sand and make castles with it. They would run after house lizards and kill them with stones or sometimes they would just sit and count the airplanes landing at the Palam Airport, which was very close to the flats. They could easily see the airplanes descending behind the flats.

Aaryan and Priya were fond of watching kites fly. Aaryan was not too keen on flying them as they left cuts on hands and secondly his father wouldn't allow him as he was too young, but he liked watching them as they soared and danced in the sky. Every year on Independence Day, everyone in the colony would get on the roofs and fly kites. The sky would burst into a million colours that day and the kites would hide the sun. Many would fall like feathers and Aaryan and Priya had a field day collecting various kites that would land on their terrace. Aaryan would display his kites in the drawing room of his home till he got bored of them and would then tear them apart to understand how they were prepared.

There were a lot of bats in the area so the children had strict orders to be inside their houses before sunset. Since air conditioning was an alien concept in households and desert coolers were ineffective during the monsoons, so numerous times the windows had to be opened for some respite from the sweltering heat. There were occasions when a bat might fly into the drawing room, circle around and hang itself in the open window. Aaryan's father would let it stay there, as it was quite harmless. Aaryan was reasonably terrified of the black shiny piece of flesh hanging from the window, which would sometimes open its wings hanging on thin bones eliciting a low shriek from Aaryan. For years, Aaryan thought that black umbrellas were made of bats and had an inherent fear of them. His mother had to buy coloured ones. At night, when the windows had to be closed before sleeping, Aaryan's father would get an old tattered cloth from somewhere and sneak towards the window. He would unexpectedly leap forward like a hungry cheetah and catch the bat in his hands and then would throw it out before quickly closing the window. Aaryan shrieked and jumped with delight. His father was nothing less than a hero in his eyes for doing that.

Doordarshan, the television broadcaster by the Government of India, started its national telecast in 1982 with a single television channel. It was also the year when Prime Minister Indira Gandhi introduced colour televisions in India in the Independence Day speech. Aaryan's father did not have sufficient money to buy a colour television but he did get a black and white one. It was a wooden *Texla* television, which had a sliding wooden panel in front of the screen. Aaryan was fascinated by the arrangement and spent hours sliding the panels. He irritated his parents by asking questions about how television worked. A few months later Aaryan's father got a refrigerator on monthly installments and Aaryan could not prevent himself from slamming its door. He asked his parents if he could sleep inside it, as the air was so searing outside. He got his first taste of cold water and thereafter refused to drink the water from the earthen pot his mother had in the kitchen. He was getting completely out of control. His mother would constantly slap him for not behaving properly. She would shout as he jumped on the wooden chairs in the drawing room or pull the dining table to make the screeching noises or upset things in the kitchen. It was a very modest two bedroom house and Aaryan had the capacity to turn it completely upside down and he was showing no mercy.

Aaryan's father wanted his son to study in a public school, so after discussions with Mr. Iyar, Aaryan and Priya were enrolled in a famous public school nearby. The fee burnt a hole in Aaryan's father's pocket. The school was an enormous transformation for Aaryan and Priya. It was a far cry from the two-room play school they went to earlier. The classrooms were huge and there were thirty students in each class. They sat on desks instead of ground and wrote on notebooks instead of slates and they now had a school uniform to wear. There were hundreds of children around and morning prayers and lunchtime was all chaos and voices. Priya's elder sisters also studied in the same school. Every afternoon, Aaryan's father would wait outside the school to pick him up on his way back home to have lunch.

Aaryan had barely started going to school when Operation Blue Star happened. The waves of unrest were imminent as the whole nation watched in horror. The seeds of abhorrence were sown in Aaryan's psyche during those months. The incident of the burning taxi happened on the heels of Indira Gandhi's assassination. It embedded a disgust, tilting his brain towards neurosis. In the following years, as Aaryan grew up, he stopped reacting to human emotions. It started very gradually as a feeble antipathy towards his parents. It was not entirely his mistake but then his father was never very close to him. He was the male figure who was taught to provide, not to be sentimental or expressive through physical gestures. Aaryan's father at least loved his wife and son; he just had no idea how to express it. Aaryan loved no one. He never expressed love even towards his mother. He had a fictile smile, the necessary smile whenever he was to address an elder but there was no way anyone could squeeze out an ounce of real pleasure out of him. He liked spending time with Priya, talking to her about a thousand indifferent things, but then that was it. She was the only person who could bleed a bit of warmth from him but he was too callow to appreciate her achievement. Aaryan had no aversion towards his parents but somehow the incident of the burning taxi that night had unknowingly snapped something inside him. His subconscious had reacted to the event much before his outer self. Any strings, whether of elation or despair, were severely damaged.

One day, while returning from the school with his father, Aaryan spotted a puppy lying on the corner of a road. His father stopped the cycle and picked up the puppy. He was sick and burning with fever, barely breathing. They took him home and Aaryan's mother fed the puppy some milk and hoped that he would survive. The family did not take the trouble of taking the puppy to a veterinarian under unfaltering optimism that led to his death on the third day. Aaryan's mother wrapped the puppy in a newspaper and gave him to the woman who used to come to collect the garbage everyday. Aaryan did not flinch a muscle. He nonchalantly read the latest edition of Champak, the children's magazine he had taken fancy to and ate the newly launched Maggi noodles.

Aaryan was an intelligent and diligent student as he grew up. His first three years at the new school were quite consequential. Other than a few stray embarrassing events like the one when he had a cold and he forgot to bring a handkerchief and wiped his nose on someone's schoolbag, Aaryan was applauded for his dexterity as he moved from numbers and alphabets to calculations and sentences. He also took part in the yearly school festivals and singing programmes in addition to winning a hardback Hansel and Gretle for his academic achievements. His parents were proud of him but all this was no consolation for his bleak behaviour in his own house. Priya was nowhere close to him in academics or extra curricular activities but was always proud of his achievements and equally vocal while applauding him. The two of them had entered a tacit pact of marrying each other and had already started treating each other as man and wife. This was their secret.

The dreams of a future alliance were shattered to pieces when Aaryan's family moved to their new house in Janak Puri in 1986, another residential colony in Delhi which was quite far away from the present one. Aaryan bawled and stomped his little feet but never got the pleasure of obtain a reason for such a rash decision. A lorry was hired to move the belongings of the family. As he sat in his father's lap next to the driver, he waved his hand staring at Priya through his teary and blurred vision as she stood with her family to bid farewell to their neighbours. They were not given any time alone but had to say goodbye amidst the crowd of their family members.

"I will come back," Aaryan told her.

He did not meet Priya again.

The new house was initially disapproving to Aaryan. The absence of Priya was daunting enough and he had to press himself to make friends at the new school, which was a bit smaller and cramped as compared to the previous one. There was no playground in front of their new house but more clusters of two storey houses. Their flat was on the first floor of a building, which was very similar in structure as their previous house and encased eight families. There was a never-ending row of such houses on both sides. Aaryan felt a bit claustrophobic in his new environs. There were fewer open spaces and parks and whenever he stood in the balcony of his house, he could see a sea of humanity going about their daily tribulations.

Conditions started improving after a few days. As Aaryan stood in the balcony of his flat, staring at everything that was moving, he chanced upon a black cloud of smoke coming from somewhere behind the houses. He could not see the train rushing past but could trace it by the bellowing sound of the steam engine and the stain of smoke in the sky. He immediately ran inside and asked his mother if he could go to the terrace at the top floor and glimpse the train. His mother would not allow him to go alone and so grudgingly went with him. He crashed open the door which led to the terrace and ran towards the front railing, amidst frantic calls of caution from his mother. He was dumbfounded to see the whole expanse from there. The tracks ran from one corner of the horizon to another, just behind the houses in front of their apartment. It was like a walled city guarded by trains instead of dragons. When the next train came, Aaryan squealed with delight. It was a rare burst of real emotion, something humans usually failed to elicit from him. Soon after, Aaryan started sneaking out of the house to go to the terrace. He used to sit there for hours and stare at the passing trains before his mother could locate him. He liked goods trains more than passenger trains. They were never-ending, connecting the two ends of the horizon.

Soon, monsoon arrived and Aaryan was in for another surprise. Once he was cupping the falling raindrops in his palm as he sat in the window of the apartment when he saw something stir on top of a house. It was a peacock and he was dancing. As the peacock fanned out his tail and quivered it vigorously to attract a female, Aaryan stood in awe of the beautiful display of nature, the flagrant arrangement of colours. Soon, as if taking a cue or entering the competition, there were many peacocks dancing on terraces of numerous houses and the whole sequence looked like an enchanting ballet performed by nature with the smoke of a passing train in the background. It was at this moment when

Aaryan knew that he had to see the rest of the world. He was delighted by the way his life was throwing pleasant surprises at him. There must be so many other astounding things at every nook and corner of the world, he thought. Yes, he had started to be fond of his new home.

Life wasn't just boorish for him; it was mundanely tawdry. People were programmed, a fact he had been a witness to at a very tender age and it was just a matter of someone pressing a switch somewhere. What really got his goat during the next few years was that everyone around him was seasoned to walk in a straight line without even blinking, just like horses with blinders. His mother had to take permission from Gods for whatever she had to execute. There were almost fifteen gods sitting on an elevated wooden platform fixed at a corner of the dining room. His father would constantly bother him with his money-is-everything talk and ask him to study with all his heart. According to him, Aaryan would never find respect amongst his family and friends if he was not financially stable. Although his parents had done nothing to displease him, he considered them idiosyncratic like the rest of the world, carrying on with their banal life without knowing why. He would listen to the banter of his family, teachers, classmates, neighbours and all the people on television with a smiling face. He flinched a few muscles on his face and tried his best not to give anyone an indication that he was enduring them. He was very successful. By the time Aaryan was ten, he had amassed a vast knowledge on various topics and was unmatched during debate competitions. Although he had no intention of waking anyone up, the fact that there was hardly any argument he could not refute made him popular amongst teachers in his school.

It was the year 1989 and colleges across India were protesting against the government for implementing the recommendations of the Mandal Commission. A student committed self-immolation to voice his protests. The images on the television were disturbing. One day Aaryan's father was discussing these protests with a colleague who was visiting him at home. Aaryan was staring out of the window waiting for a train. In the middle of their discussion, Aaryan started laughing.

"Aaryan, would you please go in your room?" His father said sternly as his colleague watched Aaryan with an amused expression.

"Sorry Dad."

"Aaryan, you don't even understand," his father said.

"I do. It's us!" Aaryan said.

"What?"

"That is what is wrong with the world – us," Aaryan said as he went inside.

"Why is the kid so bitter?" Aaryan's father asked his wife later that night. His wife did not respond. She just stared.

Aaryan never had any good friends throughout his school life but he was generally liked, just the way he was liked later when he was a lecturer in Rohtak. He was amenable with people whom he found genuine and equally vicious at the slightest hint of vanity but he never allowed anyone to cross his defenses. His school principal was very fond of him and pardoned his every foul behaviour with a warning on the ground that he was one of the most thought provoking students she had ever met. The school librarian also took a liking for him. He was probably the only student in the school at that time who regularly borrowed books from the library. He picked up abridged versions of the classics and read them after lunch at home till his eyelids grew heavy. He was a Charles Dickens fan initially and read Oliver Twist twice followed by Great Expectations, Barnaby Rudge, David Copperfield, Bleak House, The Pickwick Papers and many others. He was very pleased when he won Oliver Twist in a debate competition. By the time Aaryan finished school, he had read Classics by O. Henry, George Orwell, Hemingway, Jane Austen, Thomas Hardy and the Bronte Sisters. Years later, after he moved on to the modern writers, he always went back to the classics occasionally, just to remember those careless afternoons which he spent reading, sitting by the window waiting for a train or the peacocks to dance.

Aaryan's Mathematics teacher, a very thin middle-aged man with an equally thin moustache, hated his habit of reading books that were outside his curriculum. He believed that this would affect his marks and Aaryan could be the feather in his cap if tamed accurately. He warned him not to waste his time over useless books but all he did was infuriate Aaryan. Aaryan started devising methods of irritating the Mathematics teacher even more. He started going to the library to borrow a new book exactly before the Mathematics class, so that he entered the class just after the teacher had arrived. Aaryan could not understand how such a disgusting man as his Mathematics teacher could have the audacity to correct anyone. He was an excellent teacher but an equally filthy human being. He had five daughters and a sixth child was on the way. The man was showing no signs of stopping unless he could be blessed with a boy. It was as if he was at loggerheads with God over a son. He hated all his daughters as if it was their mistake that they existed and Aaryan felt like puking every time he saw him. The Mathematics teacher complained to the Librarian, who gave him a long look of disbelief, sighed and shook her head. He went to the Principal who laughed him away. Beaten and angered, he tried to find ways to insult Aaryan but Aaryan was too impertinent for him to handle. What amused Aaryan was that if a grown-up man, who was a father of five children, could be driven to despair by a school kid, what could happen if that man was asked to make a decision in a real life critical situation? Will he be able to make it or will he just pee in his pants? Do people really grow up, he wondered. And it was not just this mathematics teacher. Aaryan could spot such people like radar. They were there in politics making all kind of wrong decisions for personal benefits and killing thousands of people; they were there in business making substandard products and affecting millions of others; they were there as common people, selfish and self indulging to the point that it wasn't difficult to provoke someone to pick up a knife and kill another man for some petty reason. All these people were like his Mathematics teacher, a slight hint of diminishing of their power drove them to madness.

Aaryan was good at painting as well but was miserable in competitions where there was a time limit to finish it. His Arts teacher soon realized that giving him enough time would create astonishing results and encouraged him, but his parents were not interested.

"It's fine as a hobby but not a career," his father would say and that was the end of the topic and it was not as if Aaryan was too keen on it.

Sometimes, Aaryan's parents took him to Dalhousie during summer vacations where his maternal grandma lived. She was a minuscule old woman with so many lines on her face that it seems that God forgot to iron her out when he created her. Aaryan would look intently at her face when she told him stories, and follow the motion of her crisscrossed face, how the gap between the lines increased as she spoke and decreased as she laughed. She lived in a double storey house, with a stone stairway carved out of the hill to reach the upper floor and overlooking a few terrace farms below. Further down was a reserved forest full of wild animals. Beyond the forest, Aaryan could see the low-lying hills and roads snaking through them that would extend till the horizon. Sometimes, he could see a bus or a truck speeding through the roads like a small ant searching for food. Near the horizon, he could see four of the five rivers of Punjab. He would sit for hours on the stone terrace staring at the hills while his mother chatted happily with his *nani* and his father snored in the next room after lunch. At night, Aaryan could see the headlights of the cars as they encountered the narrow and dangerously curved roads of the mountains in the dark. The cars looked like fireflies. His eyes would follow the headlights and wait for them to reappear as they vanished behind a curve. On the horizon he could see many lights shimmering in the night. It looked like a mirage that mysteriously vanished in the morning. His mother told him the lights were from a town called Pathankot in another state called Punjab. He was surprised that he could see another state from his nani's hill.

Aaryan was scared of the mountains in the dark. The trees moved like ghosts as the winds blew. The lights from the houses created long shadows on the valley. Everyone who lived in Dalhousie had one ghost story or another to narrate. Aaryan had heard many of them from the neighbouring children and his nani. One night, when he was standing on the terrace staring at a distant light, the power of the whole area went off. There was no one on the top floor and Aaryan stood alone in the darkness, staring at a moving car's headlight on the mountain on the left and trying to divert his brain from creating pictures of ghosts. His mother shouted from below that she would be up in a minute with a candle. As the headlight disappeared across a bend, Aaryan looked up at the sky, desperate to find another diversion. For a second, he could not comprehend what he saw but then he moved his eyes all across the sky and gaped at the thousands of stars shimmering in the darkness. He had never seen so many stars in the sky in Delhi. He could even see the white streaks of the Milky Way splashed across the night sky. He started counting but stopped as he lost count and just stared. He stood there till the power supply was restored, conveniently forgetting the ghosts.

"Why can't we see so many stars in Delhi?" He asked his father the next day.

"It's a city. It's brighter than the sky," his father replied. Aaryan did not like the answer.

His father took the family to Panjpula, a beautiful picnic spot in Dalhousie and the resting place of the freedom fighter Ajit Singh. Aaryan's aunts – his mother's sisters – who lived in nearby hill stations of Chamba and Dharamsala would visit them with their husbands and children. All the elders would end up sitting on a huge rock near the waterfall and play a card game called flash with the 25 paise and 50 paise coins. Aaryan and his cousins would chase tadpoles in the clear water of the stream while trying to peek at the playing cards the elders held in their hands. He liked his cousins from the hills. There was no malice in them. In the evening, the family would walk to the G.P.O and have ice cream. Although G.P.O was now called Gandhi Chowk, the locals still favored the older name. Contour of the hill station had changed over the years. There were now a lot more hotels and guesthouses were mushrooming all over the mountains; tourists were returning and Bollywood movies had found a new location to shoot songs. The hill station was getting a new whiff of commercialization. Aaryan's parents did not like it. There were too many vehicles on the snaking roads and too many houses shadowed the green slopes.

Aaryan was fascinated by the Tibetan Market at G.P.O. The whole market was built on wooden planks up on a hill and gave an impression of hanging in the air. The entry to the market was through a narrow path carved out of the mountain. Half of the market stood on the slope, nailed into it, while the other half protruded out of it. The shops were on both sides of the walkway, which itself bulged out of the mountain. While roaming there, Aaryan would look at the road below through the small gaps in the wooden floor beneath his feet and gasp with excitement. He would wonder if the people were not scared to work at such a place. A slight crack in the wooden floor would land a person hundreds of meters below. Most of the items were overpriced and Aaryan's father would end up bargaining and buying nothing but he did get Aaryan a toy car from there. Sometimes while taking a walk on the roads, Aaryan would see beautiful rock sculptures and painting done by the Tibetans on the mountains and stop to gaze on them. He was amazed that someone could paint on a rock.

When Aaryan returned to Delhi from the summer vacations, he always felt like he was returning to a nightmare.

Aaryan was consistently good at studies. His results were exceptional and everyone wanted him to be either a doctor or an engineer. Aaryan on the other hand had no idea about his life.

His mother constantly bugged him to pray to God to show him the path. This aggravated him even more and led to long debates in the house between his father and himself, which eventually ended up in slamming of doors. Religion and any of its off-shoots would boil his blood. He hated the fact that his mother was too religious and would constantly pray in front of God for his health and future. Aaryan started as being an agnostic initially but seeing the state of the world around him, he gradually concluded that even if there was a remote possibility of the existence of a super power, the humans have been left to their own devices by him a long time ago. There was no divine intervention coming. He was sure that the world thrived on a fool's hope only to justify the suffering of the common man.

"How could there be a God who supposedly created us with affection and thought of us to be his children and then left us to kill each other in his name and do nothing?"

"A man leading a simple life with his family dies in a car crash for no mistake of his. How do you explain the involvement of God in this? Did he kill him? If yes, then why? If No, then wasn't it in his power to save him?"

"How do you explain the deaths of pilgrims in stampedes and bad weather? They are there to see God and what does he do? He let them die!"

"What about animals? They don't understand the concept of God and they don't kill their own kind. Don't you think they are more intelligent?"

Aaryan would hurl all these questions at his parents, which led to heated arguments. His father could not understand his reason for being so acerbic. But then, they always argued as two men, not as father and son. Maybe if he would have put a hand on Aaryan's head and asked him the reason for his unhappiness, he would have got all his answers. Aaryan was beginning to understand what happened the night he saw the burning taxi and the reason was spreading in his mind like a slow poison. As Aaryan was growing up, there wasn't a year in India when people didn't kill each other in the name of religion. Punjab was constantly in the throes of terrorism in the 80s and the early 90s and the television was always splashed with disturbing images. Aaryan's mother took care that her son would not watch any distressing news but she could not be vigilant all the time. One night Aaryan saw an interview of a 14-year-old boy from Punjab whose family was killed in their own house one night by militants. Before killing his elder sister at dawn, the terrorists raped her all night. The boy survived because he hid behind the sofa, never able to muster enough courage to help his sister, listening to her screams the whole night. That day Aaryan realized that what he saw on that fateful night when he was five was nothing as compared to what this boy went through.

"My sister's screams will haunt me but I have to live. What else can I do but breathe," the boy said at the end of the interview. That night, Aaryan's hatred for mankind grew manifold. He tried to reason but he could never understand how a country that fought tooth and nail to gain independence could end up like this? A few years later, the Mumbai riots took place immediately after the demolition of the Babri Masjid, which killed 900 people followed by the bombings that killed 250 more. Nearly 200,000 people were displaced in the wake. Aaryan was 14 years old then, and full of anger.

Aaryan's father started appreciating his son's opinion as faint signs of a moustache begin to appear on Aaryan's face, even though he did not like his son's incredible ability to detest everyone. Except for the topic of God on which both of them still did not concur, he was proud of the fact that his son had an opinion and was not just vegetating through life. By the time Aaryan completed his school and was ready to go to college, the father and son had developed a level of tolerance and deference for each other. They could now discuss topics and be in the same room. Their discussions were not heated anymore but were more like an exchange of thoughts. Aaryan's father liked the fact that even though Aaryan belonged to the Generation X, he was not like the other taking-everything-for-granted, disrespectful and living-in-a-shell men and women of his age.

Aaryan wanted to see the world. According to him, the only ability fairly tolerable in mankind was their ability to beautify Earth. Nature in itself was a beautiful sculptor, but sometimes man added to that beauty. Once, discussing this with his father, he gave the example of Machu Picchu, a relatively unknown tourist spot at that time. Then the discussion veered towards Taj Mahal.

"Yes. Nothing can prepare you for the impact. It's much more than the pictures you see of it. It instantly overwhelms you. We have created some beautiful things. I could give anything to see the Colosseum, the Sistine Chapel, the Eiffel Tower or even the Manhattan skyline."

"You find the skyline beautiful?"

"I think it's creative although it has happened gradually. I like looking at its pictures. One day I'll actually see it."

"Looks like you are shedding your acrimony," his father remarked.

The sentence flooded back memories. Aaryan was quiet for a

while.

"Not everyone is a murderer, Aaryan. There are people on this Earth who have led their entire lives without raising a finger on anyone. Why has this notion entered your mind that everyone is evil?"

"Because I have seen normal people who were leading their lives without raising a finger on anyone kill each other. Dad, we are animals. We just need a chance. We are like werewolves. We wait for the moon of hatred."

"I can only..."

"Sometimes the futility of it all drives me crazy. It's so mind-bogglingly brainless. We are on this tiny speck of soil and dirt which we call Earth, which won't even register anywhere in vastness if you start comparing it with the other objects in the universe and our existence is such a paltry blip on it, just like a blink of an eye. And, even though, all you have to do is to look at the sky to be reminded of your being so minuscule and your existence to be so worthless, we still have the nerve to make each other's lives miserable."

"It's not that bad Aaryan, but I think you will take your own time to realize that."

"How do you react when someone asks you if you are proud of your country?" Aryan asked.

"I think I am proud of it, irrespective of all the shortcomings."

"It is a shallow question. And the answer to it is equally superficial, passed from one generation to the next. And it's astounding how our body responds automatically to it. I too get goosebumps when someone talks of national pride and integrity but my brain knows better. What is there to be so proud of pieces of land? People die for them. They kill each other for them. They behave as if being born on this piece makes them superior to the people living on other pieces. Just because people who speak the same language and eat the same food surround you makes you a proud owner of the land you share, completely ignoring the fact that given a chance, the same people can slit your throat at the slightest provocation?"

"But soldiers have died defending this country. Are you saying that it doesn't signify anything? Thousands have died for the independence we so much enjoy. Have they died in vain?"

"No, I am not saying that. But if you step away and wonder why a situation arises again and again that a man has to pick up a weapon to defend his rights to live freely, that is when everything stops making sense. No reason to fight can be greater than a human's life. How can anyone even think of snatching the freedom of another man? Where does the notion come from? Why does a soldier have to die? Why does someone have to become a soldier?"

When Aaryan was in his last year of school, everyone had pinned high hopes on him. All his teachers kept pushing him to give the entrance exams for all the top medical and engineering colleges in the country. His father put him in an Institute which specialized in two months crash courses to crack IIT. The crash course was too much for Aaryan. He was not sure about what he wanted to do and there was so much to grasp that he let it go. He finished the course and gave his entrance exams but nothing came out of them. He finally enrolled in a Physics Honours course in the North Campus of Delhi University. Getting into Delhi University was a humongous task. Even though he had a 94% aggregate in Physics, Chemistry and Mathematics in his final year exam in school, he could not make it to the first list of any of the prestigious colleges.

His father was exasperated.

"In our times, getting a 60% was considered a big achievement and you could easily get into a good college. It's a fish market now. 94% is not enough! They are driving the kids crazy," his father exclaimed. Aaryan finally made it in the second list of four of the colleges. He chose one simply because it was close to the bus stop.

College life was exciting. Everyday in the morning, Aaryan would get twenty rupees from his father for the bus fares and the food. His mother would pack his lunch, so that he didn't eat canteen food and fall ill. This way, Aaryan saved the money given by his father for food and collected it to buy pirated or second hand novels from the Sunday market in Daryaganj. In the beginning, Aaryan tried to go to the college by U Specials, but half the times either the bus didn't turn up or was late and when it did come, it was always filled with over excited and loud mouthed brats who behaved like buffoons to impress girls and made Aaryan bang his head on the glass window in pity. So, to escape the torture, he started taking the local Blue line buses, which were even worse. The bus operators would fill people till there was no place to stand and people were falling on each other or hanging from the doors.

Initially, Aaryan was disoriented in the alien environment in the college and waited eagerly for the lectures to get over so that he could scurry back home. He didn't talk much with his classmates and abhorred it when the seniors called them for ragging. Aaryan had the opinion that anyone who rags was mentally sick and needed to get a life. After the initial hitch, the next three years rushed past in a jiffy and transformed Aaryan into a more sociable person, at least on the surface. He could now go ahead and talk to a stranger, a quality he was missing earlier. Also, he became more confident and more confused. Physics was definitely not his cup of tea and by the time the three years of B.Sc ended, he had no idea what to do next. There was no way he could get a decent job by just completing a Bachelors degree. He tried to give a few Masters in Computer Application exams but then he had not prepared well and did not pass in any of them. The only option left was to do Masters in Physics, which he approached the way a man would approach a snake.

"I'll figure out what to do next after I finish this," he promised himself.

M.Sc lectures were held in a separate Physics department in the heart of the University. All the students from various colleges who had enrolled in the course had to attend the lectures there. Aaryan remained a mute spectator initially but soon gathered a small group and hung out with them. He bunked classes at times and went to Kamla Nagar with his gang and sat in Barista for hours playing scrabble or reading books or to McDonalds to grab a chicken burger to which he had taken a fancy. The people who came in contact with him during those five years thought of him as a mysterious but genuine guy who never came out of his shell. He was good looking, had sharp features and always got glances from girls, but the thoughts that had accumulated in his mind never permitted him to reciprocate. Love was non-existent. He had never thought about having a woman in his life because he knew that he could never keep her content. The glances were never returned but were answered by a sharp turn of the head, sudden opening of a book or a sudden interest in the number of clouds in the sky.

"Do you know what an if-else statement is?" he asked his father once over breakfast. His father stared at him through his glasses before nodding in a negative. Aaryan took out the sheet of paper and showed him.

"It looks like a computer language," his father said, after studying the paper and giving it back to him.

"Did you notice how similar it is to life?"

Aaryan's father looked at him for a moment before grasping what his son was trying to say.

"Yes. Imagine collecting all the possible if-else statements of someone's life and feeding it in a robot. You can make it cry," his father said before returning to his newspaper.

Aaryan's father was a little worried because it has been almost five years in college and his son still did not have a girlfriend. He constantly bugged him and asked him if he had a crush on someone, but could not extract anything more than a blush. Aaryan's mother too tried to coax her son to disclose something but there was nothing to tell. Aaryan had made up his mind that he was never going to get married, but he had no intentions of breaking this news to his parents. Not yet.

The two years of the M.Sc course were marred with mugging unending theories, carrying out outdated experiments and creating equations using computer programs. Those two years were as corny as the three years of B.Sc. After acquiring a postgraduate degree in 2002, Aaryan was again faced with the dilemma of what to do next. He was just wandering through life without any aim. He was floating like a paper boat in a stream of water, flowing wherever the current took him. He could have turned into a social worker if he could muster a slightest ray of hope inside him, or maybe a teacher in a remote village if he would have been hopeful that education could change it all. He once nurtured such hopes, but not anymore.

"But don't you think education does make a difference?" His mother asked as father-son discussed the topic over evening tea. Aaryan's father was prodding him about what would interest him as a career option. Their talk steered towards teaching.

"Mom, yesterday while coming back in the local bus, I heard a conversation between two men. They were acquaintances and seemed well educated. They were wearing decent clothes and were not more than 25 years old. Would you like to know what they were talking about? One of them was teasing the other that he was going to get more dowry than him because his father has found a richer girl. The other guy was in a foul mood because he felt like a loser. This is educated, city bred youth for you. No mom, its not education. There is something wrong in our blood, in our genes, the way we are wired. We cannot differentiate between right and wrong because our superficial, brainwashed upbringing overshadows everything and the irony is that we are so well mechanized that we don't even realize it."

Aaryan was not optimistic at all. He had no resolve to transform things. He had burnt all hopes in the fire that engulfed the taxi that night.

He told his parents that he would prepare for the NET entrance exams for lectureship in colleges. He just blurted it out without giving it a consideration. His father suggested that he can go for a PhD, but Aaryan was in no mood to bear Physics around his neck for the rest of his life. He found Physics too theoretical. There was no instant practicality attached to it. With the exception of Electronics, everything was abstract.

Aaryan sat at home for a year after finishing his M.Sc and prepared for his NET examinations. This was a period of extreme anxiety for his parents. They never forced him to make a resolution because they knew that he was above average. He had done extremely well in his school and college and this thought sailed them through the one year their son sat at home. Aaryan's mother prayed to God everyday to show her son the path. She was waiting for her son to get a good job so that she could marry him with all the pomp and show and bring a beautiful bride home. Then she would have grandchildren and her circle of life would be complete. Aaryan thought that his mother was clichéd.

"Your motherboard is very old," he joked with her.

"Say whatever you want, but this is the dream of every mother," she retorted back.

"But why?"

"Why not? What's the loss in that?"

"We are not talking about profit and loss. What if I don't want to get married? What if I don't believe in all this?" Aaryan had no intentions of breaking the news so soon to his mother but the words tumbled out.

"What do you mean you don't believe in all this? What are you saying, Aaryan? Everyone gets married, has children. What is wrong in that?"

"There is nothing wrong in that. In the same way, nothing is wrong with not wanting that. What if I think that I am better off alone, that I don't feel the need of a life partner? Am I supposed to sacrifice the rest of my life to keep my parents happy?"

"Why not? We gave a lot of sacrifices to bring you into this world, to bring you up, to put food in your mouth. What is so wrong in sacrificing a bit for us and that too for your own pleasure?"

"I could never understand this emotional sword of sacrifice which parents hold to cut open their child's right to make his own decisions. No parents give any sacrifice to bring their children in the world, far from it. They were having fun when the child was conceived. Remember? And once a child is in the world, it's the moral responsibility of the parent to feed him and keep him alive. There is no sacrifice in that. So please, parents should stop turning themselves into martyrs to plunk their dreams on their children. It's cheap and disgusting."

"So what do you want, Aaryan?" his mother asked calmly.

"I definitely don't want to get married and I don't want the pressure to do so too. I can't plan my life so let me live one day at a time. That is all I want."

That was the day Aaryan's mother felt that she had truly lost her son. No, he was not like those pain-in-the-ass children who went against their parents wishes just because that was the latest in-thing or because that is what everyone does, but the end results were the same. He was going to a singular route. When she broke the news to Aaryan's father, he was not at all surprised. His son was unique but in a sad way. There were many times when Aaryan's parents discussed the possible reasons for their son's antipathy but they could never reach a conclusion. The incident of the burning taxi had now faded away in Aaryan's mother's mind and she could have never imagined that that incident had such a lasting imprint on her son's mind. He was just five then. It never occurred to her to mention the incident. And it did not matter anymore. Too much had happened after that. The stain was permanent.

Aaryan cleared his NET exam at the end of 2003. He started applying for the post of a lecturer in colleges in Delhi, Noida, Gurgaon and adjoining towns in Haryana. It was difficult to get a job in Delhi University as most of the colleges preferred candidates with a

PhD. He finally got a job in a University in Rohtak, a small town in Haryana. Aaryan moved out of his house in Delhi and settled down in a small one bedroom flat provided by the University. Initially he travelled to Delhi every fortnight but the frequency started decreasing as he adapted to his new surroundings and as his mother's frequency of prodding him to get married kept on increasing. She had started behaving in a very eccentric manner ever since Aaryan had left home. On some of his rare visits to his parent's house, she would stop in the middle of a sentence and stare at him as if she was seeing him for the first time. Sometimes, she would start a sentence and then suddenly stop and say nothing for the next half an hour. It was years later, after she died, that Aaryan understood the reason of her erratic behaviour. She was pondering, trying to make a decision and always failing to reach it. She had found a secret lying in an open trunk and was turning it in her head.

Aaryan missed his discussions with his father but the job of a lecturer was not easy. He taught Electronics, one of his favorite subjects and something he could identify with. The other lecturers and professors admired him and being a Delhi University pass out was considered an elite feat. Aaryan kept a distance from everyone and socialized enough to keep him visible. He read books in his spare time and planned out his future trips to all the places he dreamt of visiting. He did not waste a single rupee and collected as much as he could. His father had asked him not to provide any financial help to him as he had saved enough but Aaryan did send some amount of money from time to time.

Aaryan did not visit any of the places. Over the years, the aloofness and the silence of his house pushed him deeper into a depressed state of mind. Earlier, he had a vent. He could place his thoughts in front of his father or do things to irritate his mother but now there was no one. Returning back to Delhi was never an alternative, as that would have pushed him over the edge too. It was a no-win situation. He had never thought that living alone would be such a burden, but somehow he scraped through the tribulation. Sometimes, the thought of getting married did cross his mind but going back to his parents and let his mother have her way was something that would have hurt his self-esteem. As he thought more about it, he reached the conclusion that feeling lonely was no reason to get married. People marry for love and not because they feel lonely. I can get a dog if I feel lonely, he told himself.

Sometimes, he would just lie on the sofa after coming from the college and stare at the ceiling for hours as if trying to solve a puzzle. He would not even cook dinner at times and go to bed after gulping a glass of milk. Sometimes he would sit in front of the television and stare at it without watching it. The images would glide endlessly on the screen without making any sense, without instigating a flicker of any emotion from him. He was blending with the furniture of the house at an alarming rate.

The thought, which ate him away from inside like a slow poison in the end, was that he had the chance to pull out the plug, to break free and see the world, but he just couldn't bring himself to do it. The air he breathed was thick with the punishment he wanted to give himself. He was lashing himself for the crimes of others, for the repercussions of that one night when he was just a mute spectator. He hated himself, not for what he perceived in the wake of the incident, but for what he had become. He started drinking heavily and sometimes used to cry through the night without understanding why, till he fell asleep curled up on the floor near the sofa. He was in this obscure whirlpool that was sucking him in a state of self-restitution. He inflicted mental pain on himself as if the act would purify him.

✦

On the night of his death, he had unknowingly unearthed the secret, something wrapped in a yellow cloth. He was drunk and at first his mind could not perceive what he saw but then everything started making sense and he let go of a bewildered laughter. He finally understood his mother's long pauses during conversations as if she desperately wanted to tell him something and then changed her mind at the last instant. How did it matter now? Both his parents were dead and he was a rickety old man. Tears started flowing down his eyes till the time he could not comprehend whether he was laughing or crying. Would it have made any difference to his life if he could have stumbled upon the secret earlier? It might have, he thought. It might have created a big diversion if nothing else. He might have gathered the courage to travel the world after all.

"Oh! What fools!" he said as he started laughing again.

He kept the secret back where he found it and then before going to sleep, he picked up a piece of paper to amuse himself and wrote an if-else statement on it. He stared at the paper for sometime after finishing and threw it near his bed. He could not remember when he tumbled into sleep and then into death while he cried holding his hair with both hands.

# *Manohar*

It was slow, very slow, like a snail's sluggish crawl on the wall of a house leaving behind a smelly trail of glutinous liquid. It took five painful years for the journey to finish, painful not only for Manohar, but also for his family. He was not a likeable figure but then when you are a part of a family, you cannot wish to see someone wither away even when you dislike him. He is a part of your blood, he and all his idiosyncrasies. There is always a tinge of warmth in the corner of your heart, reminiscent of the good times spent together. Then there are always those moments, when you wonder why everything turned out so different. When you wonder what possibly could hold people together, if not the fact that they come from the same blood? Or are we just not born to be that way? Craving to be something that we cannot be, each with our own false ceilings to hide our true selves?

It was one of those days when the clouds were trying to be elusive. There was a forecast of rains but if you have lived in Delhi for long enough, you know that it has to be taken with a pinch of salt. His wife's cousin brother, Shailesh, had come to Delhi with his wife for a visit. They had planned to do a bit of shopping in Connaught Place, but Shailesh was not feeling well. He pushed the rest of the three to go ahead without him. So, they took a three-wheeler autorickshaw and Manohar asked the ladies to get in first. It wasn't chivalry but the plain fact that he liked to sit at the open side of the autorickshaw, slightly pushing his left leg out and holding the iron rod at the top with his left hand. He felt like a warrior sitting on a galloping horse. Little did he know that this was his last ride as a warrior.

As the three-wheeler turned left to encircle India Gate, an Ambassador car coming from the right hit it. The impact toppled the autorickshaw and before Manohar could realize, he was dragged a few feet on the road encased inside it, with his wife and Shailesh's wife on top of him. Soon the traffic stopped at the busy Akbar Road and people encircled the overthrown autorickshaw and whispered to each other as if it was an alien spaceship. Then a few of them came forward and helped everyone out. The women came out unscathed with a few minor bruises as Manohar had absorbed their impact. The driver was shaking with fear. Manohar had fractured his backbone and his left wrist. His left arm was bruised and bleeding profusely because of being scraped on the road. As people created a perfect circle and talked - hushed voices trying to figure out the next move - someone called the ambulance. Manohar had lost consciousness. As the ambulance was taking an eternity to appear, a man was kind enough to drop them at the nearest hospital in his car. The surgeons had to immediately operate upon Manohar. He was 67 years old at that time and had never thought that he had to be saved by someone when he was preparing himself to die. The ladies got a few sutures, a few bandages.

The operation saved him but now he was too contiguous to death to fall back, the taste was too engulfing. He had smelled it. He could always feel its presence, lurking in the corners of the hospital room, waiting patiently. It was a mad year. Death was dancing all around. While he lay on his hospital bed watching television and nursing his broken back, he felt nauseated at times, as he saw bodies and fire strewn all around. It was a mildly cold March of 1993, when Mumbai was shaken with several bomb blasts – more than thirteen. His wife would not switch off the television as their daughter lived in Mumbai with her husband and two children.

"Did you call her?" he asked.

"Yes. They are all right. They are all at home."

"Good. Good."

"This doesn't make sense," his wife said as she watched the horror unleash on the television.

"Try making a list of things which make sense. It will be smaller and you will waste less time," he said.

"You are an atheist, you can't feel the pain of a Hindu," his wife said curtly.

"I am an agnostic, not an atheist. I think I have spent my entire life trying to make you understand the difference, but never mind. And what do you mean by the pain of a Hindu? I can feel pain. Any kind. And believe me, I know what I am talking about. I have felt the pain of two women and a vehicle on top of me very recently. And are you sure all those who died were Hindus?"

"They were the targets."

"Ha!"

"And what does that mean?"

"I am torn between calling you obtuse or naïve. Haven't you seen enough bloodshed to understand the physics behind it? Everyone is a target. You don't need to be Einstein to understand this. It's a business like any other, like Steel industry or manufacturing clothes. We even have schools to teach it, so whom are we fooling? Earlier, there was a struggle to acquire land, to have something that we can call our own. Now there is a struggle to acquire people for a religion. It's like the Olympics. Which religion will win the maximum gold medals? And what happens after that? What happens after everyone has confirmed a berth in heaven? Something else will crop up to keep the blasts alive and kicking, something else to tear the flesh of the sacrificial lamb apart."

His wife switched off the television.

"Have some rest," she said snappily.

✦

Manohar used to be a very active old man. His hair was intact, although they had turned completely white. He was of medium built, without the ubiquitous pot belly which men of his age are prone to. He was one of those old men who give an impression that they would have been very handsome in their youth. Well, he wasn't. He grew handsome as he grew old. The square jaw was more prominent now, eyes more deep because of the lines at the outer ends, nose more perked up because of the slight hollow in the cheeks, face more proportionate because of the lines from the corner of the nose till the corner of the lips. He had a deep voice and a healthy appetite.

He went daily for a morning walk in the park close to his house. He could never sit quietly. Like a toddler, he had to keep himself occupied. Somehow, after he retired, the feeling that the inevitability of his death was looming on the horizon never left him. He had a different perspective, a positive one and too much spare time. He wanted to breathe as long as he could without leaning on anyone else's shoulder. After his morning walk, he would go to the Mother Dairy booth to collect milk in the tumbler, which he carried with him. The sight of milk filling his tumbler as he inserted the coins entertained him. Here was another reason to marvel at technology, the passage of time. From squeezing the milk out of a cow's udder to inserting a coin in the machine, he had done it all. He would also collect a few vegetables and then would go and sit with the Muslim barbers in a local shop. The shop was on the ground floor of the building where he lived, built illegally like hundreds of shops in Delhi. It had a glass door with picture of Caucasian models flaunting outlandish hairdos. The owner of the shop was a chubby middle-aged man named Anwar, with a thin mustache and a broad smile, displaying red teeth smeared with gutkha. He sat on the wooden bench outside the shop and discussed politics with Manohar as his subordinates did all the work. They had become good friends in the last five years and the fact that they belonged to religions that were constantly at loggerheads with each other had never bothered them. They were two men killing time, and nothing else.

Sometimes, he would be at the shop for hours, entertaining the younger barbers too. They were a group of six men who were never busy at the same time. They liked Manohar but then they did not exactly slit off the throats of their other Hindu customers either. They had to put food on the tables, to provide their children with an education – the plights of a common man. Sometimes they discussed religion mashed with politics and philosophy. Manohar was always cautious while discussing religion with them, especially the younger barbers. They were immature, and Manohar was of the opinion that the boiling point of blood is very low at that age. They never crossed the line, never went beyond a point. Too much had happened in the past to rake the ashes. There was always some skirting, some uncomfortable laughter.

At times his wife would wonder where her husband was and

would call him by screaming his name from the balcony of their house. They were like any other old couple, weary and bored of each other's presence but with a stashed away aura of love. At home, he would spend a major part of his day watching news on television. Cable television hit India in 1992 and the idea of having a hundred channels to watch was not balmy anymore, the only catch being that there was no remote in their black and white television and eighty rupees was still an exorbitant price to pay every month for the services of the Cable operator. But there were workarounds. The Cable television operator happened to be the grandson of a long forgotten friend and he agreed to reduce the price to fifty rupees a month and provide their preferred 12 channels, the number that their television could accommodate.

After Manohar would get bored of the news, he would switch to Santa Barbara or Bay watch. He would watch films on Star Movies with 'adult only' ratings at night with his wife. It was exciting. They had never imagined in their life that they would be able to see naked men and women copulating, drenched in the heat of passion. It was something foreign, not to be envisaged in the sexually oppressed land of Kamasutra. It was like spotting a polar bear in a desert but there he was, a spot of white fur, dancing on the sand dune in the shimmering sun.

Manohar was brought back home in an ambulance after a few weeks. He was confined to bed and there was a nurse to constantly look after him. His wife slept in the drawing room with her grandchildren. Manohar was having extreme mood swings and she was not in a mood to entertain another baby. She was done with them. Yes, he acted difficult for the initial months. It was tricky to please him and very effortless to make him cry. For Manohar, it was not easy to be in the bed for 24 hours of the day, month after month. He felt crippled, handicapped, something that he always feared and detested. The feeling strangulated him and sometimes he would bang his fist on the bed in frustration. He had tried to avoid this situation of being bedridden in old age but then life works in strange ways, you finally end up with something you have been running away from all your life.

There was always a swarm of people present to meet him. There were people whom he had almost forgotten existed. Then there were his three daughters. The one who lived in Mumbai kept coming to Delhi every two months on short visits. They were not a constant aid. They had families of their own. Anwar came to see him twice. He wasn't very relaxed in the house. Their conversations were jittery. It was as if they were able to converse in a setting only to which they were accustomed. Still, Manohar was grateful that he came, grateful that there were threads which joined him to the outer world.

The nurse left by the time he was able to stand with the help of a walker. He had not walked for the last eight months. His muscles were almost dead. It took him ten days to drag himself to saunter a few paces. With his skinless legs, he looked like a stork looking out for fish in a muddy pond. He was determined to rejuvenate himself and started walking in the balcony of his house. His wife helped him. She would give him her arm when he was too tired to walk back in his room. Within two months, he started using a walking stick. He was still confined to his house but was gaining strength and was preparing himself to take his morning walk. It was almost a year now since he last took one before the accident.

Then one bright, beaming morning, it happened. The switch

was suddenly turned off. No one was able to comprehend what went on below the layers of his brain but Manohar's interest fizzled out faster than it had fructified. Everything just drained out of him one fine morning, like the energy seeping out of an athlete who has finished a marathon and has no inclination to keep standing; who falls on his knees as he crosses the finishing line. Although Manohar's marathon was on a contrary end, he had given up even before the gun was fired. He knew his end was near but he hastened it towards him. He was in a tug of war and there was no opponent now. The rope was all his and he tugged it hard.

There were no explanations. It was as if someone hypnotized him out of it. He started to spend most of his day on his bed, watching television, munching food and sleeping. There wasn't any agony on his face but it was not tranquil either. Sometimes he would divulge in deep thoughts and stare at the fan for hours. Sometimes he would just talk to himself in sleep. His wife, who was cheerful from the last few weeks noticing his revival, again lost track of him. She tried everything from chidings to charms, but Manohar had turned into a thick-skinned rhinoceros. He started losing weight again and as time trickled away, he lost his body fat at an alarming rate. The doctors who saw him persuaded his family to drill sense in him.

"He is just killing himself. He can live for a long time but only if he wishes," one of them said.

Over the next four years, his family saw him turn from a zealot into a skeleton. His skin was fading like incense, vanishing in thin air. He was solely on soups and juices, thus adding to the effect and had lost track of any remnants of his personal hygiene and would sometimes not take a bath for five days, not even a sponge bath. His legs were now so thin that the bone joints were visible. He looked like a Jew in a concentration camp, starved and short on any hope.

Sometimes he would lie down on the bed and moan with pain. Nobody knew where the pain was and he would not bother to tell anyone. His wife would curse him and refused to sleep in the same bed with him. She would go into the drawing room and sleep on the sofa. His grandchildren were past caring by now. Such a long time had passed that everyone had developed immunity to the spectacle. It was as if the sight of the decay was deeply rooted in their lives. Everyone was now used to the strong smell of the imminent departure, the way people get used to the smell of garbage if they stand near it for too long and then suddenly you can't smell it anymore. Not a day would pass without a sound of agony, a heated argument, a flurry of tears or a series of sighs. A question, which hovered like a ghost on everyone's mind, was – How? How could a grown up man who had weathered life, crumble like an old detonated building when he was on the verge of recovery? How could helplessness come to everyone so easily?

His daughters too tried to plead with him. Sometimes, his wife would phone them and cry her heart out. The daughters would descend and try to drill some sense in their dying father. Manohar had been quite authoritative with them when they were young and unmarried and some of the traits were still present, however feeble. He would produce indiscriminating grunts, which would make the daughters quiet. They would stay overnight in the house, providing a shoulder to their mother's aching heart. It wasn't easy to see one's husband die in front of her. Her grandchildren provided solace but then they were too busy or pretended to be because of various reasons. The grandson, who was the elder of the two, was in the first year of college. The granddaughter was in school. Their age was too tender to view the dismal dissolution, the shameless, nonsensical window-shopping of death. They felt disgusted by what they saw, by the austere thrust towards deterioration. They had stopped passing through the room in which their grandfather lay spread over the bed like a live carcass, unless it was very necessary. Sometimes, Manohar would stop them and ask them to give him some water. They would have to then put a hand behind his back and push him up into a sitting position so that he could drink it. He would grunt and make sounds of pain as he gulped down the water. The touch of him, the closeness, the nauseating smell of the dilapidation would repel the young, brimming-with-zest bodies of his grandchildren. It was the fear partially, the unquestioned truth of life, the reality that no matter how conceited they felt about their youth, that was how they would end up. Crumpled. Anguished. Abhorred. Alone. There were other reasons too, some silent undercurrents of misdeeds, a few unsaid words of satisfaction. The grandchildren were not sad that this was what everything had converged to. The agony of their grandfather enthralled them; his tears satiated them.

✦

A week before Manohar's death in 1998, his brain started shifting too much in the past. He was seeing things that were lost, people who were dead and was scratching out memories that were long buried. Once, his wife saw him talking to someone whom she knew died a long time ago. He was in some other dimension, or maybe he was in transition, half here and half there. Is this how it happens, his wife would wonder. First your memories trickle out and then they drag out your soul at the end, like the coloured handkerchiefs coming out of a magician's cap, tied to each other, like coaches of a train. There was a door that was opening for his departure that she could sense, but her mind was not ready for the inevitable. There were memories, apparitions passing through that door, unattended, visiting her husband, welcoming him to the other side. The air in the house was growing very still. The grandchildren were forbidden to enter his room.

A day before he died, the doctor was called again, a burly obese man and a sharp contrast. He checked Manohar's pulse. He looked as if he was transferring his fats into Manohar, so that he could survive for a few more days. Manohar's grandson smiled. The image was too ironical not to invoke a reaction. His exams had started and there was an exam three days later but it was not easy to prepare, not with all the melancholy.

He will not survive, the doctor said.

It was then that his wife broke down with an unexpected ferocity. She started to howl and tear her hair apart. She banged her hands on her chest and screamed her husband's name again and again. The grandchildren were startled. They had not expected such histrionics as they were under the impression that their grandparents hated each other given the number of times they screamed at each other in a day. Manohar's wife had crossed the ordeal with as much calm as she could aggregate as if she was accumulating each of her emotion for this day. Her daughters tried to stop her, catching hold of her flapping hands. Manohar was unconscious. He was hardly breathing and waiting for death with bated breath. *Gangajal* was brought and put in his mouth. His pulse diminished and by the next day, nonchalantly the soul passed to the other side, quietly closing the door behind.

The house was in a whirlpool for the next thirteen days. People flocked the house to pay their last condolences to the family.

Manohar's wife was in an uncontrollable hysteria and would enter paroxysms at an alarming rate. She cried continuously for the first two days, taking breaks only to sleep at night. Sometimes, she would weep so much that her tongue would roll over in her throat and would block her windpipe. She would not be able to breathe and make chocking noises, which would spur the ladies in the house into action. A steel spoon will magically appear from the kitchen which one of the ladies would try to insert in her mouth trying to push open her teeth which had shut down like iron gates, while the other would try to hold her head steadily. As the spoon entered the mouth and pushed open the teeth, a sudden gush of air would enter her lungs, and for a second she looked like someone who was drowning and was pulled up just in time.

She insisted on going to see the last rites performed on her husband, although everyone else in the family thought that this was not a good idea. She was too panic-stricken for the ceremony. She went anyways, saw the pundit perform the rites and saw her husband burn away with wood, turning into ashes in a matter of minutes. It was then that her grandson broke down. He had not shed a tear yet, but the sight of a person he had known since he was born flickering away in fire was too much to bear. He broke open a pimple on his nose in the process, thus mixing blood with tears. His exam was on the next day but he wasn't thinking about it. The granddaughter did not cry.

The male family members went to collect the ashes the next morning that were to be dispersed into the Ganges in Haridwar, the holy city. It was a strange feeling, to see a human turned into something that could fit in a small copper vessel, like a genie. That was what was left of him, a few bones and handful of bone dust. That was the sum of his life, his 70 years of existence, boxed in a vessel.

His grandson went to take his exam that day. It was a three hour-long exam but he couldn't sit through it for even an hour. His grandmother was screaming in his head, his grandfather's skin was melting away where the professor stood, and he was crying in the examination room. A tear fell on the answer sheet and dissolved away a word. He wrote as much was necessary to pass although he knew much more. He got up drawing a series of surprised glances from his classmates, thrust the sheet in front of the examiner and ran out of the suffocating room. He passed the exam. Barely.

That night he saw his grandfather in his dream. He appeared as a spectre, walking from his room to the bathroom, with sparks appearing from behind his head. There was a glow all around his body. His legs were so thin that the glow made them almost invisible, creating an illusion of him flying through air. The dream was explicit, like an extension of reality. He was in a deep slumber and he woke up sensing a bright flash of light near him. His relatives were strewn around him, snoring unabashedly. The night was dark, deep blue and there was no moon. And there he was, Manohar, standing at the door, staring at him. There was no expression. No sadness of a ghost, no anger for a lost body. Nothing. And that is when he woke up. Gasping and drenched in sweat. This was not a dream, but he was sleeping exactly in the same position, surrounded by the snoring relatives. Surreal. Was he still dreaming? Did he ever fall asleep? He was shivering but did not have the courage to wake anyone. They will laugh at him, or maybe they will get scared too. A dog howled in a corner of the street.

Aaryan covered himself with the sheets and forced his eyes shut.

# *Vinod*

Vinod's earliest childhood memories were those of watching Mother India with his parents in the recently opened Delite Cinema in Delhi. They would take the Delhi Transport Services bus from home and get down at Bengali Market. There they would devour the famous Rasmalai and *Kulfi-Faluda* and would then go to Delite to watch a movie. As evening engulfed the city, they would then stroll into the lawns of India Gate or would sit in the gardens of the Old Fort, absorbing the cool breeze coming through the trees as peacocks performed the rituals of attracting a mate by making sonorous sounds. Sometimes they would go to Rivoli, Regal, Odeon or the Plaza to watch a movie – the cinema halls for the rich and effluent from the walled city and Lutyens's Delhi. Delhi had not spread like a wildfire at that time. East Delhi was still an uninhabitable jungle, not the mesh of discombobulation it later turned into.

Going to watch a movie was nothing less than a ceremony. People would flaunt their best attires, would buy samosa from the street hawkers and tickets that were incredulously nominal by any present standard. During the interval, the children would wait squatting on their seats, as the fathers would go out to buy some more samosas while mothers would go to the bathroom to reapply the lipstick. Vinod, like any other child of his age, was fascinated by the screen and could not distinguish it from reality. So, while watching Mother India, when Vinod saw Nargis run amidst the roaring fire, screaming to be saved, he nudged his father to extricate the damsel in distress and questioned the morality of the crowd who just sat there without showing any chivalry. His mother smacked him on his head and asked him to stop his buffoonery, as the hero was about to enter the screen to save Nargis.

Delhi was a strange amalgamation of humanity those days. The partition was still a raw open wound. There were uprooted families from across the border, trying to find a foothold, trying to absorb the absurdity that the home that they had left behind was now in a foreign land and was either burned down or occupied by a foreigner. There were those who did not cross over and managed to stay afloat, still breathing and waiting for the acrimony to subside. Then there were the hooligans, a bite of partition migrants that took up the task of being the gundas, the illegitimate offsprings of division and abject poverty. Vinod had not seen the partition, but years later, when he tried to superimpose the people around him on the people who would have fought in the freedom struggle, he couldn't. It was as if someone had replaced all of them by a single spell of black magic with a capricious, underdeveloped and narcissistic race. It was an army who fought the enemy with all their might and then slaughtered each other to divide and loot their land as soon as they won the war. Was it a sudden injection of apathy or a passing wave of barbarism or just another one of those human idiosyncrasies? It was hard to tell.

But people were in high spirits those days. There was a future to look up to, a nation to build. Things were changing; there was a constant motion. There was freedom in the air and it was fresh. It was all theirs, the whole chunk of land, their motherland. There was no fear of a bomb exploding in a busy market or a terrorist sprinkling an array of bullets on people waiting for a train. There was still time for that to happen, for events to climax to that point. At present, there was stagnation to life amidst all the drift, a stagnation to be savoured; a stagnation of freedom that was here to stay and decay. That is why, when the first general elections came in 1952, people were euphoric to see their names on the voter's lists. They dressed up as they did for the movies and went to vote and to have the indigo stain on their nail, which they displayed enthusiastically till it fell off. There was no opposition party at that time. The elections were to select various members from the Congress party to represent the people in parliament.

Vinod was the firstborn. So it was just the three of them at that time, his parents and him. His father was a dogmatic disciplinarian, a rough intense man with an immense capacity for anger and who believed in a good thrashing to make his point. Vinod was terrified of him during his growing up years, and would never look him in the eye while addressing him. The only person whom he knew was not afraid of his father was his mother. She was a beautiful woman with incredibly sharp features and was an intrepid warrior as far as her husband was concerned. She would never tolerate her husband's random caprice and was quite a tamer, both with closed and open door of their bedroom. Sadly, Vinod could never take advantage of his mother's hold over his father. In fact he never connected with his mother; he never felt the warmth, the implausible love that mothers shower on their sons in the Bollywood movies. Maybe it was just because of the movies, the larger than life dramatization of motherly love that he took to be the benchmark. Maybe it was actually the case that his mother never really loved any of her children, neither him nor her three daughters who popped out of her later. Sometimes she would look at him as if she could not place him. Sometimes, she would take him in her lap and ask him about his day in the school and shower him with kisses. She was an enigma to Vinod all his life, a jigsaw he was not able to solve till the end. One thing Vinod was sure of was that his mother lived in the past. Sometimes, she would go into bouts of terrible mood swings for days and would treat everyone as liabilities, and rant about how terrible her life had turned out to be. Sometimes she would wear a new sari and apply makeup, make some pakodas and tea and wait for her husband to return from office, sitting at the window. What an eccentric family I had, Vinod pondered years later.

Saturdays and Sundays were kept aside to spend some time with the relatives, besides an occasional trip to the cinema. Vinod was particularly fond of Satish, his father's jovial younger brother. Satish had the same features as his brother; they gave an impression of being twins. Vinod compensated for his father's inability to express himself with Satish. In a way, Satish was the father Vinod never had. He was married to Vani, a girl whom he had met in a sari shop in Chandni Chowk. He worked there as a salesman and she would come regularly to the shop for one reason or another just to have a look at him. They shared stolen glances with each other for a month before Satish had the courage to go and talk to her. It became a regular affair afterwards. They would go to the Red Fort and sit in the Diwan-i-Am, annexed with the shadow of the stone pillars as it danced with the sun. Sometimes the couple would go and sit on the stairs of the Jama Masjid, amidst pigeons fluttering around. At times, he would take her to Golcha in a rikshaw, to watch the latest movie and while the screen came alive with stories, he would take her hand lightly into his own as a romantic song breezed into the narrative. Later, Satish would go with Vani till the tram station. He would look at her, standing in a corner of a tram, her dupatta dancing in the wind, till the tram would disappear at a corner of Chandni Chowk.

There was a traditional initial resistance to their marriage, but then the parents of the girls gave in. The boy was all right, they finally admitted after meeting him. The whole ruckus was a ritual, something that had to be done when a girl dares to fall in love. Satish was married soon afterwards in 1953. Their son was two year younger to Vinod. The families met regularly, going out together on weekends. When they met, Vinod could see the stark difference between his father and Satish, and the obvious physical similarities. Satish's family was blissful. Vani was a convivial woman who lived in the present.

Sometimes, Satish would take both the boys for a tram ride. They would go till Shahar, the most famous restaurant at that time in Chandni Chowk and the boys would be asked to order anything they liked. Then they would go to the Atma Ram's bookshop, and Satish would buy them storybooks. The boys cherished his presence as he always told them funny stories and made them laugh. Vinod was really excited when Satish took them to shikar, a hunting trip, for the first time. It was the first time he had seen a rifle but Satish would not let him use it.

They crossed the river Yamuna in a boat. The iron labyrinth of the Old Yamuna Bridge loomed above as the boat crossed the river to East Delhi or Yamuna Paar as the locals called it, a jungle with a very few settlements here and there. A train rumbled on the iron bridge as the steam engine pulled it through, yielding thick clouds of white smoke. There was a thin mist hanging inches above the clean river, and the local washermen were washing clothes at the banks by hitting them hard on the stones, dispersing the thin fog engulfing them in the process. Vinod watched them with one of his hands skimming the water as the oar made rhythmic splashing sounds. He did not believe his uncle when he told him that there were jackals and foxes in the jungle till he heard one of them howl as they set foot on the other side.

"Don't worry. We are here for the partridges and quails. Jackals won't harm us and even if they try, we have the rifle," Satish said as he saw the boys getting terrorized.

They asked the oarsman to wait for them and entered the jungle. Satish was good with the rifle and within an hour they had three dead partridges. The boys were jumping with joy as they reached back to the boat with each of them holding a dead bird. They gave one to the oarsman, who thanked them with a beaming smile and the rest of the birds were used for the Sunday lunch which Vinod's father and Satish prepared, relieving the women from their duties for one day.

When Vinod was old, he often wondered what became of all the animals in Yamuna Paar? Were they all killed or were they wise enough to retreat as they saw the Frankenstein of urbanization coming towards them? I guess they were wiser than the humans; he chuckled on his own joke that his grandchild refused to appreciate. By the time lines started appearing on Vinod's face, east Delhi was teaming with millions of humans and had turned into a concrete urban jungle with no signs of the past.

Vinod's sisters were born in quick succession in 1956, 1958 and 1960. His mother had turned into a baby generator, churning out infants at a frightening rate. His father was fine with the girls, although he would not have minded another son. Vani had another boy and the couple decided to halt after that. Satish joked that he was just a mere worker in a cloth shop and not a government employee like his brother who could afford four children. Vinod's sisters were named Neela, Rohini and Poonam. By the time Poonam, the third daughter was born, the house had tilted towards mayhem. Vinod was the one who tried to maintain the harmony as his mother was almost on the verge of a nervous breakdown because of the tiresome task of juggling her four children. He helped his mother as much as he could before going to school and also after returning. He cleaned the dishes and filled the water into the earthen pots from the taps. Only then he would complete his homework and play with his sisters, giving his mother a chance to rest. She was exhausted all the time. She was also turning a bit rotund, and now had stretch marks on her stomach, something that Vinod did not like at all. His father would come in the evening and the family would gather in the drawing room to listen to the radio. Vinod's mother would put her head on her husband's shoulder and her hand on his chest and listened to the songs playing in the radio with closed eyes. That was the only time when Vinod would see a trace of emotion on his father's face, a smile on his lips.

Vinod grew up into an undistinguished young boy. He was shy and quiet most of the times unless he was with his sisters. He would bully them at times, being the only elder brother. The family would visit Satish on weekends and the six children would have a grand time together. Vinod was heartbroken when Satish told him that the trams had stopped operating in Chandni Chowk. He had always looked forward to the rides. Instead, Satish promised to take him for a ride in the tanga.

As they grew up, his father became more and more stern and

stopped allowing Vinod any privileges that he could have got being a boy. You must not set a wrong example for your sisters, he said. He was very particular about how his daughters behaved outside the house and did not give them any chance to talk to unknown boys. To set an example, Neela was slapped hard and was locked in the toilet for two hours after her father saw her talking to a boy. She was thirteen.

But these were still convivial days of Vinod's life before everything started to crumble. No matter how despotic his father was, there was always Satish to look after him. No matter how impervious his mother appeared to be at times, there were always his sisters at home and his cousins at school. He could see his mother drift away, not only from him but also from the whole family, but this was an actuality he had grown up with. It never occurred to him that he had to cope up with it. It was his way of life. And then there were times, when his mother was perfectly normal, guarding her cubs; so he preserved those moments in his brain, blocking out the gloomy, purposeless times.

Satish died in his sleep when Vinod was twenty. He plainly stopped breathing. That was the night of the blackout. The war had started. It wasn't the first war between India and Pakistan, but it was the shortest, lasting only for 13 days and leading to the birth of Bangladesh. People had put dark curtains on the windows of their houses. Some had painted them black. A siren woke up Vani that night and then suddenly the power went off. There were trenches dug outside their houses and they were supposed to leap into them in case of a bomb raid, which thankfully did not happen. She tried to wake up her husband but he didn't respond. She ran to the room in which her children slept and woke them up. The boys huddled around her and ran back to her room. Her husband was not moving. She was not supposed to light a candle. Soon her sobs fused with the wailing sirens as her sons tried desperately to wake up their father in the dark.

Satish had somehow held the families together till now but Vinod instinctively knew that they were now like a small piece of ice that had broken away from the glacier, drifting away on a desultory trajectory. Vinod was hit by a humongous void which settled on his heart like a veil. He could not understand why Satish could not have lived like everyone else, holding his hand and sailing him through. He had not witnessed death from such close vicinity and it left him more angry than miserable.

Vinod's father and mother were there for Vani, providing a shoulder but what the widow and her children wanted was a foothold and food. Satish's family shifted to Bombay in 1971 where Vani's distant relative promised her a job in a cloth mill. The cousins clung to each other and sobbed on the railway platform before the train took them to a different future. Vinod saw his cousins rarely afterwards, mostly on marriages and deaths.

✦

*March, 2017*

Vinod and his wife were an archetypal middle class Indian couple who had jostled through life to safeguard the future of their children, sacrificing too much of their own pleasures and notions, and now that all of it was over, they were left with nothing but the bare minimum to cover for the rest of their life. So there was the house, the pension and food on the table, enough to sail through a 65 year old man and his wife. There was no question of accepting aid from their children, and for what? Expensive holidays and cruise? Nah! They were luxuries. You could live without them.

Sometimes Vinod wondered that if every generation slogs to preserve the future generation then which generation actually enjoys its life. It was lunatic, a relay race that never ends. His wife was a woman who was tilting towards obesity in the absence of a driving force. She was a beautiful woman in her youth but there were too many unsymmetrical lines on her face now. Their life was prosaic, with the only source of entertainment being the maid who came in the morning and afternoons to clean up the dishes and the house. Vinod's wife circled the maid like a moth circling fire. She made sure that each and every corner of the house was sparkling clean even if it irritated the maid and amused her husband. Vinod chuckled and waved his head enjoying the spectacle and sank his head in the newspaper as soon as his wife gave him an icy glare. During one such deceptive act of hiding behind the newspaper, he read that soon robotic maids would be available in Japan who will look exactly like humans. In fact you could provide a face you would like the maid to have. He showed the article to his wife.

"Robots? They can never dust like humans. How will they remove dust from the corners?" his wife said.

"They might have vacuum cleaners in their fingers. Who knows! Anything is possible. And imagine Madonna as a maid!"

"Whatever. I will never have one!"

"Yes, I can understand. The constant bickering might not irritate them. Now you wont like that, will you? And besides, they are just going on trials. It will be decades before anything remotely similar is available in India."

Sometimes, Vinod would surf the high speed Internet wirelessly on his touch screen laptop sitting on his bed, sipping tea, and would wonder at the leaps technology had taken in his lifetime. He came from a generation when no one could have dreamt of something like Internet or a mobile phone or even a digital camera but here he was, integrated in a moment of time where things had gone from one end of the spectrum to another. The city had undergone a metamorphosis too. It was odd how a piece of land with an imaginary boundary could change with technology. Delhi was not Delhi anymore; it was NCR, the National Capital Region and included all the satellite towns around it. There was a Metro network larger than the Tube. Yes, who could have imagined? There were malls so huge that you can get lost in them. Nothing was laid-back now; there was always a rush...rush of honking cars, rush of anger, rush of egocentricity, rush of dissensions, rush of lecherousness. Did love at first sight exist anymore, he wondered? Do people even know what that means?

There were two plasma televisions in the house. They were dirt-cheap now, ever since the 3D televisions had entered the market. He craved to get a 3D television, but he was used to getting things when the rest of the world had relinquished them after savoring every ounce of it. His taste of television programmes did not equal that of his wife's and they decided to have separate rooms and separate televisions instead of juggling the channels and fighting, the remote acting as a single sword in the duel. The arrangement did not bother either of them. They had had enough of each other's company. There were no more thoughts to slice, no more albatrosses to look forward to, no more cracked Earth to water. Both of them were like two people living in an old age home, meeting only during breakfast, lunch, tea break and dinner, leading completely separate lives.

When the heart attack came, Vinod was studying female wrestling on a sports channel. His wife could never fathom what drew her husband so whimsically to this sport. This was one of the crucial reasons why the television split out like an amoeba. The sight of women punching each other, tearing apart whatever bare minimum they were wearing and uproot each other's hair with all their might had revolted her. She could still take men doing that to each other – there was something erotic in that – but women? Her husband on the other hand devoured it. In Vinod's defense, he loved to watch wrestling irrespective of the gender of the wrestlers. Vinod also treasured watching Discovery and National Geographic channels, especially the documentaries where they showed lions running in slow-motion after helpless deer and tearing them apart later on, smearing their faces with blood of the deceased. He loved to see snakes gulp down huge frogs, creating a frog-shaped bulge in their throat. He loved to see owls tearing down rats bits by bits. His wife concluded that her husband had a deep undercurrent of savageness and a sex drive that had almost diminished to nothingness but could be redeemed momentarily by watching women fight. She could never understand that her husband loved nature; the rawness intrigued him. He was a Neanderthal born in the wrong era. And then there was this emptiness around him. The television was his home.

The fact that the heart attack came when he was watching females punch each other assured his wife of her suspicions. She might not have heard him cry out her name if she had not been in the kitchen, filling her water jug for the night. When she reached his room, he was lying on his bed, panting and frantically holding the remote in one hand, as if afraid that his wife would change the channel while his heart raced to a stop.

The heart attack was massive. Vinod had an existing heart problem; his right auricle was not large enough and diabetes ran in the family. He had chest pain earlier but seeing him helpless like this catapulted his wife into a state of frenzy. She telephoned their son but the phone kept ringing. Then she telephoned her daughter who hurriedly called the ambulance. Vinod had lost consciousness. His wife sat there constantly staring at his chest, imagining that it was not stirring. Her thoughts were evading her, swimming into the past and inquiring her judgments. She had a secret, heavily guarded from her husband with no intentions of disclosure, but then life does not run wild like imaginations. Till now her adjudications were her own, but the thought of taking them alone to her deathbed alarmed her. She had never intended on telling her husband anything, but panic was taking its course, raising the skipped thoughts like a phantom from out of the ground.

What if it all goes wrong? Yes, the secret was cursed but their life had not been a bed of roses without it either. She had to tell Vinod once he gets well, no matter what the consequences. Maybe, it would be good for her children. They would not want it, maybe even Vinod would not want it, but what is the harm in telling? What could possibly go wrong?

The doctors put Vinod under a 24 hours monitoring in the ICU. He was unconscious the whole day. His son arrived next day after being constantly bothered by calls from his sister.

Vinod's wife did not cry. In fact she was anxiously waiting for him to open his eyes, to regain enough consciousness to understand what she was about to tell him. The fact that he might not open his eyes at all did not occur to her; it was as if she was sure that he would not die before she told him what she had to.

Vinod feebly opened his eyes in the evening. The children

were in the hospital canteen, eating samosa with their evening tea. His wife was staring at him from the glass door, standing alone. She glided in as soon as she saw his eyes flicker. She had a bundle in her hand. Something wrapped in a yellow cloth, which she had taken out of her bag. Her husband gave her a weak smile.

"Are you all right?" his wife asked.

He nodded and smiled again, a bit wider this time.

"I have to tell you something," she added.

Her husband looked at her imploringly. The realization that she could give her husband another heart attack never crossed her mind. She was too optimistic in the hope of making circumstances exceptional for the family; blind to the miseries she was about to unfold. She thought the news might make Vinod better.

Her husband's expression showed no signs of transitions while she divulged the events of a particular day and the specifics of what she was holding in her hand. He looked through her as he would have looked through a pane of glass. After she had squeezed out every last sentence out of her, she stood there, pressing his hand in hers and looking expectantly at him, expecting an accolade. It was then that his expressions changed like a sea studded with a sudden storm; a pain emancipated, breaking the barriers of calmness, ending up as a hoarse voice from his throat. The nurse came running into the room and asked his wife to leave. She stood outside, watching the nurse grope with the machines. The doctor came a minute later, but the situation had gone out of hand by that time. When the children arrived, Vinod had taken his last breath. She stood there, still floating in the sea of sanguineness, scantily absorbing the actuality. This cannot happen, she was whispering again and again, as tears finally coaxed themselves out of her eyes.

Meena decided to stow away the cursed yellow bundle forever.

# *Meena*

Meena was the fourth child of Jai Dev and Sujata Devi. She was born in 1962, the year of the Sino-Indian war, the war between the two most crowded nations on Earth. It could have been like a fight between two mammoths, but it wasn't.

"This is the girl who started the war!" Her father used to say when he was in a good mood. She had two elder brothers and an elder sister. Another younger sister came three years later, born during the first Indo-Pakistan war in 1965.

"And here is another girl who started the war!" The coincidence amused Jai Dev to no ends. Little did he know that his younger daughters would turn out to be the meekest of all his five children. A few years later when the second Indo-Pakistan war started, Meena asked her mother if they are going to have another sister.

"No, my child. If I start bearing a child every war, I will end up doing that for the rest of my life," her mother replied.

The family lived in a two-storey house in Dalhousie. It was an unadorned house created from wooden planks and stones and had steps carved out of the mountain to go to the top floor. Jai Dev simply forgot to add a staircase inside the house when he built it with the help of his brothers. Later the mountain was carved out when he realized his mistake. The stairs created a beautiful symmetry with the pathway to the main road, creating a V shaped structure. The stairs ended up being an embarrassing predicament for Jai Dev rather than a solution. They were faultless during the summers, when the Sun was shining and walking was perfectly possible, but the nightmare started in winters when Dalhousie was covered with thick layers of snow. They would find it extremely difficult to use the stairs and had to wear some extra layer of woollens if they had to go up and did not want to freeze to death during the ordeal. Sometimes, it would snow in the night and then the dew would turn the snow-covered areas into a very slippery and dangerous terrain. In the end, the boys always had to shovel the snow out of the way.

Meena's father worked at the post office. He had inherited some land from his father, which he never used. Instead, he kept it aside for his daughters' marriage and difficult times. Jai Dev was a tall and extremely thin man. His profile was almost non-existent, as if he lived in a two dimensional space. Sujata Devi was supposed to be obese after bearing five children, but she too followed her husband's example and remained quite thin. It was as if the children had drained out the last ounce of flesh from her body. Jai Dev, though quite articulate in front of people and specially his wife, turned out to be very tongue-tied in front of his children. He was awkward and treated them as Martians who had dripped out of the taps and had no idea about how to handle them. His wife could never understand his behaviour and compensated as much as she could. But finally, at the end, the boys drifted away faster than the girls. The eldest son was eight when Meena was born. He was already used to his father's reticent behaviour and was not surprised at his father's lack of reaction to Meena's birth other than the supposedly humorous remark about her starting the war. Jai Dev took Meena in his hands and looked at the small bundle of flesh that had just left his wife's body. There was amusement in his eyes and then just as he had lifted her, he kept Meena back on the bed without a sign of happiness or an exclamation of joy. His wife cursed loudly. Jai Dev was not heartless but contentment was a virtue he was unable to express when it came to his children. He had seen his father behave in a similar way with him and his brothers. A patriarch was not supposed to blend in his family.

As Meena started going to school, she became friends with a couple of her classmates. The gang was always running here and there and was always up to some mischief.

"Of all my children, you are the silliest, Meena! Why would you always run so fast? Do you know what will happen if your foot slips? You will end up in a jungle in the valley in the middle of ten bears and they will tear you apart," Sujata Devi screamed at her.

Meena could sprint very fast and Sujata Devi was petrified when she saw her daughter running like a horse. The mountains were dangerous and there were sharp bends and vehicles were always coming and going. She was especially terrified of the trucks and the buses and then there were the horses. There were many small villages scattered here and there in the hills. Besides terrace farming, their main source of income came from giving horse rides to tourists. Sujata Devi hated the thought of her daughter colliding into one, falling down and then being run over by a bus. One day, while buying groceries at G.P.O, she saw Meena running with her playmates on the Mall road. She was enraged. On returning home, she covered her hand with a thick cloth and carefully uprooted a few stems of a plant called Bicchu-booti from the mountainside. She had never used this plant on her children although the women in the neighborhood vouched that one beating with the leaves of the plant would create amazing results. There were thousands of tiny, almost invisible thorns all over the stems and leaves and one touch of it would send an unbearable burning sensation on your fingers that will not go unless you rub it with the leaves of another plant. On reaching home, she tied the stems together with a thread and wrapped it with a newspaper, so that it would be easier for her to hold it. And then she waited.

Later that day, after Sujata finished beating up Meena on her arms and legs with the plant, she plucked the leaves of the other plant that would ease the pain. She mashed the leaves together creating a paste and applied it on her daughter's skin as she cried.

"I am not asking you to stop running, but stop running on the road," she said as she rubbed the paste on Meena's arm. Meena cried herself to sleep that night and Sujata got a piece of Jai Dev's mind.

Meena stopped fooling around and became more conscientious after this. The pain was too much to bear again. She regularly participated in racing events in her school and there was nobody who could beat her. By the time she was ten, she had a shelf load of trophies and certificates. She started participating in district level events and she was unmatched there too. She had a great career ahead had she been given a chance but Sujata Devi was not gifted with the acumen to encourage her daughters for anything besides getting married and be of service to their respective husbands. So, letting Meena build up a career out of sprinting was nothing less than a profanity. She did not even think of indulging her husband with her thoughts.

"Look Meena, you are a girl and girls are not supposed to do many things till they are married. You have to remain in your boundaries otherwise you will be a burden on us for the rest of your life. I am not asking to give up all your dreams but wait till you get married. I am sure you will get a loving husband who will bow to all your wishes. Concentrate on your studies. No one will take a woman as a wife who runs for a living," she told her daughter.

What Sujata said that day defined and destroyed Meena's life. Meena was the best sprinter in the district and would have gone for national level championships had her mother not intervened. She was too naïve to understand that her mother had just baited her out of her dreams. Young as she was, she foolishly pinned all her hopes on her marriage. Her mind subconsciously contemplated marriage to be a doorway to utopia, to reach out to her dreams. She started picturing a husband who would let her run, who would take her to the movies and who would love her like a madman. She kept running at district level but never went beyond that.

By this time, her brothers and elder sister were married. The eldest brother had taken up a respectable position in the transport department and had moved out with his wife to another house. The second brother moved to Chamba, another hill station, to work in the Electricity department. Meena's elder sister was married to a local shopkeeper who sold expensive lampshades to the tourists. The elder sister knew that marriage will not open any doors but close many but she did not have the heart to tell her sister. And now she was too busy helping her husband at the shop and trying to get pregnant.

Meena met Vinod in 1978 at a friend's wedding in Dalhousie when she was sixteen. He was twenty-six years old and should have been looking for girls his age, but there was something about her. He followed her everywhere in the wedding, sat behind her or leaned over a little closer to hear her voice. His mother was also in the wedding but she was too busy being nostalgic that she hardly kept track of her son. Meena was aware that she was being stared at and it was only after a few minutes that she steeled herself and was able to steal a glance at him. Vinod was quite alarmed all of a sudden, lowered his eyes and turned red. Meena found him handsome. Both of them exchanged quite a few glances that night without talking to each other. They were afraid that if they would try to achieve that feat, their parents would be instantly on them like hungry hounds.

A few days later when Meena returned from school, Sujata Devi took her face in her hands and kissed her on the forehead.

"You are the luckiest of all my children. A family has shown interest in you. They want you to marry their son. My Meena is going to be a bride soon! Ah! How time flies. It's as if it was yesterday, when I beat you up with bicchu-booti and now look at you, all ready to start your own family!" She was too happy to continue and dabbed her eyes.

"Who?" Meena croaked.

Thankfully, it was Vinod. Since his mother was hell bent to find a bride for him because he was way past the marriageable age and she was tired of making excuses in front of the relatives, he pounced at the first chance he got to mention Meena. After they returned to Delhi, he whispered that he had met someone he liked when his mother was showing him photographs of a few girls she had selected for him.

"When?" His mother said with a baffled look.

"Dalhousie," he said, staring at the floor.

"What's her name?"

"Meena."

"Oh! Jai Dev's daughter?" His mother was meditative for a

moment as he nodded.

"They are below us in stature and even in caste and she is too young for you. You are aware of that?" She said finally.

"Umm-hmm."

"And are you absolutely sure? I must tell you that I am not very keen unless you are sure of this. I wanted you to marry someone from Delhi, who understands city life and knows how to conduct herself here. So?"

"I am very sure, Ma."

"All right then, I'll send a message. We will have to match the horoscopes. If they match, I don't have a problem."

The horoscopes fitted together like two pieces of a jigsaw. The pundit told Vinod's mother that they were the best matching horoscopes he had seen in a long time. She thanked him, sighed, gave him his fees and went away to break the news to her clan. She was prejudiced against Meena and no horoscope, no matter how brilliantly it matched her son's, could alter the bias. But what was she supposed to do? Meena was poor, she belonged to a lower caste but she was perfect for her son as per the horoscope. She sat in her two-bedroom apartment in Delhi and stared out of the window as she twirled her hair in her finger mulling over the turn of events.

"So be it. If nothing else, she would be of assistance to me," she finally said.

Meena's initial anticipation disappeared when she came to know that it was Vinod who had proposed to marry her. Although she was not sure if she wanted to get married at such an early age, all she was asked was whether she liked the boy. She had a choice. She could say yes and start a new life in Delhi or she could say no and end up like her elder sister, dusting lamps in a local market. She said yes. She also had a notion that Delhi would provide her a bigger platform to pursue her dream of running.

Vinod worked in a five star hotel as a staff member of the room service. His income was good especially because of the tips he received. His mother did not like his job at all and always mentioned him as one of the managers in a five star hotel in front of her kitty party friends. She hated the idea that her son changed bed sheets and cleaned toilets for other people. But this never stalled her from demanding the salary from her son on the first of every month. Vinod was quite docile when it came to his mother. He was given twenty rupees from his own salary every month for his expenses and he took them without even the slightest whimper. It was not as if he sought supplementary amount but he had seasoned himself to believe that twenty rupees was more than enough for him to spend in a month, and it was. He was even able to accumulate.

Vinod's mother was a shapeless woman who every now and then blamed her husband for turning her plump. She spent most of her daytime visiting the local market and buying clothes and other accessories for herself or playing flash and gossiping with her kitty party friends. Sometimes, she would go for a movie with her friends. As soon as her husband and son would disappear for their jobs, she would take out a number of sarees from her almirah and position herself in front of the mirror, holding each sari in front of her, deciding which one of them to wear. She would take almost two hours to get ready and then would glide her handbag elegantly on her arm and move out of the house like a queen. The family had no car. They weren't that rich. So she would either take a bus or a rickshaw. She would usually eat out at lunch and would return before her husband arrived in the evening. She abhorred cooking food and dusting and cleaning the house but she never asked her son or husband to help her in her household chores. She wanted a maid but she could not afford one, until now. Vinod's father expressed his view that Meena was not suitable for his son but was silenced by his wife.

"Your son admires her, so what is your trouble? It's not as if we are bringing a girl from another religion."

"But why can't he marry a girl from Delhi?"

"Why? What is the danger with the girls from Dalhousie?"

"Nothing."

The family visited Dalhousie again and everything was finalized. Meena was to give up her studies and move to Delhi after getting married. Her mother told her that she could continue her studies there, with the permission of her husband of course. The Shagun and Chunni were presumed to be small ceremonies but distant relatives from both sides appeared as the news travelled through the hill station. Meena's elder brothers arrived with their wives and children. Her elder sister came almost a week earlier. The ceremony happened in Meena's home where Vinod's family came with thirty relatives. A tent was erected in the open area near the house for the *halwai* to prepare sweets and lunch for the guest. A pundit performed the puja inside the house and gifts, sweets and jewellery were exchanged. Vinod's mother did not demand a dowry but she did not decline from accepting it either. She expected to receive something befitting without saying anything. Jai Dev thought that given his financial standing, a little less was expected from him.

The families were cordial with each other during the ceremony. Vinod and Meena had not talked to each other yet and were not expected to during the course of the day. Vinod sat with the pundit and all the male members in one room while all the women assembled in another room. Both the ceremonies happened simultaneously and in the end both of them were brought together to touch the feet of all the elders. That was the time when they swiftly glanced at each other. They looked extremely admirable together. Even though there was a gap of ten years between them, it somehow never showed because Vinod looked years younger for his age. The pundit consulted a plethora of charts to finally provide a marriage date. Meena and Vinod were to be married two months later.

After the ceremony, Vinod went back to Delhi with his family. There was no way Meena could have communicated with him during those two months as both the families did not have a telephone connection. The only two ways they could have exchanged a few words was either by writing letters or if Vinod could visit her in Dalhousie. Writing letters appeared a bit awkward to both of them, as they hardly knew each other. None of them was very good with words. Instead, Vinod visited Dalhousie twice during this interval. He was a bit anxious while taking permission from his mother but then the urge to talk to his future wife was too much to suppress.

"Why do you want to go all the way to Dalhousie to meet her? It's an eighteen hours journey and you are going to get married anyway in one and a half month." His mother was perplexed and did not like the way her son was behaving lovesick.

"I would like to know her a bit more before we get married," Vinod said timidly.

"Hmmm. This generation is poles apart from how we used to conduct ourselves. During my time, people got married even without looking at each other. Their parent's word was enough. Times have changed." Vinod's mother sighed.

"How did you and dad get married?" Vinod asked. He was aware of the saga but wanted to make the point that his mother did not practice what she was preaching.

"Oh! I have things to do in the kitchen. Go if you really want to. What can I say?"

Vinod reached Dalhousie and stayed at his cousin brother's house. He went to Meena's home in the afternoon when he was sure that she was back from school. Her mother opened the door and on seeing her soon to be son-in-law grinning at her doorsteps, unannounced and reluctant, Sujata Devi reacted as if she had seen a spectre. She was completely unprepared for an occasion of such massive proportions and she could not let him in with the present disarrayed situation of the house. It was just a reflex but she banged the door shut as soon as she opened it. She bit her tongue the moment she realized what she had done.

"Son, can you please wait here for a moment. The house is in chaos. Let me set things right," she said from inside.

"Please don't bother yourself. I just came here to meet Meena. Would you be kind enough to ask her to sit with me outside at the terrace?" Vinod said as he recovered from the shock of a door banged shut on his face.

"Oh no! You are our son-in-law and I have to let you enter the house and treat you with all the respect, which is a son-in-law's right. I will go to hell if I don't do that."

The door opened after ten minutes and Sujata Devi appeared with a jovial gait. Vinod touched her feet and entered the hurriedly ironed out house. There was no trace of Meena anywhere. Two cups of tea, a handful of sweets and a full plate of dry fruits later,

Vinod was finally given permission to converse with Meena. Sujata Devi chatted with him like her long lost son for almost an hour before she remembered the purpose of his visit. She went inside and shoved Meena into the room. Vinod was aware that Sujata Devi will be sitting in the next room with her ear on the door and will listen to each and everything he would say. So he motioned Meena to be quiet and tag along. The front door was still ajar and both of them promptly moved out. They ran down the stone stairway to the ground floor and further into the terrace farms below in the valley. They sat on a stone pathway next to a farm and giggled till they got their breath back.

"How are you?" Vinod asked. That was the first time he had spoken to her.

"Afraid," Meena said.

"So am I."

They talked for an hour. She told him about her school, her friends who lived in the neighborhood and her family. She did not bother to mention the topic of further studies or her sprinting abilities. She was skeptical that this was not the right time to mention all that. Vinod told her about his job, about Delhi and how big it was compared to Dalhousie. He did not mention the fact that he gave all his salary to his mother and had to take permissions from her to do pretty much everything. Soon Meena reminded him that it was getting late and she should return. As she got up and started walking, Vinod caught hold of her hand.

"I'll come again," he said.

"I'll wait."

The trepidation in Meena's mind underwent a moderate change in that one hour. They had a very orderly conversation, nothing was absurd or out of the place. In that one hour, she knew that Vinod was a trustworthy and authentic human. There was nothing despicable about him, not at least in the first meeting and considering the fact that he came all the way from Delhi to meet her. Vinod on the other hand was relieved, not only because he now had no reasons for skepticism for this relationship but also because he genuinely admired Meena more after this brief meeting. The flutter, which he experienced in his gut when he first saw her was not a farce and he was much appeased.

Meena's mother was on the brink of tears when she saw her daughter walking up the stone steps back to her home, as if she had just returned from a war zone. There was something very audacious about the present generation; they were not punctilious like hers. There was recklessness and they were not shy to display their emotions. She was more content not because Vinod had the passion to carry out his heart's desire but because her daughter had the competence to invoke such a strong emotion in someone. She vehemently bothered Meena to tell her everything about her meeting but Meena was too shy to share such details with her mother. Meena's younger sister who had been in a deep afternoon slumber during all this joined her mother as soon as she woke up and witnessed her mother's prodding.

"Did he hold your hand? Did he kiss you?" Meena's sister whispered in her ear and ran away. Meena glared at her.

It was much more exacting for Vinod to pay a second visit. His mother could not identify with what had got into her son. She could feel her grip loosen. Soon, she would have to share her son and to split him with someone who had driven him to an unacceptable level of psychosis. It was like sharing her favorite piece of jewellery with a notorious kleptomaniac. Her husband had his own reasons to stay away from her bickering and spent most of his evenings listening to the news on Doordarshan. Vinod faced some resistance from his mother when he asked for permission to go for a second time. She tried to reason but what harm could such a meeting bring? She gave up in the end but with a growing sense of uneasiness.

When Vinod knocked at Meena's door for the second time, he wasn't that blessed. Jai Dev was at home that day with a running nose and completely irritated, as his wife had not given him the ginger tea on time. Both men were dumbstruck as Jai Dev swung open the door. Vinod had the good sense to quickly bend down and touch Jai Dev's feet and hide the shadow which had passed over his face. Jai Dev blessed him but Vinod could have peed in his pants had he not seen Sujata Devi walking up the stone stairs carrying the tea, which she almost dropped the instant she saw him. Jai Dev and Sujata were completely lost. Meena was not at home so Vinod was invited inside to have a cup of tea. Although he had been inside before, he had not experienced the direct steel glaze of his soon to be father-in-law previously. For half an hour Vinod sat inside the house, transfixed by the carpet, and sized up by Jai Dev numerous times. Sujata did all the talking and kept the men entertained but Vinod was embarrassed enough not to utter a word unless asked a question.

When Meena and her younger sister came back from G.P.O with the groceries, Sujata Devi opened the door. Meena had no idea where to look and her sister giggled and ran into the bedroom as Jai Dev's stern stare followed her. Sujata called her youngest daughter back and motioned Jai Dev to get up. The trio went to the ground floor leaving the couple together.

"The boy is a spendthrift," Jai Dev said as they walked down.

"Oho! Why? Are you saying this because he got some expensive jewellery for Meena, just like you used to bring for me?" Sujata Devi lashed, her remark dipped in sarcasm.

"Look at the money he has wasted for these two trips. What was the need? They are anyway going to get married in the next twenty days."

"Do you think everything in this world happens because there is a need for it? Ah! If you could have understood this, my life would have been heaven."

Their daughter giggled and the parents realized that they were not unaccompanied.

The moment the family left them, Vinod stood up and kissed Meena on the cheek. Meena was in a stupor on seeing him again and the kiss just pushed her over the brink. She blushed and looked down.

"I told you I'd come again."

"Yes. You did."

Both of them sat on the wooden chairs and Vinod took her hand in his.

"I love you," he said.

Meena looked up at him and this time he kissed her on the lips. There was something as tenebrous as a thievery in kissing a man in her own house with her parents sitting a few paces away that Meena couldn't stop herself. She kissed him back and for a few moments both of them lost all connections to their surroundings. They kissed fervently. It was their first touch derived from absolute passion, their first amalgam.

"How will I spend these twenty days away from you?" Vinod asked later, when their hearts had attained the normal rhythm.

That day they didn't talk much. One hour later Sujata

Devi came up under the pretext of asking them if they wanted something to eat. Vinod got the cue and left soon after.

The days became extremely demanding as both the families started preparing for the marriage. There were a million minuscule details to be carried out, things and people to be arranged, a swarm of people to be invited, train tickets to be reserved. The days passed away as ephemeral wisps of time. Soon, the marriage day arrived and Vinod's family landed in Jai Dev's house with a crowd of friends and relatives from Delhi and Dalhousie. Two hundred people attended the wedding and the arrangements were impressive considering Jai Dev's social standing. Vinod's mother remained true to her snotty countenance and treated everything with mild aversion. Nothing was good enough for her. Although she had not demanded any dowry, she did not want to return empty handed either and the way things were, that was quite close to how the situation was. Except for a few pieces of furniture and some average jewellery, she found everything overtly bourgeois. She sneered at the food and Meena's tasteless wedding sari. She behaved like a pompous queen who was sacrificing her son to the deprived.

The women entered a tear shedding competition after the wedding was over and it was time for Meena to leave. Meena's mother and sisters cried as if she had died. Her brothers, their wives and their children cried too. Jai Dev remained calm and gave her a warm embrace. Meena and Vinod were just thankful that it was all over. They were bone-tired and hadn't slept well since the last two days.

Meena stayed in Dalhousie for two more days before she finally took a bus to Pathankot with the family and then a train to Delhi from there. Her own family came to see her off at the bus stand and again her mother and sisters shed copious tears. They were not going to see her for a long time now. Vinod's mother was quite distant and watched the family from the window of her seat in the bus. Her husband discussed the weather with Jai Dev.

Vinod and Meena had slept like logs during the past two days. Meena was sure that she would never be able to sleep next to a man on a bed but she surprised herself. She was too tired to notice anyone on the bed on the first day. When she woke up in the morning of the second day, Vinod was already up and had just returned after taking a bath. In the instant their eyes met, he was upon her, kissing her passionately. Vinod wanted to wait till they reach Delhi because there were too many people in the house but he had waited too long. It was not awkward and both of them were driven by the animalism lingering from their first kiss. It was a miracle no one disturbed them during those fifteen minutes, at the end of which Meena was impregnated.

The journey to Pathankot was a queer one for Meena. She had never gone down the mountains before and was surprised to see how flat Pathankot was. On reaching the railway station, she was in for a surprise. It was the first time Meena had seen a train. She was taken aback by the sheer magnitude. When she saw the steam engine pull in, she was a bit alarmed to sit in something so enormous and running on two very thin rails.

"I am scared. Are you sure this is safe?" she whispered to Vinod.

"What are you talking about? Of course it is."

Meena was amazed to see the number of people a bogie could accommodate. It was like a small town inside. She gave a short scream when the train started to move.

"What was that?" She asked alarmed.

"It's moving. That is how it will take us to Delhi," Vinod's mother said and rolled her eyes.

It took some time for Meena to get used to the rumbling, the rhythm and the deafening noise. She almost jumped when Vinod slid open the window and moments later another train rushed past. She was not able to sleep at night. She and her mother-in-law were on the lower berths while both the men slept at the upper ones.

She stared out of the window at the stagnant moon as she lay down on her berth. It was watching over her and smiling back. She was amused how the lands rush past as the train moved but the sky remained still. She comforted herself by reflecting that the sky had been following her from Dalhousie and no matter how different Delhi might be from her place of birth, the sky would be the same.

Delhi was harsh at first glance. It was like a disordered congregate of people, voices, vehicles and animals. Also, it was flat, as she had been forewarned. Suddenly, Meena did not have to press her toes to walk uphill or walk at an obtuse angle with the ground to run downhill. The roads were unnecessarily wide at some places and surprisingly narrow at some. She could not understand how so many people could drive in the same direction without bumping into each other. The family took a black ambassador taxi from the station to their home.

The house was smaller than what Meena had expected. There were two bedrooms on the same floor. The sitting room was shabby and had four wooden chairs and a wooden table to welcome the guests. The dining room had an almost rusted dining table, which could be folded away to make space and had matching foldable chairs. The curtains were very dirty and the kitchen was in tatters. She started understanding why before marriage when her father asked Vinod's mother about the furniture they would like to have, she demanded a wooden dining table and chairs, two almirahs and a divan. Thankfully, the house was recently painted.

"Your house needs some serious work," Meena told Vinod as soon as they were alone.

"Just my house?" Vinod said as he pulled her towards him.

Soon the furniture arrived and the house got its first breath of new life. Meena was particularly proud of the two almirahs which her father had sent for her. There was a false ceiling in one of the almirah. It was their small secret that she did not even share with Vinod. You could slide it off with the help of an almost invisible depression in the ceiling and it would open a compartment of the size of a thin briefcase. There was nothing for her to hide there but it was exciting. Surprisingly, she did not have a hard time in acquiring that particular almirah. She knew that if her mother-in-law would have unknowingly demanded the one with the false ceiling, Meena could not have refused. But the sizes of the almirahs were different. Her mother-in-law took the bigger one.

Two days after the family arrived in Delhi, Vinod and his father rejoined their office. The couple did not go on honeymoon and ended up sitting in the lawns of India Gate on weekends or watching a movie. Their sexual life was pleasurable and Meena started to learn how to get pleasure from Vinod without making sounds as her in-laws slept a few paces away.

The twenty rupees that Vinod got from his mother were not enough for the couple to survive now. She did not offer him more on her own. He had to go and negotiate. She mulled over it for three days before increasing the amount to forty rupees, a very generous hike according to her. Meena started setting up the house. She cleaned the kitchen and put everything in proper place, which ended up giving her mother-in-law a migraine, as she could not find anything during her rare visits to the kitchen. Meena saved some money and got new curtains for the house. Her mother-in-law did not resume her earlier activities in a jiffy. Initially, a lot of neighbours and her friends would flock the house to have a look at the new bride. Meena had to sit with them and accept gifts, money and sweets. After the initial frenzy died down and people got busy in their lives, Meena's mother-in-law started going out on the pretext of buying groceries and then she would not return till the evening. Meena had, by now, taken charge of the house. She completely transformed it. Things were clean now, in their place. It did not look like the Mughals had plundered it. She cooked all the three meals and packed the lunch boxes for the men. As time passed, her mother-in-law became more shameless. She would get up at ten in the morning, have breakfast and take a bath and glide out of the house after ordering Meena about the menu for the dinner. She never offered to take Meena with her.

It was not as if Meena did not try to break the ice. She tried to initiate conversations many times, but no matter how hard she tried, her mother-in-law would not treat her as part of the family. She was always an outsider. Moreover, her son was fading away from her life because of this new woman. He was spending less time with her mother and even demanded a raise! In the cover of false egotism, she was blinded and could not gather that her son was happy, more than he had ever been in his life. There was an undercurrent of resentfulness, which never allowed her to speak with love to Meena, who had left her house to be with unfamiliar people. Meena never complained and kept trying for months. The only thing that kept her going was Vinod. She had realized that he was under the sole of his mother's shoe but snatching him from there would have been a terrible mistake which she could not afford, not at present. Vinod was always his loving self but turned into a meek lamb when it came to his mother. Her father-in-law was a riddle to her. He was like a ghost wandering in the house. He barely spoke and opened his mouth only to eat or to fight with his wife at times.

"I am not sure how he is with Ma. They barely speak in public. You haven't seen a full-blown fight yet. It's hilarious. Once they started throwing food at each other and the next day I saw a lump of rice sticking on the ceiling. I would like to believe that they loved each other once but then time kills many things," Vinod told her once.

"How is he with you?"

"He is just my father. I don't think he believes in friendship or something like that between a father and a son. Even mother thinks like this. They have to maintain a distance; an emotional bonding would make them lose their standing. And maybe it has something to do with the generation gap too."

"But isn't that wrong? You are a family. You are supposed to love each other, know each other."

"Oh! We love each other but we certainly don't know each other."

"My father and brothers were aloof as well, and I did not like that a bit. I abhorred it. Why are fathers always like that?"

It didn't take long for the opportunity of the first big fight to present itself. Vinod's parents had a fight the next day, which started with no sugar in the tea. Both of them were restraining themselves because of Meena's presence but now that she had been in the house for sometime, the mask was too cumbersome to carry. Vinod was in the room getting ready for work and Meena was packing his lunch in the kitchen. The fight started at the middle C note and went till F. It was a symphony, which only the two of them could create and enjoy. The mother-in-law stormed in the kitchen and threw the teacups in the washbasin. There were tears in her eyes and she was loudly cursing her husband. It was like a loud, over the top performance in a theatre, done so many times and done to perfection.

"I curse the day I married you! You have made my life hell. Oh God! Take me away!"

"Oh God! Yes, please! That will be the end of my woes. Take her away!" her husband screamed from the room. Meena was afraid that the neighbours would listen but then she realized that they too might be used to it by now.

"That's it! I am leaving this house this very minute," Vinod's mother screamed back as she stormed out of the kitchen into the room and banged the door shut.

Meena was stupefied. The time during which her mother-in-law was in the kitchen, she stood there frozen, as someone would stand in the presence of a huge tornado, waiting and praying to God to make it pass you by.

"I am not taking any more insults from you! I am going to Haridwar." The mother-in-law was shouting as she opened her new almirah and started throwing out her clothes on the bed. She pulled out a large handbag and started stuffing her belongings in it. Meena was still frozen and was intently listening to the fight when Vinod came from behind, kissed her and picked up his lunch.

"Bye sweetheart, enjoy the rest of the show," he said as he rushed out of the house.

The mother-in-law did not leave the house. Vinod later told Meena that stuffing her clothes in the handbag was a part of the climax of the fight. She would clog up the bag with a few of them and then half way through, she would throw herself on the bed and cry her heart out with her head buried in the pillow.

"Ma, I want to discuss something. Meena would like to complete her last year of school."

"Why will she want to do that? We are not going to let her work in an office. Enough money comes in this house. And who is going to look after the house? I am too old to run around buying things and making food." Vinod's mother was aghast when her son came to ask for authorization for Meena's admission in a school. Meena was standing next to him, her head bowed as if waiting for a punishment.

"But Ma, I want to complete school and it's just a matter of a year," she said, raising her head suddenly. Her husband was quiet. He had no idea what to say next.

"I don't see any sense in it. Why to waste money on something which you are not going to use?"

"We can't measure everything with money. Some things are important to do in life. And I would also like to do a job after I complete my school." Meena thought it would be a good idea to slide in her ambition to have a career as an athlete in between but then restrained herself from blurting that out as it would have given her mother-in-law a heart attack.

"Enough! We have never allowed girls in this house to work.

That is the job of a man."

"Which century is this?" Meena was desperate.

"Don't try to talk like my husband. I will not suffer another of his kind. Son, take your wife to your room. I will not allow anyone to walk over my decisions in my house. If you want to do that, you have to live somewhere else."

"Why didn't you say anything?" Meena asked Vinod as they entered their room.

"Because there was no point, there is never a point. You can argue with Ma for the whole day and even that won't help. Why do you think my parents have these impossible fights? I don't know what to do Meena."

"Neither do I," Meena said as she stifled a dry laugh.

"What happened? Why that laughter?"

"My mother used to tell me that I can do anything after I get married because I will have the freedom and..."

"And?"

"A supportive husband," Meena said lowering her voice to almost a whisper.

"What do you want me to do? I can't go and fight with them. They will throw me out of the house. Do you think we can afford a house on our own? Where will we live? You have to grin and bear it Meena. At least for some time."

That was their first bone of contention. Meena had fallen in love with someone without knowing him well. She had not evaluated the baggage with which Vinod came and it was too heavy to carry. It was choking her, eroding her off. The three months that Meena had been in this house were barely hanging together because of the physical intimacy and the initial pangs of love. There was nothing else to glue her to the new relationships. She was distressed now that the hinges were loosening and the bolts were coming off. Vinod was not one-dimensional as she had blinded herself to believe. Many times, after she had finished washing the dishes and mopped and cleaned the whole house, she would sit in the window of her bedroom and stare outside.

Vinod was a coward.

The words would sizzle on the brink of her thoughts but then she would shut her eyes and shove them away. She was helplessly kicking the waves, trying to blow off a thick mist.

Yes he is. He can't take a stand.

No. No. Please. Don't say that.

Things did not turn undemanding when Meena found out that she was three months pregnant in December 1978. She wrote letters to her mother and sisters to tell them about the good news. Vinod was elated and for sometime, Meena too tried to overlook what had happened, but this was like a second slap, reaffirming the first one. Her mother-in-law was beaming when she broke the news to her and touched her feet for her blessings.

"It's good that you threw away the idea of completing your studies. It would have been impossible with the baby. I hope it's a boy," she said as she kissed Meena on the forehead.

"I hope it's a girl," Meena screamed in her brain.

Her father-in-law gave her a smile as she touched his feet. It was the first time she saw him smiling. She almost didn't recognize him as she straightened up and looked at him.

She was caustic about the way things had turned up, almost at the tip of being abrasive. She felt shamed, mocked and she blamed Vinod for it. The child was an unexpected righteous stamp on his mother's decision. Vinod, on the other hand, acted like a civilian caught in the line of fire and had no idea which way to dart. The conditions at the house did not make anything better. Meena was completely acerbic and did not turn to Vinod for any grievances she had, and she had plenty of them. Vinod, on the other hand, tried his best to recreate the initial magic. He was triumphant at times, but sometimes Meena sulked miserably and all his tricks fell flat. He could not comprehend the mood swings and the fact that Meena was growing extremely sparse and any questions related to how she was feeling were met with a wide variety of replies like I-am-fine, good or leave-it-you-don't-want-to-know.

Meena was in pain and she became frail as days passed. The primary reason was that no one in the house was taking care of her. Her mother-in-law had returned to her previous disposition. As soon as her husband and son were off to their offices, she would take a bath, wrap a sari around her and leave the house. She would order Meena about what to cook in the evening and any other specific household task that was to be performed. Sometimes there were a heap of utensils to be cleaned or clothes of all the family members to be washed. Washing machines was something unheard of at that time and everything had to be done by hand. This was in addition to the daily cleaning and mopping of the whole house. Meena did not have respite the whole day and was just eating her usual meals at lunch and dinner. Her husband was under the impression that his mother was taking good care of her and there was no one to prove him wrong. It was as if Meena wanted something terrible to happen, but then she knew that even if she raised her voice, it would be very easily hushed.

By the eighth month of her pregnancy in May 1979, Meena could not stand straight because it strained her backbone too much. She was terribly thin and by the last month, unable to stand. Vinod was alarmed and took a few days off from the office, completely disrupting his mother's routine. When Meena was finally admitted to the hospital on entering labour, the doctors were surprised how she had survived till now. Childbirth was extremely painful and she remained in the hospital for the next ten days, recovering from the loss her body underwent in the previous nine months.

There was a permanent, visible crack in her relationship with Vinod. She was not bitter. It was as if all the venom inside her was drained out with the child. She was disinterested. Dispassionate. She did her best to be polite with everyone around her. Everyone seemed to be genuinely happy, but she knew that it was not for her. She was just a carrier, like a mosquito. Her mother did not come to see her. The journey was too arduous for her old bones. Neither of her sisters came because they were too busy with their own family or studies. After she came back home from the hospital, her father came with her eldest brother and stayed at the house for two days, much to the discomfort of her mother-in-law.

Sometimes when the baby was asleep, Meena would put the last few months on a loop and play it like an old record in her mind. She could not ask her husband to move out of the house. It was not realistic. But she was not prepared to lead the life that stared at her now. She could not complete her school and even if she did, who would give a job to a senior secondary pass out? She had started to juggle between apathy for her relationships and suffocation for her situation.

"What have I landed myself into?" she would question herself numerous times. She wanted to run to her mother and shake her violently.

"You said I could do whatever I want after marriage. I could run, I could complete my studies, I could follow my aspirations. You lied to me! You had the nerve to lie to me to stop me from dreaming. Look what you have done to me. You have stuffed me in a cage!"

Then sometimes, she would blame herself for foolishly falling in love with a face without bothering to be pragmatic. But then isn't expecting love and pragmatism to go hand in hand a bit too much? There has to be foolishness in love.

Sometimes she felt like erupting in front of Vinod. But she could never gather herself to do that. She could foresee complete decay, and it was too heavy a burden to carry. In the end, she decided to relent.

✦

*September, 2022*

She was alone when the tragedy struck. She had been alone from the past five years since the death of Vinod because of the twin heart attacks, trying to absorb his absence. She was almost sixty and had too many blurred years and sad memories behind her to be enthusiastic about life. She had even stopped thanking God for letting her live for another day.

She had no intentions of keeping a full time maid since she could not trust strangers in the house as she was alone now and had heard enough stories of old, decaying men and women slaughtered for money in their sleep by the domestic help. It wasn't a trusting world anymore. There was a time when her mother would leave her house unlocked in Dalhousie without any fear of a robbery and walk to the market.

Yet, her death was outlandish. It was the cursed secret that finally finished her off.

The false ceiling jammed that day. Meena could never apprehend, why as years passed her by, she lost the ability to place things at their regular positions, to grind hinges properly, to press the right button. Why was she not able to close the lid of the pickle bottle? Why was it so difficult to lock the iron door of her house? Why doesn't the false ceiling close properly? Earlier Vinod was always there to help her and she never bothered. But now he was gone. And these were minuscule tasks. She found it exhausting to keep pace with the gizmos strewn across her house. It was a headache. Who wanted that anyway?

"I used to pick apples from trees and eat them without washing. Why is everyone so finicky nowadays?" Like any other old person, she had trepidation of handling alien things, which were not a part of her growing years.

Her daughter called every day and visited her on alternate weekends. It was then that Meena would go out of the house to a mall or some shopping centre to get supplies for the next two weeks before her daughter could pay her another visit. Sometimes, her son-in-law and grandchildren would come too. Although Meena loved the presence of her family around her, she hated the routine. She hated getting out of the comforts of the house. Her daughter was afraid that her mother would rot in that house. She had begged her mother to come and stay with her but Meena would have none of it.

"I am an old, stale woman. I don't want you to hate me, which is what will happen if I oblige. Believe me, I am unbearable," she said while munching dim sums in a restaurant.

"Ma! Will you stop that? Ravi and Sunny love you and you know that. Why are you so cutting at times?"

She used a walking stick now and dragged her feet. It was hard to pick them up each time she walked and then there was the joint pain.

"How the mighty have fallen; there was a time when I was the school champion in running competitions," she said to her daughter while they watched television.

"I know, ma. I know," her daughter said as she stroked the hair off her mother's face.

"But my mother would not allow me to run. She filled my mind with dreams. False dreams. It could have been different for me, very different."

There was a confounded look on her face, as if trying to remember if the incident actually happened or was it just an imagination. Everyone she knew was gone. Then she sighed and closed her eyes. Yes, it did happen, ages ago, in another life. The mere act of dragging the memory out exhausted her. Then suddenly she started laughing.

"What happened to you?" her daughter asked with an amused look on her face.

"Did I ever tell you that my mother beat me up once with bicchu-booti?"

"Nani did that? But why?" her daughter started laughing.

"Because I used to run and nobody was able to catch me. She was scared that I would bump into a horse and fall into the valley."

Her daughter was thankful that she did not end up like her mother. Misery of one generation always comes with lessons for the next one. Maybe it was subconscious, but her mother always pushed her into doing things she was not able to do herself. Maybe, it was the changing times. The generation leaps. Or maybe it was an angry resolve. Some things are bound to happen eventually but then there is always someone who clicks the light on. Her mother did that for her and she was grateful. She always prodded her daughter to go and find a place for herself in the world.

She looked at her mother, sleeping peacefully on the sofa, oblivious to the television. She switched it off and covered her with a blanket. She had to go to the office early tomorrow morning. She locked the main door and walked towards her car. That was the last time she saw her mother alive, breathing and dreaming of the life that could have been.

The next day Meena woke up with a start.

"What time is it?" She looked at the wall clock searching for her glasses. The digital clock blipped 10 o'clock, 26 September, 2022. She stared out of the window for sometime before searching for her stick and getting up from the sofa. All of a sudden she was seized with an itching to see the contents of the false ceiling in her almirah. Whatever was there was not important now. It was cursed but she could not get rid of it. It was tempting to have something of such a great power in your hand, just like black magic, although she had no use for it. She was ashamed of hiding it, like a woman hiding an affair, but the consequences of letting it go were extreme. She was a part of the maze now, not the one trying to solve it. She was the jigsaw; she was the monk who sat at a place for years and became one with the trees surrounding him.

She stood in front of the almirah, the almirah that she brought into the house as her dowry. It was the only other entity that had equalled the number of years Meena had been in the house. They were like sisters. Comforting each other. Keeping secrets.

She just wanted to see it one last time. She had decided that she was going to burn it, as she had decided a hundred times before. She creaked open the wooden almirah and stretched out her hand to reach the tiny, almost invisible depression on the ceiling. It was too high for her and she had to step up on the base of the almirah to reach it. She turned around and planted her walking stick on the wooden base of her bed that was inches away from the almirah. Then gently, she put each of her steps up on the base of the almirah, holding the rod at the top. The almirah stirred and creaked to adjust to her weight. She again tried to reach the depression and this time was able to press it. There was a click as a rectangular area moved slightly upwards from the point she had touched displaying a gap. She slid three of her fingers inside and tried to slide it open. It jammed. She tried again applying a little more strength but it wouldn't budge. She kept trying till the point of desperation but something was stuck and the ceiling was not moving.

"God! Let me have it. I promise to burn it," she kept saying. There were beads of sweat on her forehead. Her arms were in pain. She looked like a woman hanging out of the door of an overcrowded bus. There was something invisible stopping her from grasping the cursed bundle. All of a sudden, stars were flashing in front of her eyes and the almirah was shaking violently.

She gave the corner a maniacal push. But the shake was too enraging for the almirah to maintain its balance. It bent forward and the weight of Meena was enough to plummet it like a half cut tree. There was a surge of fear and blood on Meena's face for the few seconds which the almirah took to crash on her. Her backbone broke as the wooden foot of her bed hit her from the back as she fell upon it and the almirah closed in upon her like a coffin. It stayed on top of her after hitting the bed at an angle and scattered everything inside it around Meena's body. She died instantaneously. The false ceiling jumped back in position and closed because of the impact.

Her daughter telephoned her the whole day and did not get a response. She drove to her house with her husband and found her beneath the almirah. Her body lay at an unimaginable angle that only an acrobat could have produced. She was too shaken to touch her. Meena's son-in-law pushed the almirah back and took Meena in his arms and placed her gently on the bed. He could almost fold her from the middle like a newspaper. He could feel the body broken into two. He then picked up the clothes and a few boxes that had fallen off the almirah and put them hurriedly inside.

"Sleep well Mom," Ravi said as he kissed her on the forehead and walked back to the drawing room to console Lipi and phone the relatives.

The almirah stood in the bedroom, with open doors like open arms, watching over Meena. Mourning.

'I'll keep your secret with me, my sister,' it said.

# *Lipi*

Shakuntala was on a contour that was way off the mark. There was no reason why she should not have been in high spirits but she wasn't. Initially she was not sure if she was pregnant, but then after a series of spells of morning sickness she went to the nearby government hospital to meet the gynaecologist. She broke the news to Manu who started crying with joy and immediately sat down to write a letter to his family back in Khanna.

Shakuntala did not fancy a child. She was just eighteen and was terrified. As Manu wrote the first line of the letter, she stood over him and stared at the ink drying on the paper.

"I don't want it," she said.

"Umm-hmm. What?" Manu replied absentmindedly.

"I don't want it," she repeated.

The pen stopped. Manu dropped it on the wooden table and turned around. Shakuntala walked backwards and sat on the foot of the bed.

"Why?"

"Because it's too early, I don't want a child right now. I have to study further, get a job."

"What? When did that notion get into your head?"

"I can't sit in this house for the rest of my life, Manu. The walls will cave in on me one day. When we were in Khanna, conditions were different. There was nothing for me to do there. Here there are a lot of opportunities. I can attempt."

Manu was quiet for a moment, brooding over her reply. What has happened to her, he thought!

"What do you want to do? Abort the child? You are not thirteen. You are eighteen years old...old enough to bear a child. I was so happy, Shakuntala, so glad that we are going to have a baby. What got into you?" Manu said calmly.

"Please don't get me wrong, Manu. I.... It's...it's not about my age. I am not ready mentally."

"What is bothering you?" Manu asked.

"If I have to tell you, then I don't have to tell you."

"You have to tell me. I cannot understand everything you don't say."

"There was a time when you did."

She lowered her eyes and looked at the floor. Manu waited for her to say something. They could hear each other's accelerated breathing. Then Manu got up and left the room. Shakuntala sat on the bed like a ball of crumpled paper, lost in thoughts. Yes, what was it that was bothering her? She chose this course. She couldn't pin her thoughts. They were like fast moving dots of light on a wall. She dropped back on the bed, the way she had dropped years later when the nerve cracked. It was a discerning moment, hanging in air. Maybe my consciousness cannot stand contentment, she thought. There was something terribly wrong with her and she knew it. Her mind instinctively smelled bliss and instantly lurked to search for counter sentimentality, something to negate facts, smear them with darkness, inflicting pain when it wasn't required. She wasn't always like this, she thought as she lay there. Was it after her father's death? She could never resist putting a veil of gloom over everything. There was sadness even in her smile and invariably, she was distancing herself from Manohar, without realizing it. As she lay there and looked at the fan, she started getting angry. Why can't Manohar let her be? All she was asking for was some time. Her breathing speeded and she was fuming within minutes. She calmed down after a few moments, got up and completed the letter Manu had started to write, breaking the good news. She wrote another one, to her uncle Kulbhushan and left both the envelopes in Manu's office bag. That evening when Manohar came back from office, he brought a box of sweets.

"Thank you," he said as Shakuntala opened the door.

She smiled and nodded. He kissed her.

Shakuntala was now completely on her own. There was no other woman to help her and advise her how to take care of herself during pregnancy. Manohar's two elder brothers, Akhil and Sambhav, were now living in Delhi with their families after snatching the Shoe shop from him but there was no question of involving them.

"They are dead to me," Manohar had declared. They were actually flourishing. The shop was throwing money at them at an astonishing rate.

Two months later, Manohar's younger brother Satish arrived from Khanna with a withered away leather bag and a green jute backpack wearing a brown khaki kurta pajama. Like his elder brother, he was bored stiff of Khanna and wanted to work in Delhi. He was the youngest of the six brothers and by far, the most flamboyant product of the family. Manohar was exhilarated. Satish's presence flashed the farms in front of his eyes. He suddenly had an itch to go back once. He was amused how his coming to Delhi had started a chain reaction and now all his brothers wanted to come here and settle down.

"I'll help you Satish, but let me tell you one thing very clearly.

If you try to contact any of the traitors who took my shop, you are dead to me, just like them," Manohar told him very calmly as Shakuntala gave him a glass of milk mixed with Roohafza.

"We all know what they did. They are not a part of the family anymore," Satish said.

Manohar talked to Narayan about Satish. Narayan, the good man that he was, agreed to help.

"Did you know about the girl in our village who was in love with Manu," Satish asked Shakuntala one day.

"Yes, she came to see me," Shakuntala said trying to remember the face of the girl who gazed at her when all the ladies in the village came to see her after the marriage.

"Oh! Did she? I didn't know that! And what did she do? Pull out her hair and bang her head on the wall?"

"Nothing so dramatic," Shakuntala said suppressing a splutter of laughter, "but she was gloomy. I could see that in her eyes."

"Oh! She was an idiot. Manohar had never promised her anything. She was just throwing herself on him. Did she talk to you?"

"No. Just stared."

"Hmmm. So what is your brother doing?"

"Madan? Oh! He is still studying. I hope he too comes to Delhi and settles down here. There is nothing for him there in Dalhousie," she said.

"It's strange how everything gets concentrated in one place. I wonder what will become of this city in another hundred years."

Satish stayed with the family for two months before finally moving out to Chandni Chowk, where he started working in the sari shop. Narayan had used his contacts to get him the job. Satish's work was to show the saris to ladies and nudge them to buy them by praising them as they wrapped the sari on their shoulder and looked in the mirror. He was an instant hit with women and was promptly promoted in two weeks. The shop owner took him in as his tenant and deducted a certain amount as house rent from his salary. Satish would visit Manohar and Shakuntala on weekends and the trio would roam around in the city and go out for movies or would just simply sit in front of Shakuntala's radio listening to the songs and making elaborate dinner.

It was in the shop that he met Vani, the girl whom he married later. She came in with her mother when Satish saw her for the first time. As he praised her obese mother who discarded all the saris in quick succession, Vani gave him enough stolen glances to make him aware of her. She came with a relative next and soon she started coming with her friends whom she would force to come under the pretence of buying a sari.

Shakuntala went back to Dalhousie when she was six months pregnant. She had forgotten all about it but one fine day she got a letter from Kulbhushan asking her about her plans to return to Dalhousie. He reminded her that it was customary for a girl to go back to her mother's house when the first child was about to be born. It is my duty to take care of you and to see that you follow all the rituals, so remind Manohar and get a ticket as soon as possible, he wrote. When she showed the letter to Manohar, he promptly booked her tickets. Satish went with the couple to the station to see her off.

"Vani and I have decided to get married," Satish said as the steam engine dragged the train on the platform amidst puffs of smoke.

"What! That's great news," Shakuntala said giving a radiant smile. Manohar congratulated him.

"I want you and brother to come and talk to her parents. We will wait till you come back with the baby," Satish said as he picked up her luggage.

As Satish went inside the coach to keep her luggage on the seat, Shakuntala stood at the door looking at Manohar. He took her hand in his.

"I will see you soon. Write to me," he said. She nodded.

Shakuntala went to Kulbhushan's house. Her father's house was locked up now and besides, there was nothing but cobwebs and distant memories there. She promised herself that she would go there once while she was here. The farm did her good and so did the presence of so many known faces around. Kulbhushan's wife, Pushpa, was a bit fat now, thankfully. Three of Kulbhushan's sons were married and were living in the same house with their wives. The ground floor of the house was extended, taking up a part of the land on the right of the house. In the last six years, Shakuntala had returned twice to Dalhousie, to attend marriages of two of her cousins (although six of them had got married) but that was it. The place reeked of sadness, the past always alive to mock her presence. There were marks of her cheerful childhood everywhere and then there were marks of emptiness. The summer houses that her father made stood at every nook and corner, taken up by wealthy Indian families now. There were no British left but they had left their prints in the form of churches and summer houses in Dalhousie. The distant five rivers at the horizon always reminded her of many of the lazy afternoons she had spent roaming around with her father. She visited the convent once, to meet her old teachers. As she passed the girls hostel, her eyes fell on the lawn covered with profuse green grass, the lawn where she saw the owl. Many of her old teachers were there. They were surprised to see her pregnant, as if she was never supposed to be. How time flies, they exclaimed.

Then, finally one day, she went to the house in which she was born. It wasn't completely empty, as she had expected. The furniture was intact, covered with sheets. The paintings hung on the walls, covered with a thin cloak of dust. There weren't many cobwebs either. It was as if someone had recently cleaned it up. She went to her room, her parent's room and then to her grandmother's room. She imagined how it was, overlapping her thoughts on the present. When she opened the door of her parent's bedroom, she saw a glimpse of her father sitting at the table and writing a letter, and then he turned around, smiled and disappeared. Her mother's image had begun to fade away from her mind. She was just a blur now and Shakuntala had a sudden urge to see her. She turned towards the main hall and went to the painting that hung on the wall. She grabbed a cloth and rubbed away the hint of dust from it and there she was, sitting on a chair like a queen and smiling a weak smile. Kanshi's painting hung next to her. It was one of those moments when the present is such a far cry from the past that one begins to wonder if the past actually existed. What do I have in Delhi to remind me of this house, she asked herself. The radio, ah! The radio, she whispered.

"Someone was in the house, it seems rather clean," she told Kulbhushan when she returned back.

"I send someone up there every month to do some cleaning, in case you would like to return there for a few days," he said.

"You know I can never go and live there. This is my house."

"Yes, and it always will be," Kulbhushan smiled back.

There was a silence before he suddenly asked, “Are you not going to use it?”

“I don’t think I will ever use it. It is cursed,” she said.

“Why do you say that?”

“It killed papa.”

‘It can change your life, Shakuntala. Think about it,” Kulbhushan emphasized.

“What if it changes for worse? I don’t think I have the nerve,” she said.

“Where is it now?”

“It is in my trunk where you put it and that is where it will be till the day I die.”

“Burn it then.”

“Maybe I will.”

Pushpa confined Shakuntala to the house after a few weeks of her arrival.

“You are almost seven months pregnant now. I can’t allow you to roam around in the hills. It’s dangerous,” she said.

So, Shakuntala stayed in the house. There was something in the air of Dalhousie. She was hungry all the time and chomped anything that came her way. All the women of the house would sit together and cut vegetables and Pushpa would update Shakuntala with the local gossip from the past year. Sometimes they would knit small sweaters and socks for the baby or sew flowers on handkerchiefs. Pushpa made sure that Shakuntala was always kept occupied. She knew that the girl had a problem of going into depression if left alone for long.

She wrote regularly to Manohar, about how her stomach was turning into a balloon and how the baby kicked all the time and asked him whether his cooking has improved and how were Satish and Vani. Manohar wrote back that he was dying to hold the baby in his hands and to see her. Satish is good and cooks for him over the weekends with a hand written cookbook provided by Vani, he wrote. And is he any good, Shakuntala asked. He was a disaster initially, but he is getting there, I am getting there too, he wrote back. How is the weather in Dalhousie, he asked. It is snowing, she replied.

The boy was born in the snow covered January of 1952 in Kulbhushan's house with the help of a local midwife and all the women in the house. All the men gathered in one room and waited. After the boy was born, the pundit informed the family that the boy's name should start with the alphabet 'V'. Manohar arrived two days later with difficulty as the roads leading to Dalhousie were closed at many places because of heavy snowfall. Shakuntala and the baby were taking an afternoon nap. He tiptoed into the room.

"He is so small," he whispered.

Shakuntala opened her eyes and looked through him. It was hard to apprehend him after an absence of three months.

"When did you arrive?" she asked in a hoarse voice, clearing her throat.

"Just now. He is beautiful!"

"Yes, he is,"she said smiling, "the name should start with V.'"

"V...hmmm...Varun? Vijay?"

"I was thinking Vinod."

"Vinod. That is perfect."

Soon the whole hill station converged in Kulbhushan's house to see the baby and give their blessings. Then the namkaran ceremony happened, where in front of the pandit and the crowd that had flocked to have a free lunch, the family named the baby as Vinod. Shakuntala stayed in Dalhousie for another one month while Manohar had to return back to join work two weeks later. He again returned to Dalhousie to take Shakuntala back. When they reached Delhi, Satish and Vani were there to welcome them. Vani had lied at her house that she was with one of her girlfriends. When Shakuntala entered the house, she looked around and thought that the house had shrunk a bit. Vinod cried most of the time, but was surprisingly quiet when Satish picked him up.

"He loves me!" Satish said.

"He cries a lot. He was crying during most of the train journey," Manohar said.

"Yes, it is exhausting. Two months into it and I am already exhausted," Shakuntala said, "Wait till both of you get married and have kids of your own. You will know."

Vani blushed. Satish rubbed his nose on Vinod's nose.

When Narayan came to bless Vinod, he told Manohar, Shakuntala and Satish that he was leaving for Khanna. He had had enough of the city life and wanted to go back to the place he was born to spend the rest of his days. That is why he was so keen to sell the shop in the first place. Everyone begged him to stay. Shakuntala pleaded that the family was indebted to him for what he had done for them and would do anything to make him change his mind. Narayan blessed her and wiped a tear off his cheek. He had made up his mind.

"Besides, your brother Bhaskar needs some company," he said to Manohar. Narayan left for Khanna ten days later. The family went to the station to bid him farewell. Manohar hugged him and blinked back tears.

"You have to come back for my marriage," Satish told Narayan.

"Of course I will," Narayan said and smiled. When Satish married Vani two months later, Narayan was there to bless them, as promised.

Shakuntala had finished what Manohar wanted. The child was now a reality, a crying, hollering, and demanding-each-and-every-ounce-of-her reality and he certainly wasn't the solution to her tribulations. She blamed Manohar for her plight. There wasn't a moment of respite. Vinod slept at unusual times and would wake up in the dead of night. There were times when she wanted to scream. The family went out on weekends but going to movies was not possible now, not with Vinod. There was an opening between Shakuntala and Manohar and both of them did not even realize this because Vinod always filled it up. He was always claiming their attention, filling the long gaps in their conversations. In fact they were not having many conversations. In the night, they would put Vinod to sleep and then sometimes hungrily satisfy their carnal desires before wandering off to slumber. There was no room for exchange of thoughts. Earlier, the dinner was always prepared before Manohar came back from office so that the couple could spend some time together but now, only when Manohar returned from the office would Shakuntala get some time to hurriedly prepare the dinner as he played with Vinod and distracted him. Both of them were drifting like two clouds moving in the same direction, with the distance between them increasing with every gush of wind. In addition to the walls of the house wolfing her down, there was another abstraction in her life now – a chain tightly wound around her neck. She was not as pleased as she had imagined she would be with the child.

Vinod could never point out the precise instant when his

father turned to a stern and a vicious dictator. It was unhurried. All he could gather years later was that the relationship between his parents had turned from being amorous to the point of being pointless and this affected the way they treated him. His father subliminally blamed him for the rift. He was thrashed for minuscule mistakes and a fight between his parents would invariably hang a sword on his head. Shakuntala's butterfly stroked in and out of depressions and added to the gloom in the house. Even the birth of his three sisters did not change a thing. There was too much to handle all at once and sometimes he would hear muffled hints of fighting from his parents' rooms followed by shuffling and sometimes moaning. Vinod understood years later, that his parents could never get enough of each other, mentally or physically. Shakuntala had four abortions in the years separating Vinod and her first daughter Neela's birth, because she was not in a mood to satisfy the whims of her husband every time. Manohar, of course, could not understand the logic. He was from a village that followed the ritual of the more the merrier. Shakuntala gave up four years later and they had a flurry of daughters. After four children, Manohar understood that his present salary could not afford a larger population in the house and to Shakuntala's relief, he decided to put a lid on it. Vinod was always a handful, but three more children threw Shakuntala completely off balance. She gave in, conceding like a weak mud house throwing herself into the tribulations of taking care of her children and husband. The ordeal had started to shape her into someone else.

The family went to Dalhousie during summer vacations, when the temperature in Delhi soared to unbearable heights. Shakuntala was never able to cope up with summers in Delhi. She absolutely despised them. It was like living in a frying pan, she used to say. Earlier, when the girls were not born yet, she stayed at Kulbhushan's house. But after the three girls arrived, it was not appropriate to stay in Kulbhushan's already overloaded abode. So, the first time she went to Dalhousie with her four children, she wrote a letter to Kulbhushan announcing her date of arrival and requested him to get her father's house cleaned up for her.

It was an inscrutable sight when she entered the house with the children and Manohar for the first time. As she inserted the key in the lock and opened the door, she had a tingling feeling, and goosebumps appeared on her arms. The old smell of the house was still there, the wood still creaked beneath her feet, and it was as if the house was always alive, waiting for her to come back, welcoming her. Manohar was speechless. This was the first time he had entered the house where Shakuntala had grown up. He roamed around, staring at the paintings of Kusum and Kanshi Ram, at the woodwork on the doors, the carpeted rooms and the heavy copper and brass utensils in the kitchen with beautifully carved out designs on them. He was particularly fascinated by a copper tumbler, which had an elaborate work done by an artisan on it.

"That was papa's glass. He used to drink milk in it at night," Shakuntala said. She was standing at the kitchen door observing her husband as he held the tumbler in his hand and admired it.

"It's beautiful."

"We will take it with us if you want to," Shakuntala said.

"You grew up in a big house," Manohar said, studying her face.

"I wasn't here for long," she said and walked out to see where the children were.

The children were confused.

"If we have such a big house, then why do we live in that small house in Delhi?" the girls kept asking.

"This was my father's house. And where you live is your father's house. Children always live in their father's house. Now no more questions and let me see what food Kulbhushan uncle has sent for us."

After that, it became almost a yearly affair for the family to come and stay at the house and enjoy its luxuries. The children would urge Shakuntala to take them to the places where her father took her. During 1950s and 60s, Dalhousie presented itself to Shakuntala in various lights. There was something she couldn't place; the place was altered to a different shade every time she visited. It was changing too much for her taste. The hill station had lost its glory with the partition. With almost half of Punjab gone into Pakistan and after the end of British era, tourism took a dip. There was no more influx of British bureaucrats or wealthy Indian families; the lull was deafening enough for Prime Minister Jawaharlal Nehru to step in himself to promote tourism in the hill station. Then during the early 60s, thousands of Tibetan refugees entered India and Dalhousie landed with the responsibility of hosting them as per the directions of the Prime Minister. Over the next few years, Shakuntala saw various Tibetan paintings and rock sculptures sprout on the mountains. Her heart felt outlandish and the roads felt alien at times. And then in 1966, Dalhousie went from Punjab to the Union territory of Himachal Pradesh. It felt farcical, as if someone had picked it up and placed it somewhere else. The four rivers in the horizon now belonged to another part of India and so did the shimmering lights of Pathankot.

Panjpula was now also the sight of the resting place of the brave freedom fighter Ajit Singh who breathed his last on the day

India gained its independence. The samadhi and the waterfalls behind it became the favorite spot for children to play. Shakuntala would sit on the rocks scattered amidst the flowing water and sing songs with her cousins while their children ran after tadpoles. The water was so clear that the children could see the tadpoles hiding amidst the stones. Sometimes, Manohar would sit on a rock in the middle of the flowing water and play the flute to entertain everyone. Shakuntala would just stare at him. In moments like these, she could see the same boy in Manohar who sat under a tree just to get a glimpse of her and a smile from her lips. Sometimes, while playing the flute, he stared back and she smiled the same old smile. Manohar would let the flute fall and she would laugh loudly much to the confusion of her cousins as he got off the rock to pick it up.

Their visits to Dalhousie were the time when the children, especially Vinod, remembered later on as filled with laughter and bliss. Those were long spells when they saw their mother actually in high spirits. Shakuntala might have embedded Dalhousie in her mind as a gloomy place filled with sad memories but the truth was that the hill station calmed her although she never acknowledged this fact. As years passed and Vinod grew up, the visits to Dalhousie became sparse; the euphoria died a gradual death plunging into the abyss that separated his parents.

According to Shakuntala, 1970s was the most boisterous decade in the Indian history, not because India fought a war or signed the Simla agreement, not because there was a state of emergency without any reason that lead to the crash of a very influential political party, not because India gave birth to a handful of new states or because of the backlash on the blasphemous family planning programme and certainly not because the first Indian satellite went into space but simply because of the advent of the Hippie culture. She was glad that her children were unfazed by the wave. She was fine with the bell-bottoms, the hair bun, the *anarkali* salwar kameez to which she herself adapted with much enthusiasm. There was no harm in aping the film stars and she did that herself with a bun on her head and the eyeliner reaching her eyebrows but aping hippies was completely out of the question. Whenever she saw someone with long hair with a Hare Rama headband, weird looking orange shirts and sunglasses, she blamed it on *Dev Anand*, the evergreen star. Why did he have to make that wretched movie, *Hare Rama Hare Krishna*, and blur the line between Indian and western lifestyles? The songs of the movie were banned in the house even though they topped the chart in *Binaca Geetmala* on the radio. Shakuntala would just rotate the dial of the radio as soon as *Ameen Sayani* would announce the song, ignoring the groans her grown up children produced. She was afraid that the song would turn her children into rebels.

Vinod was almost twenty when Satish died, as the war started in 1971. Manohar could not cope up with his brother's death and Vinod noticed a sudden shift in the axis of roles in his home. His parents were exchanging personifications, like two commanders exchanging signed papers after a war. It wasn't just Satish's death that hit Manohar, but the despondency that had overwhelmed his senses grew thicker. He was in doldrums about his relationship with his wife and Satish's death gave him a concluding push. He had no idea how to set things right by discussion with someone and even when he had tried, the façade which his wife put, enacting as though everything was hunky-dory, landed him into another level of disconsolation. Manohar had given up and he was bracing himself to carry on his responsibilities, nothing more. He had to marry off his three daughters and that became the yield of his life, his reason to ignore the presence of everyone in the house. His responsibilities did not carry a face, it was a box to be filled and stashed away. He retreated in a shell of his own and his wife took up from where he left and threw away her robotic trance after almost nineteen years and became the grande dame of the household. It wasn't abrupt, and Shakuntala wasn't that stern with her children initially and was surprisingly nonchalant with her son too but she was getting there. She knew that her daughters would leave her one day but her son would always remain. It was important to keep him in her grip. Without realizing, she was turning into her grandmother Radha Devi. Her life had gone out of her clasp so many times, that to anchor it became the sole purpose of her existence.

There was no scope of a love marriage for Neela, Rohini or Poonam. The girls always knew this and always directed themselves away from controversy of any kind. Although Manohar had slapped Neela hard once when he saw her talking to a boy, she was not sure what catastrophic outcome her endeavours might have if she dared to raise her voice. The sisters were pictures of mute submission; happy in the conditions they were confined to. The fact that Manohar and Shakuntala had a love marriage was never mentioned in front of them. It would have been as disastrous as tying a burning firecracker to a horse's tail.

The girls had no ambitions of their own except for Neela. Perhaps they had molded themselves into the stereotypes their parents wanted them to be. Neela, on the other hand, wanted to be an air hostess. Unfortunately, the night she disclosed her desires in front of the family on the dinner table, an airplane crashed at the Palam Airport, crashing all her dreams with it. Shakuntala could not imagine her daughter falling off the sky in a burning ball of fire and so Neela had to take up the next best alternative – to be a housewife. Seeing her volatile nature, she was the first one to be disposed off. Manohar spread the news that his eldest daughter was ready to get married amongst his friends and relatives. Soon, the proposals started pouring in. They married her off in 1976 to a small time businessman in Delhi who dealt in nuts and bolts and had a steady income.

The next one in the line was Rohini, but Poonam was already getting a handful of proposals because of her unsurpassed beauty. One of Manohar's colleagues in office wanted her hand for his son. He approached Manohar, a bit skeptically, and disclosed his intentions. His son was an electric engineer working with the Delhi Electric Supply Undertaking and earned a handsome salary. The families met and Poonam was married two months later in January 1977.

Rohini was married to a homeopathic doctor in Mumbai with a good monthly income.

✦

"I had a 60% in my final year of school, a first division. Do you know what it meant in those days? I was able to get a seat in a college in Delhi University with that percentage, unlike your uncle who could not get through even with a 94%," Vinod chuckled in front of his grandchild.

"What happened grandpa? Why this jump?" his grandson was intrigued.

"What happened? Fission. Population fission," he said and started laughing.

His daughter laughed back from the kitchen.

"Papa. I don't think my son is old enough to appreciate the Science."

"That is what I love about talking to him. At least he will not be judgmental."

"Neither am I, and I have been around for much longer," his daughter came out of the kitchen with a bowl of soup. "Try this. This is the new one I was talking about. I just added the yellow capsule with the red one."

"Is that how soups are made nowadays? Mixing capsules? We used to boil vegetables as far as I remember."

"It's harmless and who has the time to boil?"

"I can't remember the name of the hotel I joined after I finished my college. I was about to tell Sunny."

"I think it was the Imperial, if I am not wrong. The one which is near Connaught Place," his daughter squeezed her eyes as she tried to recall.

"So what was so special about this hotel?" Sunny asked as he created another monster with Lego.

"We boiled vegetables to make soups," Vinod said and laughed again.

"But you were not a chef there, right? I always wonder how you managed to learn to cook such good food," his daughter said.

"No. I was in room service. Your grandma hated the job. So, you will be cleaning rooms of other people just like a maid, she used to say. I always loitered around the kitchen in my spare time. I had some friends there who let me stand and watch. There was a guy who would not allowed me to touch anything at first, but then one day I cooked Biryani at home and took some to work. He was impressed. I was more involved with the kitchen work from then onwards. They let me handle a few things."

"And what did granddad say?"

"Nothing. But I knew that he was not pleased. He had three daughters to marry, but the tips from the hotel kept them quiet. The money was too good to refuse."

"So why did you leave it then?"

"I did not like the atmosphere. It was a place for rich spoilt kids, drugs, drinks, women, and revolvers. I just couldn't cope with it. Then I started to realize that there was no respect for a person like me there. I was just another servant."

"Grandma was right then."

"Yes, she was in a way, but I believed in falling in the pit to know how deep it was and I was young. You are not supposed to listen to your parents at that age. You are in awe of yourself," Vinod winked as he said this.

"Too late to tell me, I guess?" his daughter asked.

"It was deliberate."

There was a slight pause in the conversation as Vinod slurped the last drop of the soup. Even though it had fizzled out of capsules, it was damn delicious and low on calories, as his daughter said. Sunny took off his shirt and jumped into the pool. His mother saw him swim to the other end with a slight knit in her brow. He was seven now and was the best swimmer in his school but she always had a knot in her stomach when he swam.

"Why are you always so worried whenever he swims?" her father asked her after studying her face for a few seconds.

"I don't know. Mother's worry I guess."

There was a silence for a few seconds. Vinod stared at the ripples in the swimming pool and then at the Lego monster, lying at the rim, knocked off and lifeless.

"We lived in a house as big as this pool," his daughter suddenly said. Vinod laughed.

"Well, I still live in that house and it is slightly bigger than the pool. You are lucky, my child. I am very happy for you. I wish your..."

"So now I know why Ma could never make Biryani as good as you did," his daughter suddenly changed the subject. She saw where it was going and she had no intention of going that way. Vinod realized this too and let her steer the talk.

"Well, she tried. Where is she, by the way?" he asked looking around.

"She is taking a bath. I asked her to try the new Jacuzzi. Papa, why don't both of you shift here with us. Ravi will be more than happy."

"I know, child, but we have often discussed this topic. I am very grateful to your husband for the offer but no father would do that."

"That is so old fashioned papa."

"Lo! There comes your mother!" Vinod said as he smiled at his wife.

"How was the Jacuzzi?"

"All I can say is that all the perks of the modern day technology can never replace the mug and the bucket," she replied.

"You didn't like it?" Lipi asked.

"Oh! I did! But my arms were not getting the exercise they are used to. I was missing my mug."

"I'll get some soup for you. You want some more Pa?"

"No. Thank you. A new capsule soup, apparently," Vinod chuckled. Sunny had jumped out of the pool by now and was busy with his new robo-companion, the latest toy to hit the market.

They were talking to each other like long lost friends.

"Sometimes I feel that I am on some other planet," Vinod remarked.

"I know what you mean. What did we play with as kids? Dolls made of cloth and filled with cotton?" His wife smiled back.

"I had a plastic car with a whistle in it."

Lipi came back with a steaming bowl and gave it to her mother.

"Before you came, I was telling Lipi about why you could never make as good a Biryani as I made."

"Of course, I could not. You were trained in a five star hotel. An aging housewife, who had never stepped out of the hill station she lived in, trained me. It is another story that your god forsaken mother did not leave a chance of turning me into a maid," his wife retorted back in-between slurps.

"Mom. Please. Can't you just forget and stop remembering everything again and again? Grandma is dead," Lipi intervened.

"No. I can't! How could I?"

Vinod let out a deep sigh.

"I wonder where Ravi is. This is 2017 but this traffic in Gurgaon is getting worse day by day. I'll call him on his mobile," Lipi said and went inside to search for the cordless.

Vinod and Meena sat there like two statues. Both were filled with animosity but of different kinds, of different variations. The sun had almost vanished now, leaving behind a last streak of luminous orange struggling with the night. There was nothing to correct now, nothing to explain. The orange streak was fast fading.

✦

Like Vinod, the earliest recollections which Aaryan had about his existence were of watching a Bollywood movie. The movie was titled *Jane Bhi Do Yaroon* and he saw it with his parents in 1983. As he grew up, all he could remember was a scene from the movie in which a coffin was turned into a car and a dead body was driving it.

He was very sensitive as a child. The smallest incident like seeing a dacoit looting a village in a movie would end up with him sobbing and hiding behind his mother. His parents tried not to show him such movies but he knew how to operate the knobs on the black and white television and sometimes when no one was watching, he would unknowingly subject himself to the agony. His earliest recollections also included his first double decker ride. He was euphoric. They looked like giant green tortoise running on the roads as the driver sat in a separate cubical compartment that was attached to the rest of the body of the vehicle. He was disappointed when the double deckers were taken off abruptly from Delhi's roads later.

He also had recollection of his mother being very thin, almost pale and tired most of the times. But all these initial memories were faint, like an ephemeral blur. The strongest initial memories were of his grandmother shouting at his mother, calling her a bitch. There were a few people in his house, relatives probably. They were sitting in the drawing room, chatting and munching. Aaryan was summoned to meet them and to touch their feet. He was too shy to walk into a group of strangers and so he rolled himself in the drapes that separated the drawing room from the dining room.

"Come Aaryan, meet Madan uncle," Shakuntala said and tried to disentangle him from the drapes. He saw his mother enter the room, cautiously avoiding herself from bumping into him, balancing five glass cups of tea on a tray. She placed the cups in front of Shakuntala, Manohar, Madan, his wife and Vinod and went quietly in her room, dragging Aaryan away with her.

"Let him play here," Shakuntala said.

"It's time for him to sleep," Meena replied without stopping or turning back.

Shakuntala got up from the chair and marched into Meena's room. She pushed open the door without knocking.

"You bitch! Who do you think you are? How dare you try to disobey me in front of my family?" she muttered under her breath.

"The kid needs some sleep. I did not disobey you and I too am a part of this family," Meena replied back without raising her voice, stroking Aaryan's head.

"Don't you dare to do that again," Shakuntala raised her finger and said. She slammed the door as she went out.

Aaryan looked quietly at his mother as tears rolled down her eyes. He was sucking his thumb and his eyes were getting heavy as his mother thumped his back in a soothing rhythm. Heavy curtains covered the windows and the room was almost dark even as the sun glared outside. He was asleep by the time the tears reached the end of her face.

As far away as he could remember, things were never rational in the house. For Aaryan, a home meant a place where people shouted at each other, where people made each other cry and never cared for the family. Sometimes, it amazed him how he got out of all that maintaining coherence amongst the various parts of his brain. It was a madhouse. Yes, that is what it was. But he was too young, too naïve to understand this at that time. He was just observing. Absorbing. Forming opinions based on how people treated him.

His grandparents were benign and affectionate as far as he was concerned. Shakuntala would take Aaryan in her lap and would tell him all the fairy tales. Aaryan would sleep with his grandparents most of the times. He would sleep with Meena only when the power of the area would go off and they had to sleep on the terrace or when his legs were paining. She screamed at him at times and slapped him when he disobeyed her. The fact was that Aaryan was a hurricane as a kid and would never let his already tired mother have a minute's respite. Shakuntala somehow enjoyed this. She would be extra nice to Aaryan the day Meena would slap him. She was pulling him towards her, slowly, one gentle pull at a time.

At night Shakuntala would ask Aaryan to encircle his arms around her breasts while she told him the story of Cinderella or Hansel and Gretle or Jack and the beanstalk. The stories that she had read in the convent were coming handy now. Aaryan would listen to the stories with wide eyes as he looked out at the flickering stars as Manohar snored lightly besides him. She would tell him how his hands remind her of her father Kanshi Ram. When you write, your fingers bend out just like his, she would tell Aaryan. In the morning, before going to school, Aaryan had to kiss Shakuntala on both the cheeks as a goodbye.

Initially Manohar mutely refused to be a part of any of the camp, but then he had to be with his wife. There was no other way. Also, the fact that he was equally affectionate towards Aaryan was helping Shakuntala in many ways. Manohar too would spend a lot of time with him, telling stories from the pre-independence era, about his brothers and farms in Khanna, about Satish and

Narayan.

✦

"Ravi is stuck in the traffic jam. It has been thirty years, but this wretched city is still a clogged drainage pipe. He is saying..." Lipi came out cursing the worse infrastructure ever designed for a city. She stopped abruptly as she saw tears sliding down her mother's cheeks. She looked at her father. Vinod shrugged.

Her mother was again going into one of her mood swings. She was amused how mood swings were passed down her family as an infectious disease, like common cold.

"Mom. Stop crying. She is dead. It's over. Why do you always have to remember the past?"

"Meena, we have discussed this a thousand times over,"Vinod said.

"Yes Vinod, and that does not lessen the pain. That does not take away the fact that my own husband never supported me, never stood beside me. That does not take away the fact that our son has left us to live alone in some godforsaken town for no apparent reason."

Sunny was staring at his grandmother. Lipi asked him to go and play in his room. He got up and came towards his grandma, wiping tears off her cheeks and kissed her. Then he ran away in his room. This, instead of soothing Meena, started a new wave of tears.

"I always stood beside you, Meena! How can you say that? I fought with my parents for you."

"Yes, when it was convenient for you to separate out, you waged the war. But it was too late by that time."

"Mom. Dad. Enough."

"What did you expected me to do? I had responsibilities. You. Aaryan. Lipi. Where would we have lived? On the road? We all suffered Meena. We all did, even our children. It was not just you."

"Why are we again having this discussion?" Lipi tried to intervene. She had heard these arguments so many times that she knew what the outcome would be. Her parents would stop talking to each other for a few days but then things would return to normal out of necessity. Somebody had to cook. Somebody had to get vegetables from the market.

"And didn't I go and argue with her about my salary as you said? That is what started it all," Vinod said.

"Dad..."

"Yes Vinod, you did as I said, something you should have thought of yourself. And what was so wrong in that? Asking your mother to spare your full salary instead of giving you a meager 40 rupees from it? Because you had a son and a daughter whom you had to take care of and all that could not be done in 40 rupees. And all she could think of was that I was trying to take away Vinod from them. I can never forget the first time she used a swearword on me. I wanted to pick up the knife and slash her throat."

"Forget it, Meena. It is not doing you any good," Vinod said,"Is Ravi still stuck in traffic, Lipi? It's almost eight now."

"Well, a few days back, a colleague of his was stuck for five hours. They designed the city like a village."

"It's not just that, sweetheart. Have you seen how people drive?" Vinod remarked.

"Sometimes I wonder why human life is so cheap in our country. Is it because we have it in excess?" Lipi said.

"That is part of the reason. And then we are brought up to be insolent towards strangers. A stranger is like a piece of furniture.

He is unimportant, non-existent. And then there are always ways to blame others for our faults."

Meena listened quietly to her husband and daughter and stared at the now still water in the pool. There are always ways to blame others for our faults, her husband said. Was this directed at her? Even if she thought it was, she did not react. Her mind was tired. It was growing numb. She could not take her eyes away from the rippling image of the light bulb, shining inverted in the pool and shivering.

Lipi was born on the first day of Operation Blue Star in 1984. As the Indian army stormed into the Golden Temple, Meena was in the hospital, struggling with Lipi and tossing in pain, trying to storm her out. She was in the hospital for almost a week now because of her condition. She was weak again but not as much as during Aaryan's birth. The doctors had warned Vinod that there might be complications but everything went well. Vinod would stay with her in the hospital, making two trips to home to collect lunch and dinner for both of them. He would plant the lunch box on the carrier of his bicycle and cycle to the government hospital. Sometimes, he would take Aaryan with him placing him on the cross bar of his cycle seat.

The day Lipi was born, Vinod came late from the hospital to collect the dinner. He went into his parent's room and was there for a few minutes. Aaryan could not hear what they were talking about. Vinod came out and asked Aaryan if he would like to come with him to the hospital.

Meena was lying on the bed, a bit flushed and relieved. The first thing that Aaryan noticed was that her stomach was not round like a ball anymore. She removed a small piece of white cloth lying besides her and beneath it Aaryan saw the smallest human face he had ever seen. She was sleeping and completely wrapped with cloth with her face protruding out like an Egyptian mummy.

"This is your sister," Meena said and smiled.

Aaryan looked at her face. It was a bit swollen, too red and the eyes were too big, even when closed. He tried to touch her eyelashes.

"You will wake her up," Vinod said calmly.

"Did she come out of there?" Aaryan asked pointing at her mother's stomach.

"Yes."

"Did you get the tiger skin like grandma?" Aaryan asked.

"How long do I have to be here?" Meena asked Vinod, ignoring Aaryan's question.

"One more day, ma and papa will come tomorrow to see you."

"What is she called?" Aaryan asked.

A few days later, as the aftermath of Operation Blue Star unfolded, Aaryan saw the Sikh burn inside the ambassador. That day, after a visibly shaken Meena returned from the terrace with Aaryan, he ran to the room of his grandparents and sat quietly on the bed between both of them. Incidentally, that night Shakuntala told him the story of Prahalad, the boy who came out of the fire alive because of his devotion to Lord Vishnu, the preserver of the world. He was disturbed that day, disturbed beyond his capacity. In his dream that night, he saw the Sikh walk out of the burning car, unharmed and much to the surprise of the crowd that was dancing around the car. They had stopped dancing and were staring in disbelief.

As Lipi entered the house and dissolved into the family, Aaryan realized that she was a bully from the very word go. She was more preferred by his mother and this shifted him more towards his grandmother. Shakuntala would compensate for Meena ardently. He was jealous of Lipi who would cry and stomp her way out of anything, would demand his things and would throw things at him if he did not obey and start screaming. Soon Aaryan started to hate her. He would spend most of his time playing with Priya and his friends from the neighborhood or watching airplanes land at the strip behind the flats. His sister would try to attract his attention by her throaty laughter or her cries for sudden consideration but he would not pay heed most of the times. Sometimes, he would play with her; sometimes he would completely ignore her and run into another room. The truth was that he never felt close to his sister. Tolerant, and that too in the later years, but never close.

Aaryan liked Salma Sultana. He would stare at her expressionless face as she read daily news on Doordarshan, with a rose tucked low in her hair. Aaryan thought that she was beautiful and looked exactly like his mother. He thought the same about *Wahida Rehman*, the famous Bollywood Actress. Once, while watching a song from the movie Guide in Chitrahaar, he pointed out in front of the family that Wahida Rehman was just a carbon copy of his mother.

"Now that I think of it, there is a resemblance," Vinod said and looked smilingly at his wife.

"If I remember correctly, you once said that I look like Hema Malini," Meena replied back as she served chapattis to the family on the dinner table.

Lipi was awake now and had started to cry and Meena ran inside to check if she had fallen off her bed (again) in her sleep. And then a sudden silence fell upon the room as the clock struck 9 and Hum Log started. It was the first Indian television soap telecasted on Doordarshan in 1984; a story of a middle class Indian family and its trials and sufferings. Aaryan was just five then, but he remembered it all vividly later. It was not technically exceptional, but it had a story, which, according to his family, was missing from hundreds of sitcoms that went on air when India got 200 channels 20 years later. Years later in Rohtak, when Aaryan sometimes, on rare occasions, met with his fellow professors and readers over a cup of tea, the nostalgia of the 80s always had a scoop of Hum Log in it and Salma Sultana's rose.

The problem began when Meena decided that she needed a larger part of the salary to take care of the children. Aaryan was almost five now and had to go to school soon. The days of the cheap playschool were over. She prodded Vinod to talk to his mother and ask for atleast half of the salary every month. Vinod took a deep breath and entered the lair. That was the first major fight in the house. Shakuntala was completely against it. Manohar nodded blankly.

"You can ask me for the money whenever you want. Why do you want to keep it?" Shakuntala asked.

"If I can have it eventually, then why to give it to you?"

"And why do you want to put Aaryan in a public school? Aren't government schools good enough? We all studied in government schools. They are cheaper as well," Shakuntala said.

"No. You didn't," Vinod replied, "I want him to get the best from the beginning. It will be a little difficult for me to manage, but all of us have to compromise. It's for the future of the children."

"I still don't understand how keeping half of the salary to yourself will help things."

"I don't understand how that wouldn't."

"It's that woman, isn't it? She is instigating you," Shakuntala said, raising her voice.

"She has a name. Mom, will you please stop blowing this out of proportion?"

"Hasn't your wife done that already? Well, who am I to complain? It's your money. Keep all of it. I knew this would happen one day. Your father and I have enough money from his earnings to live. Don't give me your next month's salary."

"I do not want the whole salary."

"You can go now," Shakuntala growled.

She was filled with an immense hatred for Meena. She knew this very well that Vinod did not have the courage to take the drastic step. He had moulded himself in the cast of how things worked in her house. First her father, then her husband and now her son; no one had stayed forever. Everyone leaves one day or another. The sand was slipping and loneliness was tickling her again.

"You worry too much. It's just a few hundred rupees," Manohar said.

"Two hundred and eighty five; it's not few."

"Our children are married. I still have two years of my job left. We will be fine. What is there to worry about?"

"She is taking away your son. Don't you see that?"

"Just listen to yourself. You are turning into someone else. No one is taking your son away. Go to sleep Shakuntala."

Shakuntala did not talk to Meena for almost a week. She

whisked past her as if she was thin air. She took up her old habit of leaving the house in the afternoon and returning back just before her husband and son arrived from the office. Meena was left to take care of the house, meals and both the children. Madan had now shifted to Delhi. He was married a few years back to a girl he met in the college. They had a son who was half the age of Vinod. Shakuntala would spend most of her time with his wife, setting up their house and taking them on a Delhi tour at times. It was a week later when Madan visited their house with his wife that Shakuntala was again infuriated by Meena as she took Aaryan to her room as the guests smiled uncomfortably. Meena landed upon a reverberating sound of a swear word, something which she could not forget for the rest of her life. More abuses came later, but they were not that effective because of the get-used-to-it tone of them. The first one was as memorable as first love.

✦

"Sometimes, I feel that I am not managing projects, but managing animals in a zoo," Ravi said as he took a sip of the wine. He had finally made it to his home amidst chaotic traffic jams because of some light showers.

"Sunny, would you please use a fork? And put the napkin in your lap," Lipi said as she saw her son digging his fingers in his plate.

"Why is it always so difficult?" Vinod asked. He was a bit restless. Ravi was always in constant tension, something he had not experienced in his decades of job.

"Inefficiency. What else? And the managers get a beating from both ends. Wine?"

"Yes please."

Ravi poured some wine for his wife and father-in-law. Meena refused with a slight movement of her head.

"I need some water," Sunny said.

"Oh! I forgot to bring it," Lipi said and got up to bring water from the kitchen.

"Where is Kunti?" Ravi asked.

"I gave her an off today. She must be in the servant's quarters. I came a bit early," Lipi screamed from the kitchen.

"What really amazes me at times is that we don't teach anything practical to our children in schools and then we expect them to be the best scientists and engineers. Just like that. Even if we, for a second, leave aside the schools and have a look at the Engineering colleges, what they teach is bullshit. That stuff can't help a software engineer write a flawless code which follows all standards.

"Thank god for small mercies like this happy family, but my life is a living nightmare. Sometimes, I just feel so tired, worn out. One thing I promised myself was that I would never rush through my life and that is exactly what I am doing since I can remember. I am not enjoying my life. Sometimes I feel like leaving all this and joining Dad's business," Ravi said and stopped eating. He stared at the food on his plate and then at his son who was busy making a smiley on his plate with the leftover chicken gravy and then he smiled.

"Private companies leave no stone unturned to suck your blood," Vinod said, "There is a boy who lives next door and he works for a private firm. I sometimes meet him when I go for a walk. A company hired him during his last semester in the college. What he tells me amazes me. He says that they are made to work like labourers. They are blamed for incompetence, for not knowing something for which they are not even trained.

"My job was the exact opposite of yours. No tension of any kind. 9 to 6 and enough time to spend with the family but both of us had one thing in common. There was something absent. And maybe it's inside us rather than outside. Contentment is an approximation. You can never reach it."

"Were you content?" Ravi asked.

"No. I wasn't and that's the whole point. There were other factors in my life that pushed me away from that. My job was not the issue; it was the rest of my life. I was trying very hard to please everyone."

"I can understand." Ravi said and looked towards Meena and then Lipi. Meena had finished her dinner and was staring intently at the plate while listening to her husband.

"They had a fight today," Lipi told Ravi later that night after she had put Sunny to sleep and tiptoed to her room.

"I could tell," Ravi said as he snuggled next to her in the bed. "Was it bad?"

"As bad as it could get. Thank god they don't have the stamina of my grandparents."

"Your parents are nice people. I wonder why they were not able to manage the situation."

"Have you ever seen my father talk about the world, the problems which various people face as they live? He sounds like my brother at times. Today we were discussing the traffic jams in Gurgaon. He is very reciprocative when it comes to problems outside our house but I think a family is never explicit. There is more to understand with gestures, looks and unfinished sentences. When you stay with a person for a lifetime, you expect him to understand the thoughts running beneath your skin. Maybe that is where we all failed. We just waited for things to fall back in place instead of moving them ourselves. I could never understand that my family which was so sensitive to the problems of the world could not even acknowledge the sufferings which they inflicted on each other."

"To be honest, I could never understand your grandma. She belonged to a rich family, studied in a convent at that time and her own granny hated her and her mother. She knew how it felt like and yet when the time came, she did exactly the same thing with her son. It was like history repeating itself and no lessons learnt."

"As much as I could figure her out, she was like a woman falling off a cliff trying to get hold of whatever could save her life. The first straw was her father. I remember how fondly she used to talk about him and how rich they were and the pony rides and the convent. After he died, she was falling again and grandpa came to her rescue. I don't know what exactly happened between them but I could always sense an undercurrent of hatred. And then it was my father. By this time, she had turned really vicious and manipulative which lead to this condition in which Ma is today. After my father, it was Aaryan and me. Do you see? How she kept shifting her hopes and kept pinning them on the next best alternative? There was always something happening in that brain of hers. I could sense that. It was as if she was weighing the pros and cons of everything but then she was a very unpredictable woman, diffident, insecure and mentally sick. I think it started after her father's death. She was very attached to him. When he died, something snapped inside her. Anyway, Aaryan and I were completely in awe of her for quite some time. We hated our own Ma."

"I hope you would be fine with our son's wife," Ravi said and smiled.

"I don't think I want him to live with us once he gets a job. I don't expect that either."

"Why do you say that?"

"Because I want you all for myself after we are through this. I have given many years for this crazy job of yours and mine. When our child is settled, I want both of us to be left alone. Then we will sit besides the pool and get nostalgic about the good old days. And besides, I think children should always be given their own space. If Sunny never has his own house to take care of, he will never learn how to do that."

They kissed each other goodnight and ended up having sex. Both of them were so busy from the last few days that they hardly got time to be together. Sunny was left solely in the care of servants at times, especially during the vacations, and that is what Meena hated. She would end up in Lipi's house more than in her own and would drag Vinod with her. Still when Lipi insisted that they shifted permanently there, both of them refused blankly.

"I am again going to be late tomorrow," Lipi sighed and switched off the table lamp afterwards.

✦

When Manohar retired from his job in 1986, the family had to vacate the government flat they were living in. Shakuntala wanted to move into another rented house but Vinod was completely against it.

"For how long are we going to live like nomads?" he said.

It took some time to convince Shakuntala that Delhi was their home and there was no point in accumulating lands in Dalhousie when they were never going to return there. Kulbhushan and his brothers had kept aside some land for all the children including Shakuntala and Madan. She had no intention of selling her father's house which was in her name now after Madan gifted his share in it to her after Vinod was born. She reluctantly sold majority of her share of land in Dalhousie, and the family bought a two bedroom flat in Janak Puri. Aaryan said his final goodbyes to Priya when the family shifted there.

Lipi was two years old now and would follow her brother wherever he went. She would run after him when he went to the terrace on the top floor of the building to see trains. Lipi could not see the train and Aaryan would have to pick her up and place her chin on the cold cement and brick railing. He would then place his own chin on her head. Brother and sister would wait impatiently for the smoke to rise from the horizon and then the frown would turn into a smile, as a steam engine would appear pulling the bogies with it. It looked like a monster, guarding the city in which they lived.

Once during monsoons, as the peacocks danced, a peahen appeared on the railing of the balcony of their house. Aaryan froze and motioned Lipi to be quiet. The peahen was huge, something very different and majestic from what he had seen in the books. She walked on the railing, as if searching for something, her head moving back and forth like a hammer. And, then she flew away, expanding her wings and making heavy fluttering sounds.

Initially, Aaryan was quite fascinated by the world that Shakuntala created in front of his eyes, but soon he started to get bored of it, the way he was getting bored of the rest of his life. But Shakuntala was always better than his mother. Vinod was still giving half of his salary to Shakuntala, an arrangement that was reached over a lot of arguments and tears followed by the initial discord. She was also very keen to cook separately and did that for a week before her son again came to her for a ceasefire. She projected herself as a martyr and finally Vinod had to give in to agree to give a part of his salary to her. Shakuntala was scared that she had to cook food on her own for the rest of her life. She was quite relieved when Meena asked her to rest as she would cook the meals. She left the kitchen without thanks. The children never noticed anything except the fact that their grandma was making food in the kitchen from a few days. It wasn't unusual that their mother and grandmother never talked to each other unless very necessary or to sometimes share a common memory of Dalhousie when both of them felt nostalgic at times. But other than that, there was no bond. The only thin thread that connected both the women was their common place of birth. Sometimes, the women would sit in the sun during winters and talk about snow. Meena hated the dry winters of Delhi. She missed the heavy snowfalls, the fog rising from the belly of the valley. She hadn't seen them in years. Sometimes the women would laugh at an old memory, Shakuntala would tell her about a husband and wife she knew and Meena would tell her about their children with whom she played. It was during times like these when Meena wondered if she could bring Shakuntala to love her. On the other hand, Shakuntala might have laughed and talked with her, but she always had an air of authority, a mild cynicism which never left her eyes. She was constantly reminding herself not to lose the layer which she had so deftly woven around her.

One day Meena took Aaryan and Lipi to a friend's house in the adjoining building. She was a middle aged, fat woman with dark circles beneath her eyes. Meena had met in the grocery shop. She had a son who studied in Aaryan's school and was two years senior to him. It was in her house that Aaryan and Lipi saw a sofa for the first time. Their house had four wooden chairs to welcome the guests that were covered with cushions filled with cotton. A black leather sofa was something they had only seen in the movies. The first few jumps on the sofa were met with a stony stare from Meena and a twist of lips from her friend. She looked like an owl, staring at the children and moving her mouth in a big O, as if trying to scare them. Meena was sweating and turned pink with embarrassment. She tried her best to continue the talk but every time a shriek or a reverberation would make the ladies jump. Finally, she had to do what she was trying to avoid. She slapped Aaryan and had to lug them out of the house as her newly found friend waved at them from her door. After she shut the door, she heaved the longest sigh she could have heaved and raced towards her sofa as if it was a dying relative. It was only after she had ensured that there were no damages that she got up and left the room.

"You rotten brats! Wait till your father hears that!" Meena was shouting at them as they entered their house.

"Grandma! Why can't we have a leather sofa?" The children ran towards Shakuntala for refuge.

"We can't because they are very expensive. We cannot afford them," Meena shouted.

"We will have them very soon. Don't worry," Shakuntala said raising her chin a bit. Meena stared at her.

That night Shakuntala opened her black iron trunk and took out two thousand Rupees from a small bag. The next morning, she gave the money to Vinod and asked him to buy a sofa for the drawing room.

"Not something fancy and definitely not leather," she told him.

She also gave him an additional five hundred rupees to buy a table to go with the sofas. Vinod was dumbstruck for a moment and could not understand what his mother was up to. He got an olive colored sofa fitted with cotton fabric. It was not comparable to the leather sofa on which the children had jumped a day before but it changed the map of the drawing room. Lipi was delirious with joy while Aaryan touched the sofa with the same caution someone would touch a rattlesnake. He was satisfied but not happy. It wasn't a leather sofa after all. The children were promptly forbidden to jump on it. A matching modest table was bought as well, which was heavier and shinier than the existing one.

As Aaryan and Lipi grew up, the drawing room turned into their bedroom. It became difficult for Meena and Vinod to sleep in the same bed with both their children lying in-between them. Shakuntala would let either of them sleep with her and Manohar but the children were now growing up and hence a few kicks from Lipi while sleeping made up Shakuntala's mind. It was not worth the pain after all. So, Aaryan would sleep on the diwan in the drawing room while Lipi slept with her parents. Aaryan would jump off the *diwan* and bundle himself on the sofa as soon as all the lights went off. He liked the way the springs in the sofa would curve under the weight of his body. He would close his eyes and imagine that he was sleeping on a cloud. Sometimes he would lie there with his eyes open and listen to the sounds coming from the bedrooms – the muffled sounds of his grandparents fighting with each other for no apparent reason or the sounds of his parents talking to each other after making sure that Lipi was asleep. Then there was the ticking of the wall clock, and the swooshing of the ceiling fan, an approaching mosquito making the sound like a bomb racing towards a city from the sky, a passing train and sometimes an occasional mating sound of a peacock. There were times when he could not sleep at all in the middle of so many noises, something everyone else was so used to.

The Texla television with the sliding wooden doors was now in the drawing room, placed at a corner, between the diwan and the sofa chair. Shakuntala's radio sat on a raised wooden mantelpiece. A desert cooler was fitted in the sole window in the room, blocking it from any outside view. Even with the motor of the cooler roaring throughout the night, pumping water up so that it could drip down the wood wool, Aaryan could hear the snores of his father. He could never understand how his mother could sleep in that clamour.

On Sundays, the family would gather together and sit on the sofa to watch *Mahabharat* and *the Jungle Book.* The television was their only solace, something which brought them together, even if all they did was to stare at the idiot box. Aaryan brought novels from the school and rubbed his legs on the sofa as he read them in the afternoon after lunch. He was thankful that he finally had a room to himself, even if his family invaded it during lunch and dinner.

It was during these lonely growing up years when Aaryan's mind deviated towards thoughts that placed his own family and the world around him on an obtuse plane. There were millions of voices around him that he noticed, but then there was also a screeching of emptiness. He was living in a house with five other humans, related to him by blood, but there wasn't an iota of awareness or any sense of convergence. Maybe he would not have turned up the way he did if there was a force at home to counter what he absorbed as a child from his surroundings. His family flared his angst, multiplied his confusion. The coldness and indifference with which his family members treated each other completely unhinged the weak connections he had with them. There was a disconcerted detachment in his behaviour, which surprisingly even Shakuntala, who was so meticulously bent upon tilting the table of power towards her, failed to notice mainly because Lipi rushed in to fill the void created by Aaryan's half-baked exit. And then, India was never out of turmoil. The 80s and the 90s were filled with assassinations, massacres, demolition of religious buildings, riots, and bomb blasts. There was not a moment's respite for Aaryan; there wasn't a moment when his brain was not hammered, when he did not feel like throwing away the television. It was during this time when he started to question the beliefs of the people around him and started having arguments with his father. His grandfather steered clear of any sort of discussions most of the time. According to him, it was improper for a father and son to argue about matters. Instead, he discussed politics with Anwar, the local barber. It was more apt.

Soon Cable television invaded the household and there was a constant tussle and discussion about what to watch. Vinod had discovered his new found love for Discovery channel and female wrestling, while Aaryan found BBC and the Indian News channels more engrossing. Meena and Shakuntala were developing a liking for sitcoms but both never liked the same ones and usually the timings would overlap. Lipi was from the generation whose memories of being served by one channel were quite bleak. She could not understand what the fuss was all about and suggested that the family buy one more television so that she could watch MTV and Channel V in peace. Manohar too nodded at the idea because it was extremely difficult to watch Baywatch and FTV in the drawing room with children hovering around all the time. He further added that the televisions should be moved into the two bedrooms. So, the old Texla television was moved to Shakuntala's and Manohar's bedroom while Vinod got a new 14 inch black and white television. Aaryan was relieved that the living room would not be clogged by people who only sat together to watch television and to eat. The television split actually split the time they sat together to have their meals. They started eating in their own bedrooms. They would spread the newspaper on the bed and place the plates on it and eat. Shakuntala would sometimes eat in Vinod and Meena's bedroom just to be with her grandchildren. No one talked much as someone was always doing that for them on the television.

Meena could count on her fingers the number of times she had exchanged a few words with her mother-in-law in the last few years. There was always something wrong with whatever she did. The swear words were common now but were never unleashed in front of Vinod and the children. Meena would not retaliate and would simply leave the room. The children were of no help and that is what completely broke Meena. There was no one she could fall back upon, no one to talk to. Sometimes, the despair was unbearable. The children would spend most of their time with their grandmother who was now openly instigating them against their mother. Especially after a thrashing or a discord, she would trick them into badmouthing Meena by her acts of sympathy. Aaryan was not quite verbose when it came to it but Lipi grabbed all opportunities and gave her grandmother enough fodder to last a lifetime. Shakuntala stacked away all the words in her memory to use them at an appropriate time.

It was during this time that Meena turned towards God, turning him into a friend she could talk to. It was not as if she wasn't a believer earlier, but her inclination towards acknowledging God's presence grew during this time. It did not occur from a need to pray in front of him to make her conditions better but from a need to find someone who would listen to her and understand her. She became overtly religious as years passed which later clashed with Aaryan's thoughts and made him extremely uncomfortable.

Shakuntala had turned obese by now. Her stomach hung like an upside down hot air balloon while her breasts sagged till her elbows. She walked with a limp because it was now hard to lift her legs completely while walking. There was no question of visiting Dalhousie in this state. Her only solace was her cousins giving her occasional visits in Delhi. She suffered from diabetes and arthralgia in her leg joints. Her skin was all dry and soggy but her face still looked beautiful. Although, it hardly bore any resemblance to her face when she was youthful, but there was still a charisma to her, a glow that a bypasser could not ignore. Sometimes Lipi's friends or Aaryan's occasional acquaintances would drop by and would drop their jaws when Shakuntala showed them her old black and white photographs.

"You were breathtaking! Did you ever try in the movies?" One of Lipi's friend, who constantly chewed a chewing gum, asked.

"I had offers but it was not considered good at that time for girls to enter show business," Shakuntala would brag.

"At that time? Ha! It's still the same nowadays Aunty," the friend replied as she tried to create a balloon.

Sometimes Shakuntala would ask Aaryan to bring novels from his school. He would bring classics and she would read them with delight. Many times, while passing through her room, Aaryan would find her asleep, snoring lightly with a novel, open half way through, moving on her stomach like a ship on a turbulent sea. At night, after dinner, his grandparents would sometimes fall asleep while watching a movie on Star Movies. Aaryan would quietly tiptoe in the room and switch off the television.

One summer, Meena developed a few rashes on her back. They started to grow into abscesses and spread throughout her back and parts of her stomach. She was in extreme pain and could not sleep. The doctor provided an extremely painful method to get rid of them. He covered her back with pieces of gauze that had to be removed only when the pus had drained out. The gauze ripened the abscesses and then broke them open. For almost a month, Meena looked like a human who had just returned from an alien spaceship, battered and experimented upon. She would cry at nights because the pain wouldn't let her sleep. The children were sympathetic. Vinod took leave for a few days. Shakuntala was alarmed, for she had to work and the household finally got its first maid to do the chores. The maid ran away in two weeks because she could not take Shakuntala's constant gaze and interference. Shakuntala considered all the people from the lower castes as thieves. She was very sure that left to herself, the maid would definitely steal something of value from the house. The maid complained to Meena and Meena talked to Vinod and Vinod talked to Shakuntala.

"Like what? What is there to steal? Your father's copper tumbler?" Vinod asked.

"Yes. That in fact is an artifact. It will be sold for lakhs a few years down the line," Shakuntala retorted back.

"Meena cannot work, mother. It would be very kind of you to let the maid be. She is good at her work if not irritated."

Shakuntala of course, took no heed and the second maid left in a week and was replaced by another. Shakuntala was a bit worried now. Her son was shouting at her nowadays, something he had never attempted before. He shouted at her when he noticed that she was watching an adult movie with the door of her room open. There are children in this house, her son bawled. What's the harm if they see a bit of kissing, she thought while closing the door of her bedroom? She wondered why everyone was picking a fight with her. Her husband was becoming unbearable too. He was the master of silent whiplashes. His words were acrid and would pound on her from nowhere. They were fighting for minute reasons like who will switch off the light at night, which would finally blow out of proportion, and both of them would end up cursing each other's families. Shakuntala would be like a raging bull the moment Manohar would curse her father.

"At least my family knew how to make an honest living. They were not like your brothers. The vampires drank the blood of their own brother," she would scream in anger.

"Your father worked for the firangi when the whole nation was fighting against them. He was a traitor," Manohar would shout back.

"Mother! Dad! Stop this madness now. There are children in this house," Vinod would run into their room when all of it became unbearable. The fights, which he used to pass on as something habitual and laughable earlier, had to be stopped because of the children.

The children were quite scared initially but soon they started to giggle and laugh at the way their grandparents screamed at each other. It was a camouflage they had to put to save their sanity. The only way out without going mad was to laugh at it, to look at it as if they were watching a movie. They imagined they were not a part of it and it was happening to someone else, in some other dimension. At times, they would pretend that they were Shakuntala and Manohar and would fight like them, bursting out laughing at the end.

✦

The breakfast was French toast and baked beans with orange juice. Ravi and Lipi had finished their laps on the treadmill in their private gym, taken a shower and were ready to leave for their offices. Meanwhile Meena and the maid Kunti had readied Sunny for his first day in school after the summer vacations.

For a few minutes, there was only the sound of munching and the rustling of newspaper.

"What is new in the newspaper?" Vinod asked Ravi.

"Oh! The same old, five killed there, ten killed here, seven robbed somewhere, rapes, molestations, scams. If someone gives me a year old newspaper to read by mistake, I won't know the difference."

"Mom, go out to the new mall which has opened around the corner and watch a movie with Dad. Take the car with you. Kunti can drive you there," Lipi said suddenly to Meena.

"I was thinking of calling Aaryan today," Meena said quietly.

The clinking of the cutlery stopped and there was a pregnant silence for a moment. Even Kunti, who was quite a fool to understand a cue, jammed while filling Ravi's glass with water and stared at the family.

"Oh!" Lipi said and that is all that was said on the topic.

Later while Ravi gave Lipi a lift in his car, he asked, "you all right?"

"Yes. His name really kills me at times," Lipi said as she tried to smile, "and the worst part is that my mother still loves him even after he abandoned her years ago. I am doing everything on my own that my brother could have done standing beside me but he is not there. He is not there at all. It's as if I grew up with a ghost that suddenly vanished one day without leaving a trace."

"Lipi..."

"I am the only one left here, Ravi, and the sooner my mother realizes this, the better."

"He is her child. What do you expect her to do?"

"Sometimes I feel like telling her the truth, to tell her that her fucking son is as good as dead and let her deal with it."

Lipi stared out of the window at the beggar who had converged on the car as soon as it stopped at the signal. She was filthy and was wearing torn clothes. She had a child in her hand and was constantly placing her hand on her stomach indicating that she was hungry. For a second, Lipi forgot all her anger.

"I am sorry," she said without turning to Ravi, "Look at her. Shouldn't I be grateful that I don't have to worry for my next meal, that I am not in her place? And here I am bickering about relationships."

Ravi smiled as Lipi rolled down the window and handed the woman a ten-rupee coin.

"You are not supposed to encourage begging. That coin will probably go to the leader of the gang who will use it to buy more children to beg on the streets after he has blinded them by pouring acid in their eyes. That is what they show in the movies, don't they?"

Lipi looked at the woman as she disappeared behind a wave of cars as the light turned green.

"Maybe. Or maybe she will use it to feed her child. If there is even a percentage of a chance of that happening, it would make me feel that I have done nothing wrong. And if you are not supposed to do anything, then what are you supposed to do?"

Lipi's house was suddenly empty as Sunny too left for his school. Meena sat besides the pool for sometime with the cordless in her hand. She tried calling Aaryan several times that day. He did not pick up the phone and did not call back. Next day, he called up and talked for five minutes, asking how everyone was.

"Everyone is fine. We are here at Lipi's home. And how are you?" Meena asked.

"I am good. Busy. Teaching takes a lot of time."

"Good. Good."

There was an uncomfortable silence for a few seconds.

"Well. I hope you are taking care of your health," Meena said.

"Yes, I am. Don't worry about that."

"Any plans of visiting us?"

"I might come on one of the weekends. Will let you know. Mom, I have to go now."

"All right Aaryan, bye son."

"Bye."

Vinod looked at his wife as she replaced the receiver.

"Didn't think it was important to talk to his father, did he?" he said.

Meena sighed and went inside the kitchen.

✦

As the abscesses faded away, Meena started having sudden chronic cough attacks and fever. She started to lose weight at an alarming rate and lost five kilograms in a week. It was 21st May 1991 when she was diagnosed with Tuberculosis, the same day Rajiv Gandhi was assassinated in Sriperumbudur. As she returned from the hospital in a three-wheeler with her husband, Meena gazed at the vehicles racing with the auto, holding her scans and reports close to her chest. She imagined her family sympathizing with her and everyone encircling her and asking her how she felt and giving her courage.

"It is curable, you know. Everything will be all right," Vinod said as he saw her lost in thought.

"Yes, it is. I am sure." She was wondering when this vicious circle would stop. Why can't she have a moment's respite? By making her life abundant with misery – was this God's way of testing her?

When they reached home, everyone was glued to the television, staring at the mangled bodies strewn across the park where the election rally was held. Aaryan intently stared at the body of Rajiv Gandhi, lying face down in a pool of blood and only identifiable by the back of his head and the clothes he was wearing. There was a stunned silence in the house. The news reporter was on the verge of crying and was holding back her tears as she announced the tragedy. Meena thought that it would be better to hold her own tragedy for the time being. She was afraid that no one was going to care, that they would wave her off as they stared at the television. No one did care anyway when she finally broke the news next day. Her children had no idea how aggravated the disease was and Meena also belittled her condition. She told them that she had to take medicines and it would be fine. She was worried, though, that she might pass it to someone in the house. She was always cautious while sneezing and started eating food alone. Shakuntala reacted much better than Meena had expected. It was as if she was very excited to unearth the exact time of Meena's death. Manohar was sympathetic. It was a long journey ahead. Almost two years of harsh antibiotics and a non-existent social interaction. As if there was already too much of it, Meena thought. In a scenario, when Meena should have been bedridden, she was still doing all the chores. The maid was removed with the abscesses despite Vinod's objections.

"There are three women in the house. We can manage the work amongst ourselves," Shakuntala said, and that was the end of it.

One hot summer afternoon when the children came back from school, they were terrified by the look Meena gave them as she opened the front door for them. She was fuming, going red all over her face. She slammed the door shut as Aaryan and Lipi entered the house. As the children went into the bedroom to slide off their bags on the table, Meena came after them.

"So you go to your grandmother and badmouth me?" She asked both of them. They were quiet. It was something completely unexpected, a betrayal. They felt like soldiers who were suddenly ambushed by the enemy because their secrets were leaked out.

"I am thirsty," Aaryan said and moved out of the room. Lipi stood there like a mouse facing a cat looming large on the horizon. She had no idea where to look.

Slam!

The slap numbed Lipi's left cheek and there was a slight hissing sound in her ear.

"Did you or did you not?" Meena asked again.

"No I didn't!" Lipi lied.

Meena stared at her daughter, bewildered and tired. She felt as if all the energy was draining away from her. The doctor had asked her not to prolong any physical strain, not that it mattered. Aaryan entered the kitchen and saw Shakuntala making chapatti. He was a little surprised because it was quite rare to spot his grandmother in the kitchen.

"What happened?" he asked as he picked up a glass.

"Nothing. She forgets where we picked her up from. Daughter of a low class farmer, she has no respect for the elders in the house," Shakuntala said and went into her room to give the chapatti to her husband who was munching his lunch while watching the latest episode of Santa Barbara.

"But what happened?" Aaryan asked again as Shakuntala came back in the kitchen.

"Nothing. You don't need to know."

The children completed the jigsaw from the bits and pieces of conversations and occasional shouts they could hear from behind the closed doors. It was years later they came to know how trivial and laughable the reason was for the fight which divided the family.

Vinod had bought a cheap, local washing machine sometime back. It was painted with a shade of blue that had started to peel away after a month of use. There was no dryer, just a motor at the back to rotate the water. Meena, apparently, was dipping combs in the washing machine to clean them while the motor whirled to create a horizontal tornado. Shakuntala objected to this as the comb might get stuck in the motor. She was a stakeholder in the machine and had provided half of the money to buy the piece of metal. According to her, she had every right to avoid any malign. Meena assured her that she was holding the comb with her hands and would not let them wash away in the flood. Shakuntala thought that she was trying to be smart.

"Please don't argue and do as you have been told," Shakuntala said and started to walk away. Manohar, who had heard the whole argument and was moving towards the toilet also suggested to Meena to do as her mother-in-law said. He moved slowly and passed the ladies with alarm. He could sense that something bad was about to happen.

"I am not a child. I really don't need your suggestion," Meena said, as she wiggled the combs furiously in water. Shakuntala stopped dead in her tracks.

"Of course you need it. Mainly because that is partially my washing machine and secondly because you are an ignorant villager who has not yet learnt the ways of the civilized world. And give some respect to the elders when you address them," Shakuntala blasted out as she turned back to face Meena.

"If you have such a refined sense of how people behave in the civilized world, perhaps you can tell me the reasons behind using me as a slave in the house from the past twelve years."

"You were never used as a slave. No one asked you to work," Shakuntala said coolly.

"And who was supposed to feed you and your family if not me? I worked even when I was pregnant, and now I am working when I am fighting with an ailment. Would you have reacted the same way if I were your own daughter? You did not let me complete my school, your son had to beg in front of you to spend his own salary on his own children and now you are taking my children away from me. Do you think I can't see it? Do you think I am blind, not able to judge what is cooking in that brain of yours?"

Meena wanted to calm herself and stop the words which were flowing uncontrolled from her, words stored somewhere deep within and which she thought were long dead. She was feeling weak again. A few words and she was already exhausted. She started coughing and held the washing machine firmly with both her hands.

"Meena! Control yourself," Manohar said. He was torn between standing there and enjoying the fight and running away to urinate first. Manohar decided not to take any chances and hurried towards the toilet. Shakuntala on the other hand was finally facing her nemesis. She too had a very common habit that usually inflicts her kind. While playing her little tricks, she had always imagined that everyone was blind to all the movements of the pieces. Being malignant requires some degree of blindness, taking others as fools and she had not escaped it. So, when Meena all of a sudden turned the glare of the spotlight on her, Shakuntala felt utterly naked, right from the hair on her head till her toenail. And then, as every thief who gets caught because of illusions of his own self-sagacity, her first impulse was to defend herself by playing innocent.

"I don't know what you are talking about. Why would I take away your children from you? They are your children," Shakuntala said as a matter of fact.

"That is something only you can answer. I have turned all the reasons upside down in my heart but I am unable to understand it. Why do you abhor me so much?"

The quintessential question, which Shakuntala had never

dared to ask herself, was now bare in front of her, wobbling like the body of a goat whose head had been severed. There was a reason once, yes, years ago, when Meena came into the house. Shakuntala had disliked her instantly. In fact she had disliked her the moment Vinod had expressed his wish to marry her. She had disliked her even more when Vinod went to Dalhousie to meet her twice. Suddenly, she could not identify with her own son and the thought scared her. But that happened twelve years ago. They had two children. What was the point of hating her now? She was embedded in the family. It was pointless, a lost war.

"Tell me! Did I offend you in some way? Was I not obedient? Did I not try to be your daughter? I worked like a maniac and did whatever you said just to please you. What was it that you could not forgive?" Meena was saying. She was crying now. Tears rolled down her eyes and mixed in the water churning in the washing machine, now turning a shade of grey. She could not hold it any longer. She was breathing huge chunks of air.

"I don't hate you. You don't have anything that I am required to hate. We don't gel together, Meena, and that is it," Shakuntala started saying whatever came to her mind.

"That is because you never tried, you never reciprocated!" Meena said, wiping off her tears.

By this time, Manohar was out of the toilet. He screeched out a chair from the dining table and sat at a corner of the room, moving his head from one woman to another, as if watching a tennis match.

"I just asked you to take the combs out of the machine. Why do you have to turn it into such a big issue?" Shakuntala said in a whiff of exasperation.

"It is not just the combs. It's the way you treat me as if I am an untouchable. It's the way you talk to your son as if he has committed an unpardonable sin by marrying me for which he has to pay for the rest of his life. It's the way you demand authority without any hint of love as if this house is a dictatorship regime. It's your demoralizing tone, the tilt of your eyebrow when you look at us; it's the way your face twitches. It's in each and every gesture of yours. The hatred just pours out of you."

There was a momentary silence when Manohar stared at Meena. He was flabbergasted with her courage. Shakuntala was standing on a fork. There was no way she could have denied any of it. It was as if she was dancing exposed in front of everyone all these years, fooling only herself. She could have embraced Meena that day and that would have been the end of it, but that was too tough for her.

"You bitch! You filthy bitch! How dare you talk to me like that? Never forget from where we picked you up. If it were not for my son, you would have been plucking potatoes on some farm by now. Yes, I hate you. I will hate you for the rest of my life and I don't think I am required to give you a reason. And why are you questioning me? Go and question your children. They hate you too! In fact there isn't a single day when they don't come to me and whine about you. You have no love for them. You have made their life miserable. Now, if you have to live in this house, you have to live according to what I say. Otherwise, you are welcome to get out," Shakuntala said to a stunned Meena and Manohar, and marched into her room, slamming the door on their faces.

Manohar followed his wife after sometime without a note of consolation. Meena cried and coughed standing next to the washing machine, holding the combs tightly in her hand, as the last droplets of detergent fell back from the combs into the water, filthy with dirt by now. If she had to tell her story to anyone, people would chuckle at her. She did not beat you up, she did not throw acid on you, she did not burn you by pouring kerosene on you while you were asleep, they would say. What are you complaining about then? But she was not blowing it out of proportion. Why does it always have to be something physical? Why does someone have to strike you or burn you for people to sympathize with you? Is it because the truth is stark only with a proof? There has to be a mark on the body, a bruise, for someone to sympathize? Otherwise it's just manipulated and exaggerated sentences? She felt as if her life was churning with the dark grey water in the washing machine. She had to get out of here, before she killed herself or put a knife through Shakuntala. After she confronted her children, there were no doubts. They had to leave.

The next month was agonizing. Vinod was suddenly all up for it. Meena, for the first time, saw a degree of furiousness that she had never witnessed before. He barged into his parent's room and questioned Shakuntala. He was not giving explanations but demanding answers. It fascinated Meena. It was as if she had entered a parallel universe all of a sudden, where the same people lived but the decisions were different, where they took all the forks which were discarded in her own universe. Her husband plainly told his mother that he wanted to separate out and would be leaving the house as soon as he gets an apartment at rent. He could afford it now. Yes, after twelve years, he could afford it. Twelve years too late. Shakuntala was fuming initially and tried her best to divert the situation to her own advantage, but there was no point now. Vinod was firm and at the end Shakuntala could not say anything except – fine. Manohar was disappointed as he was expecting more fireworks.

"We are separating," Vinod said as he returned to the bedroom. The children stared at him. Meena took a deep breath.

Vinod started looking for one-room flats nearby from the next day. Shakuntala started cooking her own food; she had almost forgotten how to do that. The children were the only link between the two couples. Whenever Shakuntala would have to convey a message to Vinod, she would call Aaryan and whisper it in his ear. Aaryan behaved like a messenger carrying a secret message from one kingdom to another. He rode his imaginary horse and made *tugdak-tugdak* noises as he ran from one room to another. Sometimes, there were numerous to and fro rides, before a consensus was reached between the two empires.

Meena had already started to pack a few things in suitcases and cardboard boxes. Her preparations made Shakuntala more furious. The children were perplexed. Aaryan tried to argue with his father and even after repeated warnings from Vinod, he persisted, and ended up with a slap on his face. The children did not interfere after that. Soon there was the question of dividing the physical things, the utensils in the kitchen, the fridge, the dining table, the sofa, the washing machine. Shakuntala refused to part from things that were bought solely by her own money.

"Give us either the fridge or the washing machine," Vinod told Shakuntala.

He had found a house in a nearby locality. It was five minutes away from this house by rickshaw. It was a simple one-room house, a studio apartment. It was small for a family of four but that was all he could afford on his present salary. It was situated amongst a dingy cluster of similar flats that might have looked like thousands of amoeba cells dividing rapidly if seen from outer space. Poor families occupied the locality; those who could not afford to buy or rent the expensive two or three bedroom flats.

When the family moved out of the house in December 1991, it looked like a half eaten meal lying on the road. There were parts of the rooms that were intact, while some parts were scraped of any sign of history. The drapes from Vinod and Meena's bedroom were gone and so were the beds, the wooden almirah and the television. They left the wooden rack that held the schoolbooks of the children and a steel almirah, because there was no space in their new house to keep it. Shakuntala finally decided to give up the fridge rather than the washing machine. She had gulped down water from earthen pots all her life. Also, she wanted to keep the washing machine, as if she was trying to reward it for being an accomplice in crime. It made her feel that she had finally won something. The sofa also stayed while half of the utensils in the kitchen were gone.

There were no goodbyes, except for a hug and a kiss from Shakuntala to her grandchildren. She asked them to promise her that they would visit her regularly.

Their new house outraged the children.

"This is not a house. This is a room," Aaryan whispered to his sister when they entered it.

The main door was on the rightmost corner of the rectangle, which their parents called the house. As they entered, they saw the double bed placed on the left of the main door while a small, cheap wooden rack was placed near the door with the television on top of it. The almirah was placed next to the bed while the fridge was stuffed into the only bare corner left. There were two doors in the room, one leading to the undersized kitchen and one to the toilet-cum-bathroom.

"What! We don't have a separate toilet and bathroom?" Lipi

shouted.

"If you can't see it, that means we don't have it," Vinod replied as he opened a suitcase to put clothes in the almirah. He now realized that one almirah was not enough to hold the clothes of the whole family, and some of it would have to remain in suitcases. There were no cupboards in the room, just the bare walls with the paint giving signs of being tired and begging to be peeled off. There were cobwebs to be destroyed and the dusty floor to be broomed. The kitchen was in worse shape and so was the bathroom. Meena and Vinod spent the day, tidying up the house and throwing things at their allotted places while the children watched The Turning Point on Doordarshan. There was no cable television.

Beyond the kitchen was a relatively large verandah. It was almost half the size of the room and was big for a house of such small proportions. What broke Aaryan's heart was that all he could see from that verandah was a snarl of similar houses randomly strewn all around him. There were no trains rushing past or peacocks dancing around the house. Sometimes, when things were quiet Aaryan could hear the faint whistle of the train. He was able to hear it very clearly at nights. The place depressed him. The local children were no good. They were from deprived families and had never heard of Charles Dickens or Star Movies. So, most of the times, the brother and sister ended up playing with each other, which Aaryan found very boring. Most of the time, they ended up in a fight with their mother screaming at them, which a lot of neighbours could hear.

There were times when Vinod and Meena would long for each other but there was no way they could even touch each other in the one room they now shared with their children. Aaryan was almost thirteen now. He understood things quite well. So when one day, Shakuntala somehow was able to push her bulk on a rickshaw and came to visit them, they knew what was in store and were quiet relieved. She looked distastefully around the house as she entered and embraced her grandchildren. The trio looked like a reunited family after the fall of the Berlin wall. Shakuntala asked Vinod and Meena how they were doing and gave them some of the neighborhood gossip which both of them swallowed respectfully.

"Half of the colony has seen both of you move out of the house. There are always people questioning me like journalists about what happened as if I am the Queen of England. Why can't people mind their own business?" Shakuntala said as she sipped the tea. "I am missing my grandchildren everyday. It will not harm anyone to leave them with me on Sundays. I hope that is fine with both of you?"

So, the children started visiting their grandmother on every Sunday and Meena and Vinod got the much-needed respite. One thing which Shakuntala was learning fast was that it was extremely difficult to continue on her own. Manohar was very active and could make the rounds of the market but not with the same frequency as her son. Then there was this whole household work, which she had to do herself and which completely killed her. The maid was back as a result. She had to do something soon. It was a mistake, a terrible mistake but she did not want to give Meena an impression that she regretted putting her own foot in her mouth. The blunt bareness of the house drove her to insanity as it used to do when she had initially came to Delhi. She was like a dipsomaniac who was trying to give up alcohol but always needed a bottle of whisky in the house, not to drink but just as an assurance in case it was desperately required. No matter how much she hated

Meena, there was a meaning to the hatred when she was around. On Sundays, she would sit with her grandchildren and listen to all their vows and imagine that Meena was still in her house and working in the kitchen. It was the closest she came to nirvana.

Neela, Rohini and Poonam were traumatized by their brother's decision to leave their old parents alone. There was no telephone in the house, so Rohini would write letters from Mumbai while Neela and Poonam would pay him a visit at times. Their mother had produced quite a deplorable picture of her existence in front of them and the daughters blamed Meena for the condition in which their parents found themselves. They did not have the intelligence to get the other side of the story. The sisters reasoned with their brother many times to return to the house but he would not budge. Meena would not take much part in the argument.

"What can I say," she would say and walk towards the kitchen to check on the daal.

Soon Shakuntala also started visiting her son's house and repeatedly asked him to return to his home. Vinod and Meena were alarmed by her regular visits. She never asked for forgiveness, just asserted her right to be with her son, to be with her grandchildren. In her scheme of things, Meena still did not figure. She was still like the refrigerator, something that would come with the rest of the things whenever the family chose to return. Vinod never responded directly to her mother's implorations. He would look at the wall and would respond with a plaintive "We would think about it". The couple had no intention of returning but there was no painless way to make Shakuntala understand that. It all changed again on another fateful day in 1993 when Manohar ended up in an autorikshaw with Shakuntala and her cousin brother's wife on top of him.

✦

Mother and daughter were sitting at the huge glass dining table supported by two beautifully carved pillars that looked as if they were looted from Rome the day Nero was fiddling. Meena had packed her bags that day. She and Vinod were leaving in the evening. Now that Sunny's holidays were over, it was time for the couple to get back home. Lipi and Ravi urged them to stay, but Vinod was quite adamant.

"I called up Aaryan today," Meena said.

"And?"

"Nothing. We talked for five minutes. How is everyone and all."

"Mom," Lipi said as she placed her hand on her mother's hand.

"Five minutes in two months, that is all my son has to offer and not to mention that we haven't seen him since last two years. Where did it all go wrong?"

"It's not your mistake."

Lipi had tried her best to make her mother happy since the day she realized her pain, but she could never fill her heart to the brim. When you get something too late, you could never enjoy it. Maybe her mother was past the threshold or maybe she longed for things that she knew to be unattainable deep in her heart. In either case, she was a picture of sorrow, a wasted life.

The bags were packed, two black light suitcases standing at the door and craving for attention. Lipi called up Ravi to let him know that she was giving her parents a ride back home despite her father's protests. She took Sunny with her. As she neared her old two bedroom flat in Janak Puri, the sight left her numb. She couldn't recall the tangling incidents separately but just an enormous lump of insanity.

What act of absurdity on the part of the Gods brought the six of us together, she wondered?

Funnily, even though her grandparents were long dead, she could still feel their presence in the house. The old sofa bought by her grandma for the drawing room was long gone. An auburn couch, more comfortable and bigger in size, now replaced it. The rest of the house was practically untouched. She went into her room, her and Aaryan's room, which was earlier her grandma and grandfather's room. It was a guest room now, hardly used, dusted daily.

"When was the last time you came here?" her mother asked suddenly.

"I think almost two years back. I don't like coming here," Lipi replied with a sad smile.

"Neither do I," Meena said.

Both of them stared at the sketches of Mickey Mouse, Donald, Asterix and so many other cartoon characters, which Aaryan had made and pasted on his grandmother's wooden almirah. There was a blue Genie too with Aladdin and Jasmine floating on the carpet in front of him. Then there was this stack of second hand and pirated books that Aaryan used to buy from the Daryaganj Sunday market and which her mother had a hard time to maintain. Aaryan was elated when his grandma died. At least, my books will have a proper resting place, he thought. Their nomadic expeditions were over. He left all the books behind when he left, like everyone else.

The suitcase-sized radio rested on the mantel piece like an old king sleeping on his throne. Lipi moved into the kitchen and took a lungful of air. The smells of spices and pickles, cinnamons and cardamoms, the weird green wallpaper smeared with splashes of oil near the stove, the window on the left overlooking the kitchen of the neighbouring flat, the mini exhaust fan on the upper right corner, the steel containers which her mother kept on the open shelves...it was all too overwhelming. It was like sitting in a time machine and swooshing down the past. It was not a well-maintained place, but it had her memories. It was the place where she had told her mother about her first boyfriend as she sat on the slab, swinging her legs while her mother prepared halwa for everyone. She remembered her mother smiling for a second before she turned stern and asked her to be careful. You are a girl; always remember that, she said. It was here when she had seen her father cook chicken curry for the first time. It was the best one she ever had, she claimed, as her father gave her a spoonful to taste. It was here when Aaryan, in one of his rare good moods, made bread rolls for everyone in the family.

Sunny was quite amused by the large wooden radio and was frantically moving its dial.

"Does this work?" he asked.

"Dad, I think you should make this thing work for once and put the question to rest," Lipi said to Vinod as the family settled in the drawing room.

"It does work but I have to put a few wires in place," Vinod told Sunny.

"Make it work the next time we come. Okay?" Sunny said.

There was a knock at the door. Everyone looked at everyone and then Meena got up to open the door. Aaryan stood there with a small backpack perched on his shoulder.

✦

Vinod had no money for his father's operation, not enough. It was at that time that his sisters came to his rescue and shared the cost. After the operation, Manohar was in the hospital for some time and Shakuntala realized that it was not possible to take care of him if her son stayed away. She again asked Vinod and Meena to return. There were no apologies.

"I can't do it alone." That is all she said.

Meena had been struggling with Tuberculosis for almost a year now. She was almost cured but the medicines had taken a toll. She was beaten hollow from inside.

"I don't want you to take up the slave's job again," Vinod said to Meena.

"They need us. We will have a maid," Meena said.

The family returned to the old house a week before Manohar was discharged from the hospital. The day he was brought home wrapped in Plaster of Paris, he hugged Meena and cried. The children were relieved. Aaryan ran upstairs to the terrace to see the approaching train. Shakuntala was dumbfounded. She had not expected her son to return, but then there was a sudden rush of relief. That day, the whole family gathered together – her son, her daughters and their families. The cousins met after a long gap and Manohar regularly came to tears in the presence of his eight grandchildren around him. Meena touched Shakuntala's feet when she entered the house and Shakuntala blessed her. Both of them knew that they had to take things forward from here.

The nurse made Shakuntala a bit uncomfortable in the beginning, but then there was no other way. She was a gift from her sons-in-law. The maid was back too and suddenly the house was buzzing with people after almost a year of silence. Meena was back in the kitchen, taking good care of Manohar and he too was upbeat about getting well. The nurse was given the storeroom adjacent to Manohar and Shakuntala's room. She was given a makeshift bed there. Although the room was a bit cold because it led to the balcony, but there was no other choice.

When Manohar finally lost the will to live after eight months, the fragile appetite of the family for intimacy and love crumbled too. Manohar's sudden callousness terrified Shakuntala. There was an imminent fear of being left alone which again pushed her to the brink. She got irritable by Manohar's dramatizations, the unnecessary references to death and his adulation for Meena, whom he thought was the best daughter-in-law anyone could get. She started snapping at the mildest of provocations and thus started a new level of her fights with Manohar that the grandchildren again started to enjoy. A year's separation from their grandparents had drilled in a degree of respect for their parents in them. They were growing up too, were nurturing an acute sense of differentiating between the right and the wrong. Aaryan was now just three years away from college. Shakuntala started to understand that it was now quite hard to influence her grandchildren. They were on a plane of their own. Besides that, the children had started to spend quite a lot of time with their mother. After coming from school in the afternoon, they would play carom or cards with their mother before taking a nap.

It was during this time when Lipi had a heart to heart with her mother. She was thirteen now and grappling with the relationships in her house, with the subtle flow of hatred, which flew beneath everyone's skin. She wanted to know why things were the way they were. Little did she realize that she was not entering a no man's land as she made herself believe. She was just switching sides. Meena told Lipi her side of the story, unbiased and undiluted. In the end, the room was filled with invisible anger and realizations. Lipi had jumped over to the other side. She wiped off her mother's tears. She tried to share the gory details with Aaryan too, but he gave no sign of any concern.

"I am not interested," he simply said.

"And why not?" Lipi asked him, giving him a slight push, "I am talking about our mother here."

"I am sorry that you have realized that you were being used as a pawn. I reached the point some years back and decided not to tread on either of the roads."

"Why?"

"Because it's stupid! It's childish! How difficult is it for six people to live in a house together? I cannot make it worse by taking sides and adding fuel to it. I have to get out of this house as soon as possible. It's a mad place and I will lose my mind if I stay here for long," Aaryan said. He got up and started walking out of the room.

"Yes. Run! That is what you can do," Lipi said.

"You want to stay and be a part of the mud slinging? Be my guest. I am out of here."

The four years after the family reunited were marked by Manohar's cadaverous deterioration, things getting back to how they were between Shakuntala and Meena, the constant shouting and fights between the four elders. Meanwhile Aaryan completed his school and joined a college in Delhi University in 1997. He could not be an Engineer or Doctor as his father and teachers had anticipated even though he topped his school in the 12th board examinations. He did not hang himself from the ceiling fan as hundreds of students did every year in India as they buckled under the pressure. That was one point when he was thankful for the mangled relationships in his house. If nothing else, they had made him immune to such trivial tensions.

Manohar died three days before Aaryan's Quantum Mechanics paper. Aaryan was then taking his first year final exams. A night before Manohar's death, Shakuntala asked her family to leave her alone with her husband for a while. Seeing her condition and the way she had reacted after the doctor confirmed that Manohar was not going to live, her children tried to dissuade her. She had been crying the whole day, thrashing her chest with her hands.

"I want to spend some time alone with my husband!" she screamed.

Shakuntala locked the room from inside and looked at Manohar. Tears flew down the dried tributaries of her cheeks. She opened her almirah and took out the key. She then sat on the bed and pulled out the iron trunk.

She lay down next to Manohar, took his hand in hers and placed his flute in it, curling his fingers over it. She took his face in her hands and kissed him. She was not expecting a miracle; she hardly knew what she was doing. She stayed like this all night, looking at Manohar buried under the flute, his breathing trickling towards a halt. In the morning, she put the flute back in the trunk. He was still breathing, no matter how erratic it was. And then she opened the door.

✦

Meena stood at the door as if she had seen a ghost. Aaryan took off the bag pack from his shoulder and touched her feet.

"You have put on some weight," she said.

He entered the drawing room and touched his father's feet. Vinod mumbled something inaudible. He was surprised to see Lipi there. She got up and gave him a cold hug. Aaryan sat on the diwan and took off his shoes. There was an unintentional caprice in the room, a lull of rarity. They were, after all, meeting after two years in that house. Even Sunny was quiet initially.

"I asked Grandpa to fix the radio but he said that he would make it work next time. Can you fix it now?" Sunny asked Aaryan.

"Let's see," Aaryan said as he pulled Sunny on the diwan and plugged in the radio in the socket just below the mantelpiece.

"I'll make some food," Meena said and walked towards the kitchen.

"I'll help you. I'll just make a call and come," Lipi said and got up. Vinod coughed.

Lipi called Ravi and gave him the news.

"What!"

"Yes, and listen, I am staying here for dinner. You have your dinner and go to sleep. Don't wait for us."

"Do you want me to come over?"

"No. Let me manage this project."

She then went into the kitchen where she saw her mother cutting beans. She pulled out another knife and started to help Meena.

"I think you should go and sit with him," she finally said after sometime.

Meena went back to the drawing room where Vinod was staring at Sunny and Aaryan trying to make the radio work. He wished that he too was like Sunny, living in the present with no baggage of expectations from the past. The radio caught a station and a Bollywood song blared in the room.

"It works!" Sunny squealed with delight.

"Yes, not the best of sound quality, but the damn thing still works even after all those decades," Aaryan said as he rotated the dial to check if some other station was available. He gave up after a few seconds and returned to the sole available station. He lowered the volume a bit and turned around to face his parents.

"I thought I'll give you a visit after I got a call from Ma in the morning."

"That is very kind of you," Vinod said. Aaryan lowered his head.

"So, how are things at the University?" Meena asked after a prolonged pause.

"It's good. I am teaching Artificial Intelligence now. I am also thinking of doing PhD while I am teaching there. I have an offer."

"Artificial Intelligence? I had no idea they are teaching that at the University."

"They have been teaching that from the last fifteen years. It is very elementary – game theory, decision networks, all theoretical. This is not even a Physics subject. I just found it a bit interesting and so took it up. I was bored of teaching Electronics from the past five years."

"I thought you were quite against doing a PhD," Vinod said.

"That was five years back, dad. It would be good for my promotion."

"And how long will it take to complete?" Meena asked.

"Anywhere between four to five years."

"Do you..."

"What?"

"Do you think about getting married?"

"Ma. We have discussed this before. No, I don't."

Lipi entered the room after leaving the vegetable to cook on the stove. She was staring at her brother.

"How will you live alone all your life!" Meena said. It came out as a statement rather than a question. She was hoping that something would have happened in the last two years to change her son's mind.

"I like to be left alone. I enjoy my company. God! Why is it so hard to understand this?"

"We understand that very well, brother. We have been enduring that statement from a long time," Lipi said.

"I have a job in another city. I can't stay here," Aaryan said.

"You could have lived here. This is not America. We live with our parents or at least near them and take care of them."

"Oh! I thought ours was the most Americanized family in India. If an Indian family is the epitome of love then, I am sorry, I was never able to grasp that element in our home. Maybe I was not paying enough attention."

"Lipi, please, stop it," Meena intervened.

"Let's not talk about the past. I don't want to run in circles," Aaryan said.

Sunny was mesmerized with the almost heated argument. He was a bit disappointed when it ended abruptly.

"Till when are you here?" Vinod asked Aaryan.

"I will leave tomorrow afternoon. I have to join back day after tomorrow."

Then after a brief pause – "Did you go to Dalhousie in your summer break this year?" Aaryan asked Sunny.

"Yes, we did! We stayed at the villa! Dad took me for horse riding and I took a bath in the waterfall!" Sunny said hopping with joy. The mere mention of Dalhousie would land him in explicit frenzy.

"It was a miracle that Ravi got an off for 15 days this year. He has been working so hard lately. It was such a relaxing break. The father-son went completely crazy, hopping from one mountain to another," Lipi said, looking at her son who was studying the dial of the radio now.

"It has been years since I last went there," Aaryan said.

"I think we have gone there almost every year and I have invited you, mom and dad every single time to come along, but somehow we do not appreciate family holidays in this clan."

The family had a quiet dinner that night. It was strange how there was so less to talk even when they were all together after such a long time. Dinner was like a train passing through a railway crossing, when everyone waited patiently for it to be through so that they could move on with their lives. The clatter of spoons was deafening and the gulps of water had a sharp audibility to it. Meena gave everyone the neighborhood gossip that was met with half-baked nods and sad smiles. She too realized the futility of it and entered a state of passive chewing. After dinner, Lipi left for her home with Sunny.

"When will I see you again?" She asked Aaryan before going. Aaryan did not reply but smiled and looked away.

Later, he went up to the top terrace of the building as Lipi went downstairs towards her car. He threw a glance down as he saw Lipi's car pull away. It looked like a firefly lost in a jungle. He sat on the terrace and waited for the train to come. The steam engines were long gone and so were the diesel ones. It wasn't the same now. There was no smoke bellowing from the horizon. That was one reason he did not miss the sight in Rohtak. It wasn't as if things were happening irrespective of his absence. Things he loved were dead, even the peacocks were not there anymore. He had not given much thought to coming back. He could not go through the same questions everyday. His sister had always blamed him for all the misfortunes of his parents. You have taken the place of our grandparents, she would say. He was supposed to be the good son, the final respite in the lives of his unfortunate parents, but this was a burden he was too exhausted to carry. He found the whole idea of taking sides and continuing the war eerily tiring. After his grandfather died, his grandmother was half dead herself. She could not bear it. Lipi had realized by that time what a terrible woman her grandmother was. She made her life miserable, stopped talking to her and replied to all her pleas with anger and a cold-hearted stare. Shakuntala could not bear it. Aaryan was already distant with everyone but Lipi's indifference was the last straw. Shakuntala felt an unbearable loneliness. She would lie in her bed all the time and cry her heart out and only get up to make food. She had separated herself completely, detaching herself from her son and daughter-in-law. The only time she got excited and was glued to the television was when some calamity of a monstrous nature unfolded on the screen. So, she faced her mundane life with the shield of IC 814 hijacking, Kargil War, and then the 9/11 attacks. The incidents were like a shot of drugs, reminding her that she was on a war of her own.

The household got its first telephone a year after Manohar's death. Sometimes, Shakuntala would call her daughters and cry. Her daughters blamed their brother for making their mother feel so lonely and despondent even when they were staying together.

As the images tumbled in front of Aaryan, he wondered if it was entirely his grandmother's mistake. Why couldn't his father take a position? Why didn't his mother take a stand? Why didn't his grandfather drill some sense in his wife? His grandfather had enough energy to fight with her when it encompassed just the two of them but could not raise a finger when the subject of her vile attacks was another being. Was it Lipi's viciousness that actually killed Shakuntala? It didn't go wrong because of one person. It was a bridge that was built on the wrong kind of soil. And it collapsed in slow motion, dancing a full frontal. Lipi's remonstration did not achieve anything. Shakuntala died without an iota of remorse five years after Manohar's death in 2003. It was the year Aaryan sat home to prepare for his NET exam after completing his Masters. Shakuntala was completely broken and tired of being alone and the only emotion, which had grown manifold, was her hatred for Meena. She blamed her for her disconsolate last years of her life. She had cursed Meena numerous times that she would never be happy in her life. The curse worked somehow.

A train appeared on the horizon and soon he could see perfect rectangles of light running in a straight line as the bogies rushed past. How incredible trains looked in the night. It was like a whole town moving in one straight line, people sleeping as their bodies ran from one city to another. And then, the lights of the whole colony went off. For a moment, Aaryan could only see the train moving rapidly in the darkness and then he raised his head. The stars were shining like diamonds and suddenly he was transported back to Dalhousie, the day he had seen millions of them beaming with an undiluted ferocity. The memory came with such sharpness that before he could realize, he was crying. The stars melted away as tears ran down unchecked on his face for perpetuity.

He sat in the dark till the power came back and the colony was illuminated again. He looked up at the clear sky, filled with light dispersed from all the surrounding buildings, with a handful of visible stars. He tried to superimpose a sky teaming with glittering stars on this one – the one he had seen minutes ago. It was like superimposing an exceptional life on a semblance of the one he was leading. No, it was not possible, not possible at all.

# *Life of the Secret*

Seconds before the nerve ruptured in Shakuntala's brain, she had a sudden impulse to forgive everyone. She was surprised at the emotion as much as she was surprised because of what she had done. The hatred receded the same way as ocean recedes before a tsunami hits. She wanted to give her son the happiest shock he could have ever received. But then, wasn't it cursed, she thought?

As she pulled out the black trunk from under her bed, she justified her previous decisions and actions once more to herself, like she had done millions of times before. Yes, Manohar did not deserve to be told of the secret. She had decided this the day she had kept the two letters in his bag to post, announcing her pregnancy to their families. In a fit of rage, she had vowed that no matter how hard life turns out, she would never allow Manohar near what she had kept unrevealed for such a long time. This was one of the reasons why her bitterness for Manohar reached incomparable heights over the years as her son and daughters were born. If he would have understood what she actually wanted, then life would have been different. She dragged him down and in the process was dragged down herself.

At first it did not register with Meena that there was something terribly wrong. Then she had a look at the open trunk. Her mother-in-law guarded that trunk like a vulture guarding a piece of flesh. She could not possibly go to sleep with the trunk open between her legs. And then the house was filled with a nauseating stench of urine. She entered Shakuntala's room and called her. Shakuntala moved her eyes and looked at her but the rest of her body did not respond at all. There was something lying wrapped in a yellow cloth in the open trunk and Meena was tempted to have a look. She unwrapped the cloth and looked at the contents inside it. Shakuntala was fighting a battle herself, but then she decided to tell Meena.

"It's cursed," She whispered and that is all she was able to say. Yes it was, she thought, otherwise her body would not have crumpled by just touching the wretched thing. She would not have been dying like this.

Meena was horrified not only because of what her mother-in-law had hidden away all these years but also because of its reverberations. Suddenly she felt like vomiting. Then she wrapped the cloth back and ran towards her room. She opened her almirah and gently pushed open the false ceiling and stashed away what she had fallen upon by mistake. She stood in front of the almirah for a few seconds, inhaling the truth, creating an alternate life that could have been. Over the next few days, Shakuntala's deplorable condition confirmed her last words and glued them in Meena's head forever. Meena was too religious and quite superstitious to let go of such a vivid display of the power of the curse. Earlier, she had decided to hand over the bundle to Vinod, but after seeing Shakuntala's roving eyes pleading for death for days, she did not dare to open the false ceiling.

Seven days later, Shakuntala's death was a relief, a final sigh, and end of a painful journey. Tears welled up in Meena's eyes when Shakuntala's body was brought back home from the hospital. She was not able to hold them back, now that it was all over. Vinod, Aaryan and Lipi did not cry. They went through the rituals with a straight face, as if the day was nothing different from their daily life. Shakuntala's leftover property in Dalhousie passed to Vinod. There were a few acres of farms and her father's house which went to Vinod after his sisters signed the necessary no objection certificate and relinquished their share.

Aaryan and Lipi moved into Shakuntala and Manohar's room. At first, it was a bit scary to sleep in a room in which two people had died, but the children were happy to get a space of their own. Both of them changed the profile of the room in a few days. Meena donated all the clothes that belonged to Shakuntala and Manohar. Aaryan painted and pasted cartoon characters on the almirah while Lipi put a few dolls and teddy bears on her bed. Aaryan stayed in the house for a year preparing for his NET exams. That was the only year that Meena remembered as fulfilling since her marriage. There was calmness in the house. No one was screaming, crying or tossing in pain. Of course, there was an undercurrent of indignation between her and Vinod and the almost daily heated exchange of ideas between Aaryan and his father, but it was the mildest version of undercurrents and exchanges the house had seen in years. Lipi knew what her brother was up to; he had made it sufficiently clear to her. She was afraid that the calmness was short-lived and her mother would not be strong enough to take the next blow. The next year Aaryan gave his NET exam and was out of the house as soon as he got the job in Rohtak. He was finally free and out of the cage and Meena felt abandoned. She had never imagined a life in the absence of her son.

Lipi was not as bright as her brother but she was above average. She finished her school and did a course in Interior Decoration. She was soon hired by a firm in Gurgaon and did quite well. That is where she met Ravi. The firm in which she worked was hired by Ravi to redo his entire bungalow in a new modern pattern. Lipi had no idea that she would end up living in the house she was designing, but halfway through, she was getting some definite strong vibes from Ravi. They went out for dinner frequently and it was during their third dinner that Ravi proposed. The next two months was the most blissful time for Lipi. In fact she was surprised that her life was capable of throwing someone so affectionate towards her, although it took an awfully long time for Ravi to ask her out for dinner. When Lipi would return home after spending an ecstatic evening with Ravi, she would feel like an actress returning to the dull and cold greenroom after a thunderous applause from the audience. She was living two lives, just like Cinderella. They went out together for almost a year before they finally decided to get married. There was no reason why Vinod and Meena would have objected and Ravi's parents were too smitten by Lipi to complain. They got married in a court despite some resistance from Vinod who thought that Ravi and Lipi did that intentionally to save him the embarrassment of falling short of expectations for arrangements to receive an extremely rich family during the wedding. Ravi's father assured him that he and his family were left winged and there was no need for a martyr in the whole affair. Aaryan attended the marriage in the court and seemed reasonably happy for his sister.

The couple went for a month-long Euro tour for their honeymoon ten days after their marriage. Initially, Lipi thought that she had buried the past behind but she soon realized that things were not that easy. Her mother, for instance, was not ready to handle both her children's absence and her father was not helping either. Vinod never had any idea how to handle his wife and so it was always Lipi's responsibility to keep her mother happy as much as she could. She would invite her parents to her home at times and spend as much time as possible with them. They obliged but would not stay for long. Sunny was born two years after the marriage in 2010.

✦

Vinod's heart attack in 2017 was completely out of the blue. There were no before-shocks. It came a few months after Aaryan had given the family a surprise visit when Lipi came to drop her parents with Sunny. Like Shakuntala, Meena too had her moment of truth and the yellow piece of cloth came out with disastrous results. Vinod had no idea of the degree of hatred his mother nurtured and the degree to which his own wife went to guard the secret, just because of a line of curse from a dying woman. The incredulity of it all gave him a second heart attack that finished him off. Meena was devastated. She thought that the secret would have the power to bring her husband back. In a bout of desperation, she completely forgot the dying words of her mother-in-law. Soon, the cursed secret went back to where it came from. There was no need for the children to know. There was no need to pass on the curse to them. They were blissful and content in their own lives.

✦

After Shakuntala's death, the secret bundled in the yellow cloth lay in the false ceiling for nineteen years in the almirah in Meena's bedroom. It came out once to kill Vinod and then it got stuck in the false ceiling to kill Meena. Meena could never come to terms with its presence. She would take it out at times and study it. When Vinod was alive, she had to make sure that he was not around while she indulged in her secret but after his death she almost had a peek every day. Whether due to a senile decay or any other reason, the idea of keeping the secret somewhere within her easy reach never occurred to her. It was always the false ceiling and that it what sealed her fate.

The almirah caved in on Meena and broke her into two in 2022. The impact closed the false ceiling back into position and thus, the secret was again buried.

Kanshi Ram's house in Dalhousie which was in Vinod's name had passed to Meena after his death. She immediately wanted to transfer it to Aaryan and Lipi but her son was in no mood to carry the burden, hence a few signatures later, Lipi became the legal owner of the house a few months before Meena's death. She named it 'The Villa' and turned it into a modern holiday home for her family.

✦

The almirah passed on to Aaryan who wanted to keep it after his mother's death. Lipi wanted it for herself but she let Aaryan have it. She took the radio instead. Aaryan hired a moving van to shift the almirah to his house in Rohtak. He went into his old house in Janak Puri one last time to get it. As two men picked up the almirah and took it down to the van, Aaryan looked around the house. All rooms were stripped of humans now. The furniture was covered with clothes. Aaryan felt a bit uneasy about taking the almirah, which killed his mother, but then someone or the other had died in this house on some piece of furniture. How did it matter? It was strange to breathe in the silence of the house, something that was quite rare. There was a clock ticking somewhere. He went into his and Lipi's room and looked around, as if scratching off the memories from the walls. Then he went into his parents' room and sat there for a while. What a crazy place to grow up, he thought. There was a photograph on the wall of the drawing room. It was taken a year after Manohar's accident, when he had barely started walking. It was on a Diwali that the whole family had gathered together. Neela, Poonam and Rohini came down with their husbands and children and they had called a local photographer to take a family photograph. Manohar and Shakuntala sat on chairs in the middle with Neela, Rohini, Poonam and Meena sitting on either side. Vinod and the sons-in-law stood behind while all the children sat in front. Aaryan looked at the photograph and smiled. How happy everyone looked. Anyone could have taken a look at that photograph and felt jealous of not been a part of such a happy family. No one could have seen the phoniness, the contempt brimming under those skins. Photographs were always a mean to fool others and sometimes ourselves. Aaryan hated them. He did not take the photograph with him. Those were the faces he wanted to forget.

As he closed the door of the house, he knew that he was coming here for the last time in his life. He had a strong urge to go to the upper terrace and have a look at the railway tracks one last time. The men had loaded the almirah in the van and were waiting for him. He motioned them to wait for five more minutes. He walked upstairs but as he huffed and puffed towards the final steps, his feet became heavy. He remembered the time when he used to run upstairs without a sign of fatigue. He was 43 years old now; his legs were showing signs of weariness. He wanted to go back but somehow pushed himself to shove open the door. A gush of strong cold wind hit him and he closed his eyes for a second as he walked into the copious open terrace. When he opened them, he saw the most extraordinary sight; something he could never had imagined he would see again. A peahen was walking over the brick railing, taking majestic steps and staring at him as the sunlight bounced off her crown. Aaryan was so stunned that he did not realize that he was crying. A few seconds later, the peahen flew away, expanding her wings as if trying to grab the sky in them. Aaryan buckled and sat on his knee, surprised at the flood of tears, and cried his heart out. He could not remember for how long he was there. When the two men came upstairs searching for him, they found him lying on the floor and sobbing, with his head in his hands and his legs curled up to his stomach.

✦

The almirah stayed in Aaryan's house for twenty two years. It stood in his bedroom and was dusted regularly. The wood was very robust and stood the tests of time. Aaryan used to keep a few things in it but otherwise did not use it much. The Almirah saw him turn from a middle aged to an old man, getting more and more biting with the passage of time, taking up drinking heavily and talking to himself. He sometimes went to Delhi to meet Lipi but the visits were not frequent and very short. Lipi called him up once a fortnight to check if he was all right.

Sunny had turned into a nice young man and had joined his grandfather in his business. He had no intentions to carve out a niche for himself like his father. He did well and took over the whole responsibility when his grandfather died. He married his college sweetheart and had twin boys after three years.

The Almirah had a life and a mind of its own like the ring of the dark lord and hence one day in 2044, it decided to reveal what it had so artfully hidden. It was on the fateful day of his death when Aaryan discovered a slight unevenness of the size of the tip of his finger in the ceiling of the almirah. He had noticed it several times earlier but was always either too drunk or sulking to bother to touch it. He had finished his dinner and was about to get a glass of whisky when he decided to check a few answer sheets as he drank. The answer sheets were in the almirah and he opened it to get them out. This time the unevenness did not brush past him. He stared at it for a moment as if deciding whether to go ahead and explore it or not. Then he reached out and pushed the bulge and a compartment popped up in the ceiling. The whole sequence had a dreamlike quality and he could not believe what was happening. He slid open the false ceiling and something fell out wrapped in a yellow cloth.

In the end he laughed out loud till tears fell down his cheek. He thought that he would never stop and then he started crying and laughing in quick successions. He ransacked the whole almirah, trying to find if it had any other hidden enclosures. During all this time, tears flew down his cheeks and laughter erupted from his throat every second. He finally wrapped the secret in the yellow cloth and put it back inside the false ceiling and closed it shut. No one needed it. It was a piece of garbage. Then in a fit of amusement, he wrote the if-else condition on a piece of paper and laughed again till he finished off half of his drink and let the glass tumble on the bed before he went to sleep. He was found dead the next day.

All of Aaryan's possessions passed to Lipi. She was sixty years old and had no intention of keeping her brother's suitcases in her house. She donated everything but kept the almirah with her. The radio and the almirah were the only two things that reminded her of her past, and so, they remained in her room despite Sunny's objections. Sunny's wife was one of the managers in his company.

She worked twice as hard as him and this left Lipi and Ravi to look after the boys who were now six, of course with the help of half a dozen servants.

"They say, when you grow old, each day passes with the speed with which a tortoise walks. Do you feel that way?" Lipi asked Ravi one evening after dinner when they were alone in their room.

"I think it is quite different with us. I feel old age rushing past me," Ravi said. He came and stood behind Lipi as she combed her hair.

"You used to say that when you were young."

"Did I? I guess, I want this life to go on."

She watched him in the mirror and smiled.

"What is it?" She asked.

"It has been a good life," he said as he smiled back.

"Yes it was. For me, my life started when I met you."

He kissed her gently on the neck, the skin around his lips wrinkling with the motion.

"Wish I could say the same," he said. Both of them laughed.

"I want to always remember this moment, when we stood old and crumpled in front of the mirror, staring into the eyes of each other's images."

They stood there silently, staring at the mirror as Ravi put his arms around Lipi.

"I always had a fear that I would end up like my mother or grandmother," Lipi said.

"But you didn't."

"Yes, and I would always thank God for that and you. You can't imagine how relieved I feel when I think about this. I wish Aaryan..."

She was not able to complete the sentence as her voice trailed off.

"He had his own reasons," Ravi said.

"Yes I am sure he had. I could never understand the reason of his death. Something terrible happened that night."

"The way he ransacked the almirah, maybe he was drunk and he did that in a fit of rage."

"I wish this piece of wood could speak. It has seen everything."

The almirah never spoke. It guarded the past like a serpent sitting on a treasure. Ravi and Lipi went on with their lives as the almirah stood in one corner of their room. Both of them were a part of an NGO from the past ten years that dealt with woman empowerment. When they were not juggling with their grandchildren, they were busy attending conferences and sometimes visiting remote areas. Ravi had a lot of money to throw around and usually made heavy donations and saw to it that it all went to the needy. Although he was getting too old to carry on, he nevertheless maintained a level of vigour and energy to inspire the younger lot in the organization. He and Lipi were icons there and were highly respected.

Sometimes Lipi wondered if things were ever going to change in her country. It was 2048 and they still needed such NGOs; they were still talking of women empowerment. There was a wide abyss between the cities and the smaller towns and villages. They were like two different worlds not even trying to meet since the hundred years India had gained independence. To flush out the old school of thought, maybe we have to wait for time to flush out the old generation, Ravi used to say.

"And what if the older generation passes the germ to the next one? Do we wait another generation?"

Ravi knew she was right. It was like AIDS of the brain, passed on so subtly that it did not surprise him when the NGO still got cases of dowry, physical abuse, rapes and mental tortures. It was as if time had stagnated. We replaced everything with things flashier, except for our rusting thought process. Do scientific achievements compensate for the lack of morals? The world had taken giant leaps in the past years but there were areas which refused to move ahead, rooted to the ground, deep into penury and filled with sheep pretending to be humans. India was now the most populated country in the world and that was a part of the problem. That had always been a part of the problem. Sometimes, when Ravi and Lipi would discuss all this, Lipi would ask him to take it easy. They were not his problems. Let the Prime Minister do some work, she said. Sometimes she would get frustrated herself. Maybe Aaryan was right when he told their father once during an argument that we were all werewolves, waiting for the moon of hatred.

On their 50th anniversary in 2058, Sunny gifted them a water-driven Lamborghini and tickets for a world tour.

"We are too old for this," Ravi said.

"Nonsense! We will go," Lipi said.

"I was talking about the Lamborghini," Ravi said as he winked.

It was after they returned from the tour that Ravi started to complain about pain in his chest. He was immediately hospitalized where he remained for almost a week. It was a mild heart attack, the doctors told. He died in his sleep on the seventh day.

✦

Lipi now spent most of her time in the house. She was too tired, now that Ravi was not around. She resigned from the NGO and was given a touching farewell by the people with whom she had worked for so long. Suddenly, her own battles were too hard to fight now. She realized that she could not function without Ravi, they were like two cogs entwined together. She would stay in her room and listen to the radio. It still worked, and it was nothing less than a miracle. Sometimes, her grandchildren would bring their school friends to show them the 120 years old radio. Most of them would laugh hysterically because of the sheer size of the machine, especially when now they could carry a 1000GB music player on one ear. Sunny and his wife Divya would spend as much time as possible with her, and Lipi too put up a brave front, but she was caving in, slowly and gradually.

"It's comical how we turn into each other," she told Sunny once, "my grandma turned into her grandma as she grew old. She turned into someone she despised all her younger years. She told me once that her grandma hated her when her father put her in a convent. It was unheard of in those times."

"She studied in a convent?" Sunny was surprised.

"Yes, she did. I used to be so proud to display her to my friends. A granny who can speak and read English, everyone envied me. She lost the will to live after granddad died. And now, I think I am turning into her."

"Ma," Sunny said as he embraced her and kissed her, "you are doing fine."

"No I am not, sweetheart. I pretend, but I am tired. I can't bear his absence."

"Neither can I."

It took four years for Lipi to wither away; almost the same time it took Shakuntala to wither away after Manohar's death and Meena to wither away after Vinod left.

She died silently, sitting on her chair while listening to the radio on a warm summer day in April 2062.

# False Ceilings

Sunny kept the radio. It was an antique piece and a way to remember his mother. He gave the almirah to a local carpenter whom he knew very well as he was a frequent visitor to the house, making many of Lipi's self designed pieces of furniture and who was elated to lay his hands on something made of wood. A few days later, the carpenter returned and handed over something bundled up inside a worn out and dirty piece of yellow cloth to Sunny.

"I found this inside the almirah when I was cutting it open. Did you know that it had a false ceiling, a hidden compartment?" he asked.

"Really? And you found this inside it?" Sunny was surprised. His mother had never mentioned it.

He unfolded the cloth and inside it was a file. His heart was beating loudly.

"What the hell is that?" he whispered.

The file contained a few legal documents for a property. He read through them. The paper was crumbling and he had to be very careful while turning the pages.

"Who the hell was Kanshi Ram? These are some papers of a property he bought in Delhi in 1941. God! This is old. And so much land! Anyway, thanks Balram uncle, I'll look into this. Just double check if it had anything else hidden inside it."

"I will."

The carpenter went away and Sunny almost forgot about the papers when one day, Divya took them to the office and asked her secretary to run a check on them and see if the property still existed. It was on a prime location and an enormous piece of land. The secretary came back to her a few days later with the news that there was a shopping complex on the land now.

"Maybe someone forged the papers. I also ran a check on the price. The land is almost worth 500 crores now. It was a very expensive land from the beginning," the secretary said.

"Can we challenge the present owner?" Divya asked.

"The papers we have are from the pre-independence era. I'll run a check and let you know."

That night Divya told Sunny about the price of the property.

"Holy crap!"

"Exactly."

"What the hell was it doing in that almirah? Imagine something like that lying there for all these years and nobody knew about it."

"Someone did. Someone kept it there."

"Fuck!" Sunny said as he moved his head in amazement.

His mind was racing back. He was joining images, piecing up stories and incidences. There were bits and pieces about his mother, her life before she met his father, which were missing. She had told him about a few incidences and her hatred for Shakuntala, but it was not very streamlined in his brain. Lipi usually avoided mentioning her growing up years in front of him. He remembered Meena crying by the pool as sun gleamed in her eyes. He remembered Vinod's gloomy face counting the ripples in the pool. He remembered the day he met Aaryan when they fixed the radio and the tension hanging in the room that day. But some pieces were missing.

"They lived in a two bedroom flat and all this money was stacked away right under their nose all these years. It could have changed their lives."

"Who?" Divya asked.

"My mother, my grandparents, everyone. I am sure at least one of them knew about this, otherwise this would not have ended up in the false ceiling."

"Whose almirah was it anyway?" Divya asked.

"My grandma's. She brought it from Dalhousie when she got married to grandpa. You know, the night Aaryan uncle died, he ransacked this almirah. People heard him laughing and crying. And then my grandma's tragic death...the almirah fell over her."

"So they knew about this property."

"Maybe. It wasn't a very happy household. Mom was always very reluctant to talk about it. But can you imagine the undercurrent of hatred that would have existed in the family if they would have been hiding a piece of land from each other for more than hundred years? Clearly, more than one person knew about this. And who the hell was Kanshi Ram? I have read that name somewhere," Sunny said.

"Who knows what happened? You are judging people you hardly knew. It doesn't take much for a lifelong hatred to stagnate and rot a family. I have seen it. And the reason can be incredibly stupid, something that won't make sense. No one cares about the magnitude of a reason, as long as there is one. Sometimes people go through a lifetime of pain by holding a secret that could have changed everything. It is an intoxicating addiction, an act of dominance to know that you hold something in your grip that could have changed the life of a person you detest," Divya said thoughtfully.

"It was just money."

"It could have been worse with the secret out in the open. Don't strain yourself. Go to sleep now. Let's see if we can get a hand on that property," Divya said taking off her glasses.

"You know that its peanuts compared to the revenue of our company but yeah, what's the harm in trying. Well, good night baby," Sunny said as he kissed his wife and ordered the lights to switch off.

"Good night Sweetheart."

Sunny knew that he would not rest till he could find out who Kanshi Ram was. He had a hunch, but he was not sure. Before he closed his eyes, he knew he had to visit Dalhousie. His answers were in the Villa.

✦ ✦ ✦